KILLING REALITY

BOB HENDERSON

Well Mom, I finished.
I dedicate this book to you.
I know you would be pleased.

CONTENTS

1. BIG ASS, BIG HAIR, AND BIGGER TROUBLE

"HEY, you little shit, who the hell do you think you are?"

That's what I heard as I regained consciousness from the whack to my head.

———

As my eyes gradually focused with the blood dripping down my face, all I could see was this big Kurt Russell wannabe pointing a freakin' gun at me in my own living room. The worst part? The son of a bitch looked like he was enjoying himself. So, I killed the bastard. Not really. Well, I did kill him, but it was self-defense.

Hold on, I'm getting ahead of myself here. Let me set the stage for what resulted in me being tied to a stained coffee table in my apartment, as this fucking animal named Petra Stronge waved a gun in my face.

I wanted to be in the movies—like a million other

L.A. teens who walked around Hollywood wearing wool caps and sipping five-dollar mocha Frappuccinos, thinking they were cool. It's as simple as that. A buck-fifty could get you into a noontime double feature at The Cinerama Dome, with its curved screen and dome top that resembled a giant golf ball. Oh man, I loved that place and all its futuristic glory. And I loved the movies that were shown there. They were vintage classics filled with timeless talent, not this brain-numbing crap that's churned out now.

But life has a way of taking unexpected, demoralizing turns. I never made it as an actor (big surprise), so I went to school for set design and production. I figured if I couldn't act, at least I'd still be around the action. After graduation, and then a lot of low-paying temp jobs, I finally landed a decent freelancing job as a grip for a slew of second-rate TV shows. Since I was the low man on the totem pole, I also had to be the gofer for some pretty reprehensible people. Initially, everyone played nice. They'd smile and give a "hello" or a "thank you." They actually acknowledged that I was a human being with a soul. But it wasn't long before the claws came out, along with the monstrous insecurities and egos, making life on set intolerable.

Not many people know what a grip does—it's not like we're given a lot of credit or publicity for the work we do. We're invisible. How many people do you think stick around to watch the credits roll to see the list of grips and gaffers? That would be a very small amount. It isn't easy being a grip; we work on complicated elevated equipment that supports the cameras and lighting. Sometimes we even have to support the overweight director who's had too many three-martini "working lunches." Yup, hard work for sure. Most of the time, I convinced myself I was doing something worthwhile, even if it was a thankless job.

My job as a grip was all about the camera working perfectly for every shot. Where the camera was, so was I. Which meant that with every close-up, romantic gaze into the lens, or last dying breath, the actor had to look at me as well. There wasn't anything I didn't see in front of the camera or behind it. And *that's* where all this shit went wrong.

Turns out, I should never have accepted the grip gig on the set of *Being Stronge,* one of TV's rating winners at the time, which meant it was also one of the most cringeworthy reality shows out there. The show should've come with a warning that watching was harmful to your mental health. The Stronge family made the Osbornes look like churchgoers.

Petra Stronge, the show's biggest star, relied on his nearly obsolete fame as a former hockey player for the Detroit Red Wings. He was six feet tall and still in decent shape, but he was far removed from his playing days. Petra had a mountain-like, chiseled face with a prominent jawline and ocean blue eyes that pierced anyone who got in his way.

He had brown, longish wavy hair with a five o'clock shadow that failed to hide a jagged scar on the left side of his jaw. He claimed it was a souvenir from his playing days, when he was sliced by a hockey stick. Anytime someone mentioned his scar, Petra would launch into an embellished version of his injury and how he had insisted on playing through the pain, which led to a Red Wings victory in the playoffs.

His oversized, bloated vanity also meant that the stylists and makeup crew were often kept working overtime. No doubt, he still had swagger. People often turned to watch and whisper as he strutted by.

Everyone on set called him "Pet," not so much like a lovable family pet, but because he was a salacious pervert who couldn't keep his hands from petting other women on and off the screen. He was a well-known womanizer. To Petra, if a woman was breathing, she was fair game.

The nickname stuck, and the disturbing part was that it didn't even bother him. In fact, he wore it like a badge of honor, even though he was married. Most women couldn't help but find him irresistible, although deep down they knew he was despicable.

His wife Sandy was the stereotypical big-haired, Botox-lipped former supermodel. She was also an incredible bitch on wheels with an ego that could, and did on many occasions, match her husband's. Of course, Petra and Sandy loved to act like their marriage was filled with rainbows and roses, but just like so many other couples, they had only married out of convenience. Both of their careers were dwindling, and they needed each other to stay relevant and to keep their good press and publicity checks. Petra didn't let a little thing like a marriage vow keep him from straying, nor did it keep Sandy from using Petra's image for her own benefit. They were perfectly self-absorbed and soulless together.

New Jersey Governor Chris Christie didn't help the situation when he dubbed the historic East Coast hurricane of 2012 "Superstorm Sandy." From that time on, Sandy was known as "The Hurricane" or "Stormin' Sandy," and boy, did she wring every drop of publicity from that nickname for all it was worth. Her behavior became even more outrageous. Adding fuel to her fire, the *other* reality show she appeared on, *Want $um*, was winding down, leaving Sandy worried about her lack of visibility (I swear, you can't make this shit up). *Want $um*, according to a press release, "follows current and former supermodels in their daily lives, giving viewers unprecedented access to what goes on in front of—and behind!—the cameras." Translated, this meant viewers got to watch women behaving very, *very* badly. When they weren't on photo or commercial shoots, they fought like tomcats and drank like fish. They constantly took turns at creating drama between each other and then they would make up by the end of each episode.

If the constant bickering and preening Petra and Sandy did for the show wasn't enough to push a director over the edge, their three kids (aka, The Spawn of Satan) would. Spoiled, volatile, eternally adolescent, and always aggravating, this unholy trio came complete with three ridiculous names. The oldest, Army Stronge, was twenty-one years old and excessively tattooed and rigid like his father. He was followed by his nineteen-year-old pot-smoking brother, Navy Stronge. Then there was the baby, Ranger Stronge, who was seventeen, gay, and unconcerned with who did or didn't know his sexual preference. These gun-toting, steroid-abusing brothers, who looked more like hoodlums than young men, made a compelling argument for birth control. Everyone on the set avoided these boys like the Plague. As much as I tried to stay out of their paths, they were destined to become a part of my very big, very public downfall.

It wasn't the family's collective arrogance, rudeness, or ability to suck all the air out of a room that started pissing me off, and it wasn't that they made every day on the set feel like a school trip to Guantanamo Bay; it was that they treated me and everyone else who was low on their food chain like a doormat—all for the fun of it. They would find someone's weak spot and then go in for the kill. They'd play cruel jokes on them, laughing at the poor victim's embarrassment and humiliation. Grips and gaffers, the makeup crew, wardrobe and hair stylists, and not to mention the food service people, we were all easy prey.

Even though this dysfunctional family was receiving lots of attention from the show's hit ratings, most of the crew (including yours truly) thought the show was dreadful. I admit, it didn't take long before I was burnt out and ready for a new job. I had become tired of having to arrive on set by 5 am every day, sitting in the I-10 traffic all so the Stronge family could hurl insults and crass remarks. I needed a change, and I got one; it just wasn't the one I had expected.

The day when it all began to unravel started out like every other tumultuous workday on set. Activity on the set would gain steam around 6 am, with an endless flow of strong coffee and sugar-laden assortments of jelly-and-cream-filled donuts, powdered pastries, and monstrous chocolate-filled croissants to rev up everyone's engines. The cast and crew would stuff themselves silly. You could time your watch and see their sugar highs hit before the first take, leaving them to bottom out into cranky, sullen moods by the middle of the day. It wasn't a pretty sight. Word to the wise: make sure that after the celebrities indulge in their hypoglycemic nose dives, there are no sharp instruments within reach.

As everyone crammed their faces with sugar and downed the high-test coffee, big-haired Sandy crawled out of her trailer and claimed her territory over the last French cruller. I quickly gulped down my cup of coffee and passed on the donuts to avoid hearing Sandy rave to her personal stylist about those stubborn three pounds she "just had to lose."

I meandered my way towards the storage room to get a longer cable for one of the menace arms to rig the lighting for the day's shoot. The door swept over the lightly dusted tile as I turned into the back aisle, where all the electrical equipment was stored. To my surprise, I swiftly collided into everyone's un-favorite "Pet" Stronge, doing what he did best: copulating. Since I had just seen her emerging from her trailer, I knew it wasn't Sandy whose faux leather skirt was up to her navel, with her lace panties halfway down to her knees. It was Andrea Milk, one of Sandy's much younger predatory co-stars on the show *Want $um.*

Andrea was a total "hottie" (as we on the crew called her), and her smart remarks were even hotter. Her catty attitude didn't keep men from lusting after her. Not only was she a looker, she could kick the ass of almost every female on set, and probably half the men. Andrea was a total gym rat, and no one wanted to cross her or make her angry.

When Petra realized someone had interrupted his thrilling escapade with the very flexible Mrs. Milk, his eyes shot open in what I guessed could only be fear. As soon as he recognized it was me, however, there was a palpable sense of relief in his eyes. He growled in my direction as he reluctantly dropped the handful of breast he was fondling. I was standing directly behind Mrs. Milk, who was frantically tugging at her now wrinkled sheer blouse and faux leather skirt, trying to put her clothing back together as quickly as possible. As she turned to face me with complete embarrassment, I noticed her dark crimson lipstick smudged haphazardly across her cheek. When my head pivoted back, I stole a look at Petra. His face was turning an ugly shade of red and his upper body shook, like he was going to blow a fuse. I wished I could become invisible at that moment, wanting to escape and fast, but I was frozen stupid.

"What the fuck are you doing, Henderson? Get the fuck out of here!"

His usual piercing blue eyes had narrowed into nearly black slits. He didn't even bother zipping up his fly. My mind couldn't totally comprehend what I was witnessing. Somehow, like when a hypnotist snapped their fingers, I came out of my shock, grabbed the spool of cable, and bolted like a scared rabbit out of the storage room.

I ran back to the set as fast as my out-of-shape millennial body would take me. After I calmed down and got the rig wired up and the light mounted properly, I realized the absurdity of the situation and started to laugh. Petra must have noticed, because the aging hockey defenseman suddenly slithered up behind me. I tried to ignore him, feeling his moist breath on my neck, hoping he would go away and retreat to his dark hole, but that wasn't gonna happen.

"Listen, you little prick, you didn't see a *thing*. Catch my drift?" I could smell Binaca on his tart breath, mixed with a splash of scotch—a wonderful sensory bouquet. "If you say a fucking word to *anyone*—the media, your shit-for-brains friends, or my family, *especially* my wife—you won't have any hands to grip your nuts with!" he spat through perfectly capped, clenched teeth.

I didn't move a muscle, because the menace and intensity in his voice cut right through me. It was no laughing matter now. I knew that Petra Stronge meant what he said, even though he was a lying, cheating prick. And if I breathed a word about this godforsaken "incident," I would not only be dead professionally but dead *period*; I'd heard stories about Petra's mob connections and how he'd taken a handful of bribes during his mediocre hockey career.

I was about to calm him down with assurances that I had no intention of saying anything to cause him or Andrea any trouble. Everyone who knew me best, like my mother or my next-door neighbor Mrs. Fox, would tell you I was the last person who would go looking for trouble. I was the peacemaker. But as Petra continued his spewing, I suddenly caught a crystal-clear picture of how the rest of my time on *Being Stronge* would play out: being routinely bullied and threatened by Petra. It was what I envisioned Hell must be like. *Fuck this*, I thought.

In a split-second it came to me. There was only one logical thing to do: quit! So, I did. I abruptly turned and left Petra standing there like an angry gorilla, ordering me to come back. I made a beeline for the HR Department. Looking back, it was a stupid decision. But at the time, I was in a state of panic—not to mention, sheer terror. I could only think of getting as far away from Petra's death ray stare as I could, and as fast as humanly possible.

I took a few days off before filing for unemployment. I slept past 5 am for the first time in forever, and it felt glorious. But then, reality of life reared its ugly head, so I combed the local Variety ads to look for my next job. I checked out websites like *Indeed* and *JobMonkey.com*. I wasn't seeing many opportunities. After a few weeks of fruitless job hunting, I started to feel depressed. I had been so sure that there would be more jobs available, considering how strenuous the role of a grip can be. Maybe it was time for me to desert reality TV altogether. I had paid my dues working on second-rate shows hoping to eventually land an exclusive gig on *American Idol* or *America's Top Model*, but they had never come my way. It would have been a considerable improvement to work on a show with actually talented actors instead of the plastic, Botox-injected Barbie and Ken wannabes on *Being Stronge*.

As the days wore on, I became more and more fed up with phony reality stars who were getting all the attention, and big pay to boot. Unsurprisingly, the viewers weren't turned off by their shady and scripted behavior.

In fact, it increased their popularity. It gnawed at my inner core as I became more and more obsessed with how unfair it all was. People like Sandy and Petra Stronge didn't deserve their immense Hollywood mansions and front-page headlines in every rag in town.

After a few more weeks of self-imposed exile, slumped in the sunken cushion of my threadbare couch, I glanced around my meager living room floor that was littered with laundry. The dining room table was piled high with newspapers with job leads circled that had led nowhere, and the whole place was making me feel claustrophobic.

Afraid I would turn into a Howard Hughes-like hermit or worse, I hauled my sorry ass out of the apartment and headed for the nearest Starbucks a couple of blocks away. Grabbing the latest *Variety*, I parked myself at one of the outdoor cafe tables. After blowing on the steam from my triple espresso, I sat back and crossed my legs. Moments later, I found myself choking on my espresso when I opened the paper to a startling headline, a headline that almost knocked me off my chair: "*Petra Stronge Scores.*" What the bleep?

The article stated that pervy Petra was about to win a big countersuit against Kyle Milk, the estranged husband of long-legged, mini-skirted Andrea Milk, Petra's playmate in the storage room. The lawsuit alleged "defamation of character," which was laughable seeing how Petra had no morals to begin with. Kyle had declared in court

—and to the tabloids, naturally—that he'd known Petra was sleeping with Andrea for some time. The problem was that Kyle had no evidence to prove it. Andrea swore on a stack of Bibles that she was a faithful wife, and the judge would have no choice but to rule in Petra's favor. If Kyle lost the case, the poor schmuck could be forced to file for bankruptcy.

Wiping up the coffee I'd spilled, I threw the newspaper into the trash. Something inside me snapped as loud as a giant limb falling from a tree. *How could this happen?* The SOB was going to win again—screwing the justice system while screwing somebody's wife. No fucking way! Fuck reality TV, to hell with Petra and the rest of those fake stars. I knew I had to do something and do it fast. Maybe I was finally fed up with all the poisonous bullshit that Hollywood injected. Maybe I was hopped up from the triple espresso. Whatever the reason, I pulled my phone out of my jeans pocket and called Petra at home. And in the middle of a beautiful L.A. Saturday morning, whether good, bad, or stupid, I sealed my fate. Petra answered the phone with his usual snarl: "What?"

I summoned whatever courage I could to try and sound intimidating and matter-of-fact, but came off sounding more like a bad Arnold Schwarzenegger imitation: "Petra? This is Marc Henderson. You know, you fucking creep, the grip on *Being Stronge*. Remember me? I'm the one that saw you screwing Andrea Milk in the storage room. Well, you can kiss that lawsuit goodbye. You're not getting away with your shitty behavior any longer. Enough is enough! Drop the lawsuit or I'll let Kyle's attorneys know that I walked in on you and the very limber Mrs. Milk doing the horizontal mambo. I can just imagine the headlines, can't you?"

I stopped and waited. All I could hear was *College GameDay Football* with Kirk Herbstreit blaring in the background. Then he hung up without a word.

Holy shit. What the fuck did I just do?

2. THE SLUGGER

IT FELT PRETTY good to blow off some steam, but I couldn't shake the nagging anxiety that stalked me the whole way home from Starbucks. With any luck, Petra would come clean and lay off of all this lawsuit nonsense and that would be the end of it. I was certain he didn't want his dysfunctional home life to become even more screwed up than it already was, nor would he want his public persona trashed in the media any more than it already was. He had to understand how his idiotic actions could affect the show's ratings and most importantly, his revenue. Surely, he had enough intelligence to drop this lawsuit, didn't he? I convinced myself that the decision to confront Petra was the right thing to do, tamping down the warning bells going off somewhere in my head.

After working with these wannabe celebrities for all those years, I'd finally figured out their Achilles heel, the one element their narcissistic fragile egos couldn't handle

—cheating on their spouse press, which was one tiny step up from no press at all. Anyone who'd been in the Hollywood game as long as Petra had, had to know it wasn't in his best interest to have pictures of his face Photoshopped in Andrea Milk's ample assets, plastered all over the tabloids. Even the Great Petra had to face the facts: he couldn't afford to lose his meal-ticket reality show. A *little* bad press could help boost show ratings, of course, but there was some news that could sour an audience's taste and flush the ratings down the toilet. This news would definitely poison the "happily ever after" image he and Sandy had so carefully cultivated for their fans.

I retreated to my apartment and flopped on the couch; I figured a little TV therapy would soothe my mind. I watched reruns of mind-numbing shows for hours to no avail; my nerves were shot. I needed to escape and get as far away as I could. Where would I go and what would I do? My salary as a grip forced me to live a simple life. There was no upscale community for me, no cordial doorman at a North Hollywood high-rise, and certainly no high-tech alarm system (except for Daisy, my next-door neighbor Mrs. Fox's hyperactive Bichon Frise).

Mrs. Fox, my still-sexy septuagenarian neighbor, often asked me to take Daisy out for her walks so she could "do her biz," as she liked to say. She'd hand me Daisy's leash and a plastic bag, pat my cheek, and give me a quick peck as Daisy and I would head out for a little green grass.

When I first met Mrs. Fox, she wanted me to call her "Aud," short for her first name Audrey. At the time, I thought she was a harmless, slightly ditzy, yet colorful senior citizen with too much time on her hands. That myth was quickly debunked.

Oh sure, there were a few senior moments when she might call me one of her (several) late husbands' names, but for the most part, she was a sharp, fascinating lady who didn't suffer fools gladly. Initially, some of the stories she told me seemed too outlandish to be true, and later she confessed she was testing me to see if I was paying attention.

Soon thereafter, when I'd come home from a long day at the set, we'd often share a beer on her back porch. She would then tell me her *real* stories, regaling me with adventures from her glory days when she was, in her own words, "a hot babe." Mrs. Fox had left a small town in Ohio for big dreams in Hollywood. She'd been only seventeen and never looked back. She was a quick study and learned how to dance, act, and even sing a little through sheer will and determination. She worked steadily until she met her first husband, whose name I've forgotten. (There were three more husbands after him, so it's understandable.) The marriage didn't last long, and she was back to working before the ink dried on her divorce papers. Husband No.1 was wealthy and very good to her financially in the divorce, so she didn't have to work, but as she told it, she got a "high" from being part of the biz and had actually missed it when she was married. I never said so aloud, but I had become very fond of Mrs. Fox, and she knew it.

Since I was on edge, I figured some time with Audrey would be just what I needed, but when I went to knock on her door, no one answered. Then I remembered it was Thursday, her weekly night out with her "peeps," a small but boisterous group comprised of fellow divorced/widowed ladies who could drink a crew of Teamsters under the table. I silently thanked God for Uber.

As a Plan B, I called a few of my work buddies and met them for a low-key night at our favorite bar. To my surprise, I only had three Cardinal Sin Red Ales before calling it a night. The night out didn't have the results I was looking for—I still felt uncomfortable and my anxiety was escalating.

As I parked my car on the street in front of my unit, my car lights exposed the shrubbery lining the perimeter of the retro '70s apartment complex I called home. The place was starting to look shabby; the exterior needed new paint, the windows were beyond ancient, and the entire building had a neglected air about it.

As I locked my car and headed to my front door, I noticed my feeble-at-best porch light was off. *Great, I'll have to call the landlord in the morning*, I thought. My hands were fumbling with my keys as I tried to find the keyhole in the pitch-dark. I worked gently to keep quiet so as not to trigger Daisy's barking. Finally, it connected, but I noticed the key turned too effortlessly, raising my suspicions. Usually, it took a few times for it to catch. *What the hell...?* I thought as I opened the front door and flipped on the light switch. Brightness flooded the room—there was nothing out of place. Whew. I sighed with relief, feeling a little foolish that there would be anything worth stealing in my apartment to begin with. The most expensive object I owned was my car, and even *that* was a stretch. Then I secured the double-bolted door lock my mom had given me when I'd moved; I felt safer knowing I had a little extra protection, even though my apartment was on the first floor with a sliding glass door that anyone could shimmy open from the outside. For me, security was mostly a state of mind.

I tossed my faded Dodgers jacket on the couch and checked my cell to see if I had any calls, especially from Petra—zilch. Maybe he'd decided to let well enough alone.

Exhausted, I headed for the shower. Afterwards, I headed to the kitchen to grab a bag of chips. But something made the hairs raise on the back of my neck, stopping me cold in my tracks. As I slowly passed the couch, I noticed the sliding door to the patio was slightly open. The faint reflection of someone standing directly behind me came into focus. *Oh shit!*

I stared blankly at the glass for a split second, then my brain cells thankfully kicked in. I knew I was in trouble and my body moved on instinct, searching for anything to defend myself with, when someone swiftly slid behind me, beating me to it. All I could feel was a hard *thump* on my head and I immediately blacked out.

When I came to, I had a hard time concentrating. I wondered how long I had been laying on the floor—was it minutes...hours? I tried to lift my head off the floor but winced with pain as a massive headache pulled me back down, like cement blocks in the ocean. My hands searched my body as my eyes adjusted and examined my surroundings. I was tied tightly to the leg of my mom's antique oak desk, one of her many donations to my apartment.

Squirming, I saw there were cords holding my wrists together. I also saw a pair of boots next to my couch and my eyes followed the boots up to the person they belonged to, who was sitting there, slouched, pointing a gun at me. Surprise, surprise—it was Petra Stronge. He was smoking one of his beloved ecstasy herbal cigarettes. He only smoked them to make himself feel cool. *What a poser*, was my first thought. My second thought was that *I* was the one tied up and Petra wasn't. I quickly regrouped. I had to do something about it.

Petra looked—and smelled—like he'd been partying pretty hard. His lids were half-closed, while his phone was pinched between his ear and his shoulder. "Yeah, I have him. No hurry. He ain't going nowhere," Petra snarled in the "stage voice" that he used when shooting the show.

Becoming more alert, I desperately realized I needed to loosen the cords that pressed tightly against my skin, causing burning friction. Blood trickled down my throbbing forehead, an annoying result from the blow I'd received earlier.

"Yeah, you can bring the car around now," Petra said, chuckling as he hung up the phone. He turned his piercing eyes to me. "Didn't I say you would be sorry, you little prick?"

Then he smiled and started laughing. I had never noticed Petra's menacing laugh before. I knew he was up to something dangerous. He extinguished his cigarette on my coffee table and kept grinning at me as he got up and walked into the kitchen. Even in my panicked state, I knew what Petra was capable of doing to me. It was well known on the set that Petra was more than a little OCD, and he *especially* disliked any lingering touch or scent on his hands. We'd discovered this on the very first episode of *Being Stronge* after shooting a scene where the Stronge's met their new neighbors, where there was a lot of handshaking and backslapping going down. When the director yelled "cut!" Petra held up both hands like a surgeon going in to operate. We all just stared—except his personal assistant, Mandy, who came in running like a madwoman with wet wipes, as if she were going to administer CPR to a heart attack victim. After the initial shock wore off, it quickly became an inside joke with

the crew; we made daily bets on if and when Mandy
and her wet wipes would make an appearance.

Lost in his germaphobia, Petra lathered up in my sink,
allowing the silence to fester in the air. He reached for a
kitchen towel to dry his hands, but there wasn't one.
Thank God, I hadn't gone to the store yet. As a result, he
started opening drawers to find something to wipe his
hands on. While Petra was busy searching for a towel, the
cobwebs finally cleared from my brain and I seized that
moment to make my move. I had no idea what that move
was, but I didn't dwell on it. "What the hell, Henderson!
Don't you own one goddamn towel?" Petra yelled from
the kitchen.

I used this distraction to find a way of getting myself
out of this ugly situation. Being a grip, my habit was to
always have a tool on hand, 24/7. I wriggled my hands into
the back pocket of my jeans, where I kept my trusty Swiss
Army knife. With a practiced flick of my wrist, I cut into
the rigid chords and quickly slipped them off. I hopped to
my feet before Petra realized what had happened. I
dashed to the bedroom and grabbed my old school safe-
guard propped up against the wall: a Louisville Slugger,
autographed by the infamous Sammy Sosa.

Petra caught on and raced to follow me into the
bedroom where we suddenly came face to face. My eyes
widened as I glanced at the gun he was holding in his wet
hand. Without warning, Petra lunged like a snake
attacking his prey. I twisted out of his grasp and then

swung the Slugger like my life depended on it, connecting with the crown of his head.

There was a loud crack, followed by a copious amount of blood. Petra dropped like a 220-pound sack of potatoes, ending whatever plans he had in mind for me. All the blood in my body froze as I watched the Slugger drop next to Petra on my now sodden floor. I knelt down and placed my fingers on Petra's creepy neck, hoping I'd only given him a bad concussion. My face felt flush as my stomach tied into knots. I searched for a pulse but there was nothing, only the cool beads of sweat on his skin sliding through my fingers. There was no more fiery anger in Petra's eyes. They were glassy, open, and void. I imagined them staring right at me. I immediately felt sweat pool under my arms and my stomach beginning to churn with nausea. I scurried to the bathroom, making it just in time for the bean and chicken burrito to make its grand debut in my grimy toilet.

I was heaving, and my heart was pounding heavily. *What the hell just happened? Shit!* These were the only words my mind could process. I kept repeating them like a mantra.

I had never killed anyone before. *What did I just do?* I was in full-on hysterical mode now. My brain scrambled to piece information together. You would think that with all the CSI shows I'd watched over the years, I'd have an idea of what to expect when you killed someone. Nope. Time crept. Numbness slithered through my tired body.

White noise rang loudly in my ears, masking any sound that tried to come through. I think I was in shock. I became paralyzed by the overwhelming, life-changing reality of the situation. Suddenly, I heard a buzzing vibration. A cell phone ringing on the kitchen counter broke the chilling silence. It was Petra's. The jarring tone snapped me out of my stupor, and I raced to see whose name came up on the caller ID: UNKNOWN.

It had to be the person Petra had asked to bring the car around. I hastily answered. "What?" I gruffly spoke, trying to mimic Petra's voice. The caller must have realized it wasn't Petra and quickly hung up. *Damn.* Seconds later, I heard the jarring sound of squealing tires outside. I rushed to the front window to see the back of a vintage Mercedes 250 SL turning the corner. I hurled the phone into the kitchen garbage and ran back to my room. I stopped in the doorway, examining what I began to think of as the "crime scene."

Crimson-colored blood formed streams along the floorboard. Petra's eyes were still open. Resting my hands on the door frame, I started freaking out. *Holy cannoli, what am I going to do with a dead Petra on my bedroom floor? I should dial 911. No wait, the police will arrest me, won't they? But it was self-defense. But would they believe me?*

The thought of being trapped in a jail cell for even the briefest period of time had me hyperventilating. I quickly moved on from any feelings of remorse or moral responsibility and into survival mode. Without a backward glance, I began to strategize my next move. I went to my end table and grabbed my MacBook, carefully skirting the blood and Petra's rapidly rigor-mortising body. I sat down at my desk, opened up the laptop to Google, and typed: *"How do you get rid of a dead man twice your size?"*

No, that wouldn't work. I erased that and tried again: *"How to get rid of a dead body"*.

To my surprise and immense relief, there was a ton of search hits. I scrolled through pages and pages of useless articles until I finally stumbled across a forum that seemed more like a community filled with knowledge-able, helpful citizens. Not sleazy criminals.

Patricia C. wrote, *"In this day and age, DNA evidence is everywhere..."*

"Thanks, Patricia," I said sarcastically. It sounded like she was posting a thesis to one of her criminology college essays.

Jenna W. offered, *"Every time I put my comforter in its duvet cover thingy after laundering, I think to myself, what a great way to wrap up a dead body!"* followed by laughing emoji's. My eyes darted to the wool blanket draped over my bed.

Caitlin W. mentioned the good old wood chipper from the movie *Fargo*, but she warned: *"Just make sure to get every bit in the clean-up. Target has some good ones on sale now."*

Hmmm, sounded like Caitlin was going to be

featured on an episode of *The First 48* soon. And besides, I wasn't sure if Target was the solution to my very urgent problem.

Mike C. from Nebraska suggested, *"Pigs will eat anything. With enough time and enough pigs, you are good to go!"*

Maybe I could have taken Mike's suggestion at face value, if only I were on a fucking *farm*. I was in the middle of Los Angeles, who had time for that?

Stephen F. said he would *"...marinate the body and let it slow roast for 10 hours."*

What the hell? I rolled my eyes. I wonder if he and Caitlin knew each other—there really are some weirdos on the internet.

Then Kathy T. chimed in with: *"...walk the L.A. River Bikeway and dump the body there. It will slowly drift downstream in the urban wetlands and eventually get caught on some flora. A walker, biker, or skater will discover it at some point, but it will be too late to identify the body."*

Ha! The L.A. River Bikeway! Why hadn't I thought of that? I closed my laptop and glanced at Petra's body, calculating how I was going to haul his heavy ass out of my apartment—and out of my life—once and for all.

Four exhausting hours later, I arrived back home after carefully dumping Petra in the river. Initially, I'd been worried that the location might be too close in proximity to my apartment, but my worry dissipated as I watched Petra float for a while in the cool water, drifting until his body was sucked beneath the current with the help of some stones I'd put in his pockets.

Back home, I suddenly felt very dizzy and grabbed my emergency stock of Grey Goose out of the freezer. I cracked it open and drank straight from the bottle. The chilled vodka was just what I needed. I took another pull, swallowed, and caught myself smiling. My smile turned into giggling and then uncontrollable laughter. I began laughing so hard, the vodka splashed out of the bottle, dribbled down my shirt, and onto my hands.

I began to entertain the thought that maybe I was a natural at this. It had been a no-brainer for me to kill Petra, even if it was by accident. *I mean, who will miss him?* I justified. His family would miss his paycheck, but there was no love lost there. Although I was nervous, the rest of the process had kind of fallen into place, like using my wool blanket to pull him into the trunk of the car without being seen (thanks, Jenna W.!). It hadn't been as difficult as I thought it would be to throw Petra over the Claremont Bridge and into the water. It was almost peaceful as I watched him bob up and down, eventually floating away.

All I could fathom was the possibility of being looked at like an unsung hero and how Sandy Stronge would be better off in the long run without her slimy, cheating husband. In fact, she might've even hit the jackpot on his life insurance policy! And poor Kyle Milk would now be a free man due to Petra's no-show at court. Better yet, when everyone finally realized Petra was missing, life would be better for a whole slew of people.

What gave me the greatest satisfaction of all was that with Petra Stronge gone, his reality show would soon disappear with him. The more I rationalized, the more I daydreamed that I had just done everyone a huge favor. In the end, the whole country would be better off with one less reality TV show. With that crazy conclusion, I shook my head and sighed. *What a night!*

Grabbing the remote, I clicked on the TV and lo and behold, my favorite movie happened to be on: *Goodfellas.* I thought that was kind of fitting.

3. BOTOX BABE

I COULDN'T PRETEND that I wasn't nervous as I sat deliberating my next move. What would happen when word got out that Petra Stronge was dead, or at the very least, gone missing? This was a huge deal, and I wasn't sure if the public would realize I'd done them a big favor by dumping Petra's ass into the lake of oblivion.

Unfortunately, the momentary delusion I had of myself as a public guardian quickly dissipated under the weight of reality, as I hibernated for days, hardly leaving the couch, causing a permanent dent in the already sagging cushions. Although it was clearly self-defense, I couldn't help but wonder how the trail of Petra's murder might trace back to me.

I kept replaying that night from every possible angle in my head to see if there was anything that could point the police in my direction, but I couldn't find a thing.

After days of racking my brain trying to find any uncovered tracks, I exhaled, believing I was in the clear.

But then, a detail popped into my head: Petra had someone driving the getaway car that night, and that "someone" knew Petra was going to kill me, or at the very least, render me unconscious for a few years. It wasn't just a tiny afterthought; it was a huge detail that could determine my fate. As quickly as I began to relax, I slunk right back into despair and desperation, convinced it was only a matter of time before the mysterious co-conspirator came calling for me.

My rampant thoughts were interrupted by a notification on my cell phone. *The LA Times* banner popped up with the tagline, "Brutally Murdered Body of Reality Show Star Found." Pain twisted in my chest. I immediately clicked the link to the article, which stated that the reality star's body had conveniently washed ashore in the Long Beach area, in the vicinity of Kyle Milk's bungalow. *Holy Shit!* My eyes were glued to the screen. It was being reported that Kyle, who had been expected to lose a major lawsuit to Petra, was considered a "person of interest" in the reality TV star's death and had been taken into police headquarters for questioning. The article went on to say that Kyle's "unfaithful" wife, Andrea, was the one who implicated Kyle as the potential suspect.

In all the wild scenarios I'd imagined while laying low in my apartment, this one hadn't crossed my mind once. Suddenly, my guilt lifted, and I felt my muscles releasing all that pent-up tension. In theory, this new scenario was perfect, except for one glaring fact: an innocent person could be sent to jail for a murder he didn't commit. I was the only person who knew who really killed Petra Stronge. Unless, of course, the mysterious 'someone' who was driving the getaway car for Petra that night came forward and fingered me as the real killer.

A wave of panic drowned me again, so I rushed to the fridge and took a hefty gulp of vodka. "What now?" I sighed into my hands. How could I live freely knowing that Kyle, who I had wanted to vindicate, was now in deeper shit than he was before? There was no way I was going to turn myself in and plead self-defense knowing that the cops had found those rocks in Petra's pockets—the rocks that were supposed to have kept him cemented to the bottom!

I fell into a stupor of sorts. I couldn't recall how many days had passed. But every day, all day, I was hunched in front of my laptop, unshaven, drinking coffee liberally laced with vodka, reading every news article I could find for more details about Kyle's fate and if he would be formally charged. Most importantly, I was scouring for potential facts about where Petra had washed up and possible motives the police had attached to the killing. Then I saw it.

It was an article published by a knock-off TMZ tabloid reporter who did an in-depth "exposé" on the behind-the-scenes antics of the Stronge family, going into great detail about how their real behavior was a far cry from their TV personas. The story had been in the works well before Petra's death, and the tabloid's timing couldn't have been better. It showed the egotistical family as they truly were: the epitome of everything wrong with society. I read the article twice, trying to find any positive angles in the exposé, but there wasn't one good thing said about Petra or his dysfunctional brood. The public, at least for this brief moment in time, hated the Stronges. They had categorized them as a family corrupting America's youth, devoid of any conscience or morals, and worse—they had absolutely no taste.

Soon after the article's publication, Kyle Milk began receiving kudos from the public for killing the reality star that everyone loved to hate. It quoted industry insiders, TV viewers, and even some of Kyle's so-called friends, stating that Petra was always playing with fire and that he deserved what he'd gotten. The media made it seem like Kyle was the valiant hero who saved humanity from the evil Petra.

While I didn't want Kyle to go down for the murder of Petra, part of me also didn't want him getting all the credit and glory for saving America from one more wretched-season of *Being Stronge*. Yes, I realize I was being incredibly petty, not to mention more than a little irrational. After all, I was practically in a fetal position about the possibility of going to jail, and then, in the blink of an eye, I was bitching and moaning that I should be the one in the limelight. The irony does not escape me now, but at the time, my judgement was sketchy at best.

The article made Sandy Stronge's blood boil, but not for long. Sandy being Sandy, quickly found a way to make the bad press work for her. By promoting herself as a blameless victim, Sandy turned herself into a hot new commodity, opening the door for numerous talk show features. TV wasn't her only media salvation. She also appeared on radio and social media platforms sobbing into her tissues as she shared the anguish she was experiencing because of her loss. She seemed more distraught over the cancellation of *Being Stronge* than she did about her deceased husband. For Sandy, a terrible event had turned into self-promotion gold. In addition to all the interviews and having her picture plastered across every newspaper and magazine, Sandy was in talks to star in a new reality show.

Meanwhile, Andrea Milk continued to perpetuate her role as the lonely and sad soon-to-be divorcé as she waited for Kyle's arraignment. She could go toe-to-toe with Sandy when it came to turning a bad situation into something very good for herself. The insane amount of press coverage on the murder caused the ratings for *Want $um* to skyrocket. It was no surprise really, since both Sandy and Andrea were regulars on the show.

After my weeks of research, my unemployment ran out and I knew I had to get back to work, and fast. I decided to take whatever job I could get, at least until the

heat cooled down. When the union finally called and
gave me an opportunity on the show *Primed Minister,* I
wasn't in any position to turn it down.

Primed Minister was a typical reality show (what else?)
that starred ex-pastor Justin Prime, who had turned in his
collar and left the church to be with the woman he loved,
a stripper named Better Luck. By all accounts, the Primes
were a happy couple throughout the years and had three
grown children. The oldest was Peter, age 34, who had
been married for 7 years to his wife June. Next up was
their daughter Mary, age 31. She was the first woman in
the state of New Jersey to legally marry another woman.
She and her partner Sophia had been together for about
5 years and Mary was now pregnant, but no one was
talking about how or by whom. The youngest was Paul,
age 29, who was married to the very buff Lync Sherman.
Their union was getting even more press than Mary and
Sophia's Immaculate Conception. Paul and Lync were
newlyweds, and it was their relationship that turned the
heads of executive producers and had gotten the show on
the air in the first place.

Paul had a very popular blog entitled: "Straight Talk
from a Gay Man." It had begun as a way to help the
heterosexual community better understand the gay
perspective. It had a so-so following until he started
writing about his ups and downs in the gay dating world.
When he met Lync, Paul would blog and post photos
about their budding relationship on a weekly, sometimes

daily, basis which clicked with the millennial crowd. It wasn't long before it went viral and became a *Sex in the City*-type column for the gay man, turning Paul into a quasi-celebrity. When producers approached Paul with the idea for a reality show and learned the backstory of his family members as well, they knew they had a gold-mine on their hands. And so, *Primed Minister* was born.

The show revolved around the family led by the former pastor and his hot former stripper wife (who had long ago ditched her professional name for the more demure *Paige*) and their children. It depicted the unique challenges facing same sex relationships, and the trials and tribulations that ensue. I wasn't keen on taking the job, and I was quietly hoping the show wouldn't last more than a season or two. But I consoled myself that the Primes couldn't be any worse than the Stronges, plus my rent was past due. So I thought, *Ready or not, Primed Minister, here I come.*

4. SUCKER PUNCH

FORTUNATELY, I was settling in smoothly on the set of *Primed Minister.* I was glad to be working with Greg, my best friend and fellow grip. He had a wild demeanor that could comically help even my anxieties. Greg was the hurricane in our friendship, while I was the more conservative one. Together, we were a team.

It was my third week on the new job when the storm clouds started forming. I still couldn't escape Petra, even if by association. Apparently, Greg had gotten word that Andrea Milk was looking for me and planned to stop by the set. I thought, *Oh boy, what the hell does she want?* Then it hit me—of course she wanted to see me! Andrea knew that I knew she and Petra had been doing the "nasty," and she needed me to stay quiet.

My palms started to sweat and I panicked. I decided to beat her to the punch and picked up my cell. I had to call her before she had a chance to just show up and corner me without warning. There was no telling what the crazy bitch might do.

"Hello?" Andrea answered after a few-rings.

"Hello...is this Andrea?" I asked as innocently as I could.

"Yes. Who is this?" Andrea asked.

I hesitated. "It's Marc Henderson. I hear you wanted to speak with me."

There was the briefest of pauses. Then Andrea's voice came back, "Oh! Yes. Marc, I'm so glad you called. I have a few things I wanted to talk to you about, if that's okay?" she said with a syrupy sweet voice. "You know, well, I just feel so lost and confused. I was hoping I could come by your place and talk to you about it. How would tonight be?" she paused, expecting a positive reply.

"Sure, but wouldn't it be a lot easier if we just met on the set sometime?" I was stalling for time and was hoping to grab some details she might accidentally let loose.

"Oh, you know how fast rumors can start! With everything going on, I don't need that kind of publicity right now." *Who's she kidding? If Andrea had any kids, she'd sell 'em in a heartbeat if it meant even five more minutes of publicity.*

"I think it would be better to discuss this in private," she continued.

"Well, sure Andrea, I guess that'd be okay. You can stop by my place around 7:30 tonight, if that works for you. You know where I live, right?" I asked.

"Yes—" she paused and caught herself short "—I mean, yes, 7:30 works for me. But no, I don't know where you live."

I tried to remain calm and played along, "I'm in the third apartment complex building in Canoga Park. Number 304. See you then," I said as we hung up.

Now I had a few more ideas twirling in my head. At the very least, Andrea needed to nip any talk of her and Petra's relationship—if you could even call it a relationship, given her ex was a person of interest in a murder. Or maybe she knew of Petra's little surprise visit to my house. Or, worse yet, maybe she was in on Petra's plan to silence me. Whatever the reason, Andrea needed to distance herself from anything that could be related to Petra. The $64,000 question was: how far would she go? She was one cool customer—just ask poor Kyle. Thanks to her deceit, he was sitting in a cell, worried about getting measured for a nifty new orange jumpsuit.

I had to be careful and cautious. Andrea could turn out to be more of a monster than Petra ever was. As crazy as Andrea was, it wouldn't be surprising if she gave Nancy Pelosi a run for her money.

The doorbell buzzed right at 7:30. I had spent the few hours leading up to her visit going through all the possibilities, hoping I was prepared for anything she might throw at me—literally and figuratively. I opened the door and there she was, looking very different off-screen than how I usually saw her on set. She was wearing faded, figure-hugging jeans and a hooded grey sweatshirt. She had on very little makeup, except for the mascara that was running down her cheeks. *Nice touch, those tears.* She may have been "crying," but she still looked pretty damn good—which was not a good thing for me. Women like Andrea had always been my downfall. I was constantly blindsided by good-looking women. Even with her fake tears, enhanced chest, and Botoxed who-knows-what-else, I had to stay focused.

She quickly brushed past me and landed in a heap on my couch, sniffling and giving her all to the "woe is me" act. I pulled up a chair and sat across from her. "Are you alright?" I asked, trying my best to show concern.

While Andrea dabbed at the corners of her eyes, trying for some well-practiced composure, she was surreptitiously looking at the burns made by Petra's cigarette on my coffee table. As she reached for another tissue, she fumbled and knocked her purse over, spilling its contents onto the floor: a compact, assorted lipsticks, a Bic lighter, a sticky note pad, and tons more "girl stuff."

I bent down to grab whatever had rolled under the chair I was sitting on. And lo and behold, there—snuggled right up against my foot—was a freakin' syringe! Andrea stopped mid-sniffle, her eyes becoming big as saucers. As I sat back up, gingerly holding the syringe, I shot her a *"what the hell?"* look. She rushed to snatch it from me, then quickly scooped everything back into her bag and clipped it shut.

"Oh, Marc. *Please* don't tell anyone about my little secret," Andrea said, in a hurry to explain. "You know what the papers would do with a story like this. Oh, and don't get the wrong idea! That syringe is not filled with any of those horrible drugs. It's just a little Botox, that's all. Harmless, right? Women my age have it rough. I mean, you know how cruel the camera can be. And if this got out, I'd be the butt of even more jokes on the set!"

The crew had regularly joked that you could never tell if Andrea was mad or happy, because her mouth couldn't move very far in either direction. I had never paid much attention to their snide comments, chalking it up to the typical gossip you hear on any set. But now, as I took a really good, close look at her face, their comments seemed true—she really did use too much Botox. Inwardly, I relaxed and realized the pendulum had just swung a little in my direction.

While she slid across the couch to get closer to my chair, she gave me one of those adorably sweet, cat-eyed innocent looks she'd perfected as a model. "I didn't know what to do, Marc," she said. "All this unbelievable mess— I'm under so much stress and pressure! I mean, who can I trust? Petra's been killed, Kyle's been identified as a possible suspect, and it's been a constant battle with Kyle in divorce court. Every thought I have, every move I make —it's all over the media! But then I thought, I'll go to Marc—I can be myself with him, share my worries and concerns and not worry about it getting out. I mean, I came to you because, well...I know I can trust you since you kept the little secret about Petra and me hush-hush."

She batted her eyelashes at me. I didn't dare move a muscle. *Well, in for a penny, in for a pound.* "No worries, Andrea. So, what's the news you had to come all this way *back* to my place to tell me?" I slipped in, figuring what the hell, it was time to cut to the chase and see if she took the bait.

"*Back* to your place?" she repeated back to me, doing that puzzled look pretty well.

She stalled, taking her time as she removed the compact mirror and a tissue from her purse. She carefully wiped off the mascara from her face. I watched intently, waiting patiently to see what was next. Suddenly, as if a thundercloud had moved across her face, she looked deadly serious as she tossed her compact back into her purse, this time closing it with force. I thought I was watching a cut from the movie *Sybil,* the one about a woman with a multiple-personality disorder who had 16 people crowded inside her brain. That had been scary, but not as scary as the abrupt change in Andrea.

"Well, Marc. Let's cut to the chase, shall we? *I know who killed Petra.*"

I froze. She was all business now. She glared death into my soul, giving me the evil eye, or "malocchio," as my Italian grandmother would say. It chilled my spine. Then, just as suddenly, Andrea shifted gears and launched into her well-rehearsed sob story of how Kyle had abused her and that she was glad he was in jail. My God, this woman changed personas fast—I had no idea where she was going with this, or which "Andrea" would pop out next.

"I'm glad Kyle's behind bars," she said. "That's where he belongs. And you know, everyone knew he had it in for Petra from the start. So you're off the hook Marc and I'm free. It's a win-win for both of us, don't you think?" she said very matter-of-factly.

The tears had been turned off and she morphed back into full Ice Queen mode. There it was. Out in the open. Andrea knew that I'd killed Petra, regardless of it was accidental or not. But, she wanted to pin it on Kyle to get him out of her life once and for all. Narcissistic results were all she cared about. This meeting was just another business transaction for her. Andrea was telling me, in no uncertain terms, that she would let Kyle take the blame and keep me out of it. *But at what price?*

"It's a win-win," Andrea repeated with a sly smile. "Don't you agree, Marc?"

This conniving and deranged bitch was tossing aside a guy like Kyle, who everyone knew had *never* laid a hand on her, for three reasons. First, for a sleazy affair with that scumbag Petra. And second, as an easy way to get rid of him, the whole divorce process mess, and take all his money. And lastly, for the publicity and another shot as a TV star.

My long-neglected conscience finally made an appearance. *So, it's the kettle calling the pot black, eh?* Yes, I was responsible for letting Kyle rot in prison for a bit. But at least I *felt* badly about it. Unfortunately, I had no ace up my sleeve, so the mutual benefit from letting Kyle take the fall was crystal clear to both of us. Andrea wanted a new life; I wanted to stay out of prison. We both knew she was lying about everything, but if I didn't cooperate with her, I'd have a lot more to lose and would be royally screwed. Yet I didn't want to roll over so conveniently. Somewhere down this slippery slope, Andrea would just as effortlessly throw me under the bus as she had with Kyle if she (or one of her other personalities) ever felt threatened.

So, I decided upon a new tactic. I placed my hands on the chair's arm rests, supporting myself as I stood up and walked over to the garden sliding door, opening it and leaving it slightly ajar. I walked back into the kitchen to open a drawer and removed a picture of Petra's phone that I had taken before disintegrating it into a million pieces. I had known that his phone was the last thing I needed to get caught with. But I'd also known that having a photo of the text message his accomplice had sent might come in handy.

I paused for dramatic affect and tossed it onto the coffee table, where it landed right next to the cigarette burns. I watched her intently as she looked at the screen-shot. She was thinking hard, trying to formulate a response. Saying nothing, she looked up at me.

"So, you think I killed Petra," I began, "and I think you

were outside when Petra broke into my house. So far, Even Steven. But you also knew Petra was going to kill me, and you were the getaway driver, which makes *you* an accomplice in a murder that didn't go as planned. You also probably figured that any evidence of your affair with Petra would never come to light with me out of the way, right?"

I leaned towards her. She was still looking at me, her eyes turned into narrow slits. She was seething. "That's *one* story, you little shit," Andrea hissed, "but it's not the story I would tell!"

The changes back and forth between lovable airhead and Ice Queen was making me dizzy—if only her TV viewers could see her now. Andrea's voice brought the temperature in the room way down, but I wasn't about to flinch.

"You can't prove shit, Andrea, since you'll only implicate yourself if you breathe a word to anybody. As for me, I can tell the world about you and Petra and how you set up your poor chump of a hubby for murder, which the newspapers would devour. So, I think we both have a few bargaining chips now, don't we?"

I stood, feeling a little surer of myself now. Andrea went from looking confident, to confused, to stunned, all in mere seconds. Before she could say anything, I went on, "I'll tell you what. Let me think about my options and I'll get back to you tomorrow."

With that, I quickly scooped Andrea off my couch and

hustled her out the front door before she knew what was happening. Then I bolted the door and double-checked the lock. She was one very scary person, or *persons*. But I was satisfied up to a point with how it had played out. She wasn't holding all the cards anymore *and* she might've been even a little scared. For my part, I needed to keep my cool and play my cards to my best advantage. I mimed a basketball hoop shot with a three-pointer at the buzzer. *It's a 3-pointer and the crowd goes wild!*

Much later that evening, getting ready for bed, I replayed the scene with Andrea over and over in my head. No way would she try to screw me now, since I could blow her out of TV Land with a few well-planned leaks to the tabloids. With any luck, *she'd* be sitting in a jail cell instead of Kyle. Sweet. The media would eat her alive. I let out a chuckle as I pictured the headlines: "*Botox Bimbo Sours Milk.*" That night I fell asleep like a baby for the first time in weeks.

Sometime after midnight, I woke to a whiff of some sickly-sweet perfume. The scent was all too familiar, all too recent. *Andrea!* As I bolted up in bed, I could see the faint outline of Andrea in her hooded sweatshirt standing at the bottom of my bed with her arm outstretched. A scene from *Kill Bill* with Uma Thurman flashed through my mind. But I shook out of that thought fast, because Andrea was not only beautiful, she was a kick-boxer and a pretty damn good one at that.

My instincts took over and I frantically slipped off the

bed to the floor. No good—she was quicker and more awake, and she was instantly on top of me. I felt her overpowering me since, well, I hadn't been to a gym in forever and she had muscles like steel. Unbidden, a picture suddenly came to mind: years ago, People magazine had photographed her kickboxing in a mini skirt, her thighs the size of a pole vaulter's.

Andrea had something gripped tightly in her right hand and when she pinned me to the floor, she put her knee firmly in my crotch and grabbed my jugular. Headlights from a passing car showed a glint of a syringe. *Uh-oh.* I was pretty sure this was no Botox. As I tried to wriggle free, I managed to throw her off balance long enough to scramble towards the bedroom door where my trusty Slugger stood.

In what seemed like slow-motion Déjà vu, I grabbed the Slugger and swung with all my might. The bat made contact with the side of Andrea's head with a horrifyingly familiar crack. Andrea went limp. The syringe slipped from her hand, landing on the stained floor right next to her. And like Petra, she dropped like a rock.

Then, there was only silence. I leaned heavily against the bedroom door, trying to catch my breath. All I could do was watch her blood flow, crimson rivers seeping deeply into my carpet.

Are you fucking kidding me?! My mind raced, thoughts swirling. I thought my head was about to explode. I couldn't form a coherent thought, but somehow my brain remembered I had been here before and sent me straight to auto-pilot. I had to get rid of yet *another* body, just as I had with Petra. But I couldn't do it the same way. Or could I? Why not? Same river. Same game plan. It may not have worked the first time, but with Andrea's smaller size, and using a couple of concrete-filled bricks instead of stones, surely her body would get well past Long Beach before she got snagged on any debris in the river, wouldn't it? Who knew, if I was really lucky, she would stay hidden in the water for a very long time.

Three very long hours later, exhausted, I crawled back into bed. My Slugger was cleaned and standing at attention next to the bedroom door. There was no sleeping like a baby this time. I gazed at the ceiling, grateful there weren't any more predators popping up. I felt depressed, confused, and scared out of my mind. *What the hell am I doing? Who am I?* It had all happened too smoothly. Too cleanly. And the most alarming part of it all was that I had never thought of any other option but to grab the Slugger and swing like DiMaggio. I couldn't turn away from what I had done. Maybe it was time for me to face who I had become.

5. LOSING MY GRIP

OVER THE NEXT FEW DAYS, I became a complete hermit again. I took a leave of absence from work and glued myself to the TV, sitting and scrolling through as many news articles as I could. I just knew that, at any minute, my guilt would be splashed across the headlines: *"Grip Loses His Grip!"* or *"Reality Show Showdown!"* I was sweating so much, I felt like what my menopausal mother must have felt like during one of her hot flashes she'd always complained about. In short, I was a total wreck.

Suddenly, a notification popped on my screen. I had subscribed to all kinds of news and gossip sites waiting for any inside scoop, and there it was! My eyes landed on a headline that read: *"Want $um Star Gets Hers?"*

The article speculated on the highly suspicious disappearance of a yet another reality TV star, following so closely on the heels of another. It hinted none too subtly that the two murders were linked. And, as before, there were vast numbers of people commenting on how the world would be better off without *Want $um* on air. Not to mention that viewers didn't want or need another narcissistic, two-timing bimbo like Andrea parading around on television.

The article didn't seem to be concerned over Andrea's well-being or whereabouts. No colleagues or family and friends had come forward to pray for her safety. No, it was Andrea's turn to be raked over the coals by a very fickle public. Wherever her final resting place was (and I assumed it had to be in a pretty warm climate), she'd be thrilled with the obscene amount of publicity—good or bad—that was coming her way.

I scanned through the article a few more times and was struck by the public consensus that no one really cared about Andrea's (or, for that matter, Petra's) well-being. Then it came to me: I hadn't just killed two reality stars, I might've been killing *reality TV* itself! Without intending to, my desperate acts had affected ratings in a way no one had expected. The tide of public opinion was turning, and the "good-riddance" attitude extended not only to these so-called celebrities and their bad behavior, but to reality TV in general. This sentiment hit producers where it hurt the most: their holy grail of ratings, which translated to money—lots and lots of money. I did a quick Google search and learned that several shows were losing point shares every week. Without any forethought or planning, I was finally getting what I had wanted all along...the end of reality TV!

This unexpected but very welcome demise of reality TV was like a jolt of adrenaline to my system. I rallied from the black hole I'd sunken into and was back in the game with a renewed sense of purpose. At the moment, there was literally no evidence that I needed to worry about. I felt the weight of the world come off my shoulders. Even returning to work on *Primed Minister* felt like a much-needed change of scenery. But somewhere buried in the far corners of my mind, I must've known these feelings of relief, optimism, and security would eventually run their courses.

Rumors were rampant on set the next morning, as the previous night's news broadcast led with the story that the police had released Kyle Milk due to insufficient evidence. The crew shared common feelings that Kyle was innocent all along, and co-workers were placing numerous bets on who the killer might be, and more salaciously, which reality star would be the next target. Still, there was a general unease and tension on set, as everyone realized a psychotic killer was still on the loose.

On social media, a Facebook survey entitled *"How to Get Away with Murder"* was even making the rounds. *How sick is that?* I thought. Then, I sobered immediately, vividly remembering that I'd been the one who'd started this whole mess in the first place.

While blameless Kyle had spent months stuck in

some cold, invasive jail cell, I had remained untouchable when it came to laying blame for Andrea's disappearance. And while I was relieved to see an innocent man go free, the police had since intensified their investigation, which meant I still needed to keep under the radar.

I halfway convinced myself that if I kept my head down and my mouth super-glued shut, the dust would eventually settle and the whole thing would blow over. So, I focused on what I did best: working as a grip.

After work, I'd go home and fall into a heap on my couch. I'd surf channels I'd never even watched before. But one night, I landed on a show called *Dexter*. *Dexter* was about a sociopathic killer who curbed his blood lust by killing only people who had committed their own full-blown murder for no reason other than the sake of killing and greed. Dexter spent his sun-drenched days on a Miami CSI crew helping to solve murders, while moon-lighting at night committing them—all for the greater good, of course.

The protagonist Dexter really caught my attention. Maybe in some sort of bizarre way I was like him! Maybe I was doing the world a favor by effortlessly taking out the bad guys of reality TV. It reminded me of Batman defending Gotham City from the Joker. All I lacked was a mask and cap. Okay, maybe I lacked the six-pack abs too, but I convinced myself that was just a technicality. By day, I hid behind the bland colorless life of a camera grip, but by night, I was the self-proclaimed champion of the public. I was ridding society of these greedy, narcissistic low-lives! I gave in to this wild delusion with glee. I immediately began plotting how I could bring justice to the sick world of reality TV. As the saying went, killing was definitely not the answer. But unfortunately, in my case, killing both Petra and Andrea had been *my* answer.

6. ONLY THE FAKE MAKE IT

ONLY A FEW WEEKS had gone by and already I was fed up with the job on *Primed Minister*. I tried my best to deal with phony celebrities who were treated like royalty, but who in no way deserved the honor. It didn't take long for their plastic personas to get my blood boiling, yet I knew I needed to hold it together. I couldn't ignore them in order to keep my sanity, but I'd have to in order to keep this god-awful job.

After each work day, I couldn't wait to get home to my refrigerator filled with ice-cold beer. It was the home-made happy hour I couldn't get enough of. My nightly ritual consisted of making a beeline to the fridge as soon as I got home, grabbing a beer, and sitting down in front of my laptop. I'd take a deep breath to steady myself, then I'd start scouring the headlines. By this time, the Kyle Milk story had fallen off the front page, relegated now to the lonely back page of the *LA Gazette* and was dimming in the public's memory, just like the Andrea and Petra stories. Speed-reading as much as possible, I found a few articles about some concerned citizens who were afraid for their lives with a "crazed serial killer" in their midst. I smiled at some others who commented that the deaths of these "pathetic posers" were a study in karma. What goes around, comes around. It never fails. There were even some folks who depicted me as a lone anti-hero, lurking in the star-studded shadows of Hollywood, ridding the city of its "trash." There was even an online community forum started by a strange lady named Adele R., who thought the killer was "...a total hottie, yet a sensitive guy who needed a girlfriend." Who knew I'd have groupies sticking up for me?

One night, after closing my laptop, I discovered the media websites still seemed to miss the most crucial point, that *reality TV was a cancer. Period. Stop.*

Since my second career choice was to be a writer, well, a screenwriter, I figured this was a chance to test my skills as an "auteur" and draft a letter to some high-profiled editor about the lack of sensibility, common decency, and most of all, REALITY across the entire reality TV landscape. I mean, someone had to point out the obvious—why not me?

One of the ways I got my creative juices flowing was to simply watch reality TV. I'd watch it while cooking my ever-so-bland nighttime meals. Can you even call nuking a frozen pizza for five minutes cooking? Old *Jersey Shore* reruns had me screaming obscenities and throwing a perfectly good can of Coors Light at the screen. And *Real Housewives of Beverly Hills* gave me an actual migraine. But no show sent me over the edge quite like *Keeping up with the Kardashians.* It stopped me in my tracks, and more often than not, put me off food altogether.

The Kardashian-Jenner family invaded every home, turning viewers into voyeurs who lusted after their power, fame, and material possessions—not to mention all the cosmetic surgery they'd lied about not having. I started thinking of *Keeping Up with the Kardashians as Throwing Up with the Kardashians.*

But as much as I loathed it, the show was a great incentive for my writing process. My letters got started, but I scrapped most. I eventually crafted a final draft and emailed it to a few targeted newspapers and online news sources. Nothing happened. Zero, zilch, zip. No responses, no standard rejection letters, nada.

Crap. What was I missing? Maybe I lacked conviction. Did I not have the hard facts to back up my arguments? I quickly began gathering "ammo" from published articles and online news reports about the troubling effects of reality TV on a crucial population: the millennials.

Then it was time for more research. I'd watch rerun after rerun, trying to dissect the core of the show's appeal or what I liked to call "pathological mass psychosis." *Keeping Up with the Kardashians* heavily emphasized being famous solely for the sake of being infamous. A sex tape goes viral—*oops!*—and that's all it took, folks. How convoluted and distorted was that? Yet the show brought in very high ratings for the network, which led to the creation of spinoffs, including *Kourtney and Kim Take Miami, Khloe and Lamar, Kourtney and Khloe Take the Hamptons,* and let's not forget *Dash Dolls.*

Anything with Kardashians in the title became an obsession for so many women, with the majority being teenagers and naive early twenty-somethings, who would gladly forfeit exploring who they were or could be, to model themselves after the K crew. The more I thought about that sad fact, the more I despised them.

Instead of a young female generation growing up secure and confident with aspirations of becoming the next Sally Ride or Madame Curie, they chose to worship on the altar of unpromised fame. A fame that was attached to having a personal stylist, personal shopper, and doing the fashionista routine, complete with a boutique-sized closet of clothes you didn't need.

Suddenly, being a reality TV star was on par with winning the lottery, or becoming an instant "hero." Once I slipped down this reality rabbit hole, I furiously started drafting a new letter.

"Fame is *poison.* Who the hell wants to be a Kardashian?" I glanced at the TV and then typed some more. But I soon hit *delete* and sat there staring at a blank screen. I went back to reading more data. One report suggested that reality TV was, to a certain degree, employing subliminal message techniques to influence viewer behaviors and attitudes. Made sense to me. After all, the reality shows were exposing celebrities who were sociopaths, just like Petra Stronge and Andrea Milk. And the masses loved it. They craved it. It dawned on me that maybe, just maybe, the networks were *purposefully* looking for every crazed C-list actor, steroid-hopping ex-athlete, and alcoholic socialite they could find. But it didn't stop there. No sir.

They beat the bushes in Appalachia. They went down every back road in America to find some wannabe trying to scour local media. They desperately needed to find a nobody and turn them into a somebody, until they found the next somebody. All those nine-to-fivers who were stranded in their cubicles all day would rush home to see if they could find some new adventure to vicariously live through. It didn't matter if it had hijinks at a trailer park, or moonshiners on the run from the local police. Reality TV was an opiate of distraction for a society heading down the screwed-up path of moral bankruptcy. This had to stop. People needed to see the truth. And I needed to pull out all the stops. My earlier diatribes about the evils of reality TV didn't lead to one response. So, I decided to step up my game.

To: the Los Angeles Daily News

Dear Editor-in-Chief,

I am writing you regarding the-largest, fastest-growing national product known as reality TV. And like its predecessor cocaine, it's just as profitable, dangerous, and addictive. Before you laugh at this comparison, think of the networks that distribute these shows as a cartel, the Hollywood Cartel. They offer what on the surface appears to be something fun and harmless— an opportunity to indulge in socially, certainly not anything a person could get hooked on.

But it's time to face facts: isn't it obvious that nothing about reality TV is real, and that every episode is scripted down to the last detail? More importantly, not only is the cartel offering up this hot mess of bad behavior to the lunatic fringe, it's also rewarding that behavior with fame, money, and power. In effect, it's saying to a very young and highly influential population that being bad is good—no, it's great. Sadly, it appears that the viewing public loves nothing more than to watch this garbage, week in and week out, rather than be informed and actually do something of their own.

Did you know that 47% of teenage girls consider

watching countless reality TV episodes to be one of their primary "activities," instead of being on a team sport or a member of a school club? Young women are glued to the TV (or phone, iPad, whatever—take your pick) day and night, comparing their own hair, nails, and fashion to that of the celebrities they watch. They do this instead of going to the beach with friends, volunteering, or sitting down with a good book.

Were you also aware of these troubling statistics? Teens who watch reality TV on a regular basis have low self-esteem, are more insecure, have a higher incidence of bullying, and experience more emotional highs and lows than what is considered "average" in their age group. Not to mention the disturbing number of abusive relationships they are associated with. Is there even one redeeming attribute of the shows that are turning an entire generation into vapid zombies? The facts suggest not. Then why do you constantly plaster these poor excuses for celebrities all over your news features rather than highlighting real-life and meaningful issues?

Could it be that you get some sort of kickback for supporting the atrocities the networks are committing? To that point, if somebody decided to take out the whole lot of loser reality dimwits by whatever means necessary tomorrow, most people would probably give that person a medal.

Don't believe me? Everyone not living in a cave has heard about the Petra Stronge and Andrea Milk cases. If the networks were made to understand that by putting this trash on TV, they are in part responsible for people getting killed, would they stop airing such immoral and mind-numbing schlock? Which, in turn, would enable news outlets like yours to concentrate on real news and real people, gaining back some credibility in the process? Not a chance in hell. Every network exec would run over their own mother to keep those ratings up. My recommendation? Death to reality TV!

Signed,
A Concerned Citizen

7. WHO'S PLAYING WHO?

I WAS *this close* to submitting my "new and improved" letter. But after proofreading it a couple of times, I quickly came to my senses. I could only shake my head in disbelief. With one click of a button, the police could've hauled my sorry ass off to jail. *What was I thinking?* All because of my skewed sense of righteousness—so I decided to put my letter writing on hold for a while.

Since I stopped pouring my energy into writing letters, I tried to keep myself and my mind occupied by working diligently on *Primed Minister*. But it was the same old routine—delusional reality stars thinking they were so important—and I had to struggle to keep a grip (no pun intended) on my frustrations. It felt like a recurring nightmare, as one day exhaustedly blurred into the next.

Then, late one Thursday morning, things went from bad to worse. I had downed one too many energy drinks early in the day—to counteract another late night of obsessing over getting caught and brainstorming how I could stay out of jail—and I desperately needed to take a leak. But as I entered the nearest restroom, a sound stopped me in my tracks: the unmistakable sound of frenzied-sex coming from the last bathroom stall. *Ugh. Is nothing sacred anymore?* I thought to myself, rolling my eyes in disgust. Not only did I have to piss, but I was actually *pissed* because now I had to track down another bathroom because some horny idiot couldn't keep it in his pants long enough to find a nearby Motel 6.

I turned to leave but was caught by a movement reflected in the mirror. It was Lync, the oh-so-happily hubby of the gay son, struggling to zip up as he quickly left the stall. Needless to say, he seemed quite happy and content. I turned again to leave, but another sound, this time of the stall door slamming, kept me frozen to the spot. I braced myself to see Lync's hubby, Paul, join him at the sink when, Stella, the gorgeous red-headed woman who regularly catered lunch for the crew, emerged instead. I couldn't believe my eyes—a woman!? Not his husband or even a token boy toy groupie, but Stella? All I could do was shake my head in disbelief. *So, Lync likes to play both sides of the street*, I thought matter-of-factly. *What a con.*

My mind flashed on the conundrum of whether a gay man having sex with a woman was considered cheating —or did it only count if it was with another man? I shook the thought away and refocused. This would turn into an extremely awkward situation if I didn't move fast.

I tried to escape before they saw me and I nearly made it, but Lync caught sight of me as he looked up from washing his hands, and it was too late. Things went from bad to worse, because as soon as Lync realized he and Stella had an audience, he moved in a flash and grabbed me from behind by my collar.

"Marc, what do you think you're doing? Were you spying on me?!" Lync demanded, acting like a petulant school kid who thought rules were for everyone else.

Before I could plead my case, a memory came rushing back, unbidden, as I recalled nearly the same words from Petra the night he died. I froze as if I had seen Petra reincarnated. My heartbeat pulsed through my veins. Busted yet again, in a perpetual Groundhog Day moment. *How do I get into these situations? Will this torture ever end?!* I silently asked the heavens.

I stalled for time, trying to think carefully on my feet. I slowly rotated and turned to face the fury of the duo. I made sure not to say one word. However, Stella, whom I could never have wild fantasies about again, hastily arranged her clothing and shot out of there like a bat out of hell. *Damn. The gay guy got her first. Where was my game?*

And then there were two. I warily looked Lync in the face, expecting for him to knock me shitless, verbal or otherwise. But his anger and bravado disappeared. In fact, with Stella gone, he looked downright nervous, like he was about to curl up and cry. "Hey, can't a man experiment occasionally? I mean, no harm done, right?" He tried to laugh, giving me a nudge.

He was going for the *we-guys-gotta-stick-together* approach. I immediately relaxed, sensing where this was headed. It was a soap opera unfolding before my eyes. "Listen Marc," he pleaded, "I'm in a bad spot here. Please don't say anything. Otherwise people will talk, and the ratings will bomb, and we'll be dropped from the network." He was nearly stuttering now.

I almost laughed, but the comic relief quickly faded because I felt myself bubbling over with anger and rage. I tried to choose my words wisely, but I couldn't help myself. "Really, Lync?" my voice rose, "You're not worried about your husband, or that you were cheating on him—and with *Stella* of all people? All you care about is the show and those stupid ratings! What's the matter with you?"

After seeing that I wasn't dismissing his actions, Lync dropped his friendly approach and changed tactics. "What are you, dumb or just incredibly stupid? This shit goes on all the time. You know it, I know it, and everyone else knows it too! Who are you to be holier-than-thou? Give me a break!" He was breathing hard now. Either he needed to do some cardio, or his guilt had his heart rate rising to a dangerous level.

"I'm not the one who's intelligence-challenged here,

Lync. Let me put this to you as simply as I can. Be a fucking *man!* Who gives a shit about you being gay or straight? Just be a stand-up guy for a fucking change. You know, the kind who has values and won't sell himself out for the almighty dollar?"

Enough was enough and I didn't want to face him anymore. But when I turned to leave, Lync grabbed my arm, again trying to plead his case. "You're right. Come on. Let me clear this up, will you? You keep quiet and I'll tell Paul and set everything straight. I mean, Stella's nothing to me, really nothing. Just a jump off, ya know? Anyways, that whore came on to me!"

So much for his sincerity. He was already twisting things around to dump all the blame on Stella. Obviously, he hadn't heard one word I said.

"Lync, you wannabe stars think nothing of other people, only of your pathetic selves. You will use any and everybody if it satisfies your needs and that insecure ego. You're all cream of the crop, Grade A shitheads as far as I'm concerned."

I wrenched my arm out of his grasp and headed to find another bathroom. After I found another, thankfully empty bathroom, I returned to the set, and started thinking back on the scene I had painfully witnessed. Even though I was initially shocked, I was already fairly numb to what made reality TV stars do the crazy stuff they did. I shrugged it off and tried to move on. I figured

Lync was contributing to a new medical term in the *Diagnostic and Statistical Manual of Mental Disorders*:

"Alter-telepath. A condition that affects reality TV stars who become delusional and are dangerous to themselves and the general public. There's no cure or antidote other than a total lobotomy or a permanent dip in deep, cold water."

Reality TV stars were their own cheap brand of "One Flew Over the Cuckoo's Nest," and anyone who was ever unfortunate enough to work on a Hollywood set could and would testify to that in a heartbeat.

The crew set up the lighting for the next scene between Lync and Paul—the one where they would openly talk about finally becoming a family and adopting a baby from a foreign country. I silently said a prayer for that poor baby. Then I noticed the sounds of what seemed to be an argument and looked to its source. Behind the set monitors, Lync and Paul were having a shouting match. Paul gave Lync a much-deserved hard shove and burst into noisy, melodramatic tears like a three-year-old boy being scolded by his daddy. Paul tossed his highly hair-sprayed hair and stormed off set.

Oh boy, I thought, wincing. Lync's face was cherry red and his eyes bulged, his throbbing veins running down his forehead. Everyone on the show knew Lync had a short fuse. Since finding out he was going to be a main character on a reality show, he'd started doing extreme weightlifting to get in poster-boy shape for the camera.

There hadn't been much lead time before the pilot taped, so Lync had supplemented the training with, you guessed it, steroids. A lot of steroids. He'd been overjoyed with the results, but they'd come with some nasty side effects, including serious mood swings. Lync was a walking, talking, muscular ball of anger. Just about anything could blow his fuse. And in this particular moment, Lync was fired up and ready to fight.

His incredible Hulk-like body came barreling my way. There was no place to hide. He scooped me up by the throat and pinned me against the wall like a school bully. I glanced behind him and saw Paul cowered behind the big boom with the crew, watching and soaking it up.

Lync got in my face and hissed so only I could hear: "You just zip your fucking mouth! You hear me, you little asshole? Say one word and you'll never work again. I'll make sure of that."

His face contorted in anger. It was as if he'd need an exorcist at any given moment. "You destroy my show, my marriage, or my reputation, and you will be royally screwed in more ways than you could ever imagine. *Do you fucking understand?*"

Lync couldn't have cared less about Paul or Stella. His only concern was the inevitable fallout if the story got leaked to the press. I knew how freaky and uncontrollable people who use steroids could get, but his wild behavior took the word *scary* to a whole new level. All I could do was nod my head in agreement and look for the nearest exit.

The crowd began to disperse, sensing their entertainment was ending. My heart was beating fast and I could feel my disgust rise when I felt Lync's grip loosen. Something inside me snapped. Maybe Lync's stupidity was catching, because I couldn't seem to stop the words from tumbling out of my stupid mouth.

"What are you? A fucking Arnold Schwarzenegger knockoff? The joke's on you, bud. Nobody gives a rat's ass about *Primed Minister*," I scoffed. "You'll be lucky if you get another six episodes out of this piece-of-crap show before they pull the plug."

I smirked, aiming for nonchalance, but was unsure if I was pulling it off. I stood my ground and waited. Lync started to shake with fury and leaned into my face. Nose to nose. "You naive little prick. You think I care what you think about my show? But since you're so opinionated, here's something you might think about before you go tattle-telling to the press." Paul, sidled up to join Lync, in an apparent show of marital solidarity.

"Word has it that this isn't your first rodeo. You know, being in the wrong place at the wrong time. Am I right, *scumbag?*" Lync poked his sausage finger into my chest. "You breathe one word about this and I'll deliver you to the cops on a silver platter, got it? Whether it's true or not, they come down pretty hard on people like you."

He leaned in a little further, whispering, "Have you

ever seen *Scared Straight*, shithead? I don't think you'd do well in jail, little man." Lync roughly patted my cheek as he smiled. "You'll be someone's bitch by day two. And I don't think you want that, do you?" he said, continuing to poke a burning hole in my chest.

I hated Lync to the core. He let go of my neck and I dropped to the floor. He happily strutted off, leaving me there, gasping for the breath I hadn't realized I was holding in. *What the fuck am I going to do now?*

8. OUT WITH THE OLD

THREE DAYS after Paul and Lync's episode entitled "Looking Through the Cracked House of Glass," the set returned to its usual rhythm. Still, tensions ran a little higher than usual, with new stories circulating that the couple was overly stressed due to a private, undisclosed family crisis. And since many of the crew members had witnessed Lync and Paul taking out their pent-up aggression on me, I was on the receiving end of a shitload of well-meaning, unsolicited advice. I got everything from "Don't pay them attention, they're just looking for sympathy," to "I heard Lync just got tested for herpes. You know Hitler had that, right?"

People were actually telling me not to take Lync's vicious attack too seriously. *Too seriously?* Yeah, right. I'd like to see one of them get attacked by a raging steroid addict and then see what they have to say on the subject.

The only serious thing I wanted to do was get the hell out of there.

You might think that after all the recent turmoil—the accidental killings, the fear of being exposed, the emotional rollercoaster of dealing with crazy reality stars, and the threats on my life—that I should've had already purchased a one-way ticket out of California. But nooo. After catching a bit of Paul's stupidity, I pitched my stake in the ground and was determined to continue with my plan to expose the rapidly growing cancer that was reality TV. I may have gotten distracted from time to time, but I always came back to my most pressing goal: surviving this debauched world of reality television.

I kicked back on my couch, nursing a now lukewarm beer, thinking not only of survival, but also protection. I knew I couldn't conveniently carry around my trusty Louisville slugger like it was a pocket knife. So, I made a decision. I ran to my bedroom, grabbed some well-hidden cash and a few other goodies I had stored for a rainy day, put on my hoodie, and headed out the front door to hail down a cab.

"West Hills, Sherman Ave.," I firmly directed to the cabbie. My hoodie was big enough to (hopefully) cover most of my face. I couldn't afford to not behave discreetly. Without sharing a word throughout the short ride, I quickly thanked him as he dropped me off at the dimly lit corner of Sherman and Topanga Canyon, right in front of a Sher-Way Pawn. I tried to look like I knew what I was doing as the door buzzed and notified the sales clerk that a new customer had arrived.

I examined my surroundings, observing the nooks and crannies of the worn-down store. The place looked like I was stepping back in time. It also confirmed that their reputation for having a personal arsenal of guns was spot on.

"I need a gun," I blurted out as I approached the counter. I internally kicked myself. I had already blown the whole Clint Eastwood cool vibe cover I was going for. *What an idiot! I sound like some raving lunatic.* I calmly slid a fake gun license across the counter, a gift from a former roommate who couldn't pay his half of the rent one month. He'd been a major drug addict, but he'd also been a skilled forger who'd operated a decent hustle making bogus IDs. *Thank God for small favors.*

The pawnbroker was obviously having dinner when I arrived, because I caught a whiff of garlic when he reached for my ID. He had to be anywhere from 70 to 90 years old, and he looked like a cross between Carl Reiner and Rod Steiger. He was a bulky man, with droopy jowls and a voice far too high for his size, as I discovered when he squeaked out a "hello."

"Hello," I responded in kind, trying to keep my head down as much as possible. I could feel his eyes lingering, waiting for me to say something else.

"I'd like to buy a gun," I said as I cleared my throat.

"There was a break-in at my place, and I need some protection."

I tried to sound like I was a man about his business, but I wasn't a very good liar. "Sure, slick. A break-in. Whatever you say," he said, questioning me with his eyes. "So, what kind? I mean, no gun is the same, like no woman is the same. You get what I'm saying?" he said and chuckled, laughing at his little joke, one he probably told all his customers. "What can I show you? Let's take a look."

We both leaned over, gazing through the glass counter. At first, I paused. I was trying to look like I was an educated gun enthusiast. Then I recalled a scene from a TV movie I had worked on a few years back. "How about a 357 Magnum for starters?" I stood up straight, elongating my spine as much as my five-foot-nine body would allow. Looking the pawnbroker straight in the eye, I thought I had impressed him. But he started laughing. Did I really look that lame?

"Go ahead. Make my fuckin' day," he said, giggling again and trying to hold back tears. I laughed feebly, trying to exude nonchalance, but I had obviously failed, because the broker just looked at me pathetically and shook his gray-haired head. "You kids. Sheesh—doesn't anyone remember the good movies anymore?"

Since he seemed to be talking more to himself than me, I kept my mouth shut. He continued, "I don't get those big boys in here too often, but I do have something that's pretty sweet for your little *home protection.*" He winked. "Take a look at this baby."

He fished under the counter and came out with something wrapped in a red velvet cloth. He laid it reverently on top of the counter and unwrapped it. "This baby does whatever you need for home defense. It's a CZ 75 pistol out of the Czech Republic and a semi-automatic with selective fire variants."

Huh? I stared at the burnished black gun on display, in all its glory. All of a sudden, my trusty Louisville Slugger looked like it was from the Prehistoric Age compared to this stealth fighter. It was sleek, smooth, and most importantly, lethal. I could feel my testosterone levels rising just looking at it.

"I tell you," he said assuredly, "this is one of the original 'Wonder Nines.' It even has a staggered-column magazine, all steel construction and a hammer-forged barrel. A piece of fuckin' art. Definitely for a pistol shooter."

He leaned in closer. "It'll get the job done, and then some, without breaking the bank."

I was sold. All I could say was, "I'll take it!"

The broker smiled the smile of a used-car dealer and was probably thinking, *There's one born every minute.*

My wallet was significantly lighter as I walked out of the pawn shop, but I didn't care. I was a new man with some semi-automatic power. I felt so much relief. And truth be told, it put a little swagger in my step. I was feeling a bit like Dirty Harry himself with a new gun tucked neatly into an interior pocket of my jacket. I waved for another cab and went back home.

As the cab made its way down Topanga Canyon, I let my fantasies fly, dreaming of new triumphs and glory: "Superhero Brings a New Kind of Justice to LA." Being too caught up in a sorry man's fantasy, I had no room to think about another, more reality-based headline: "The Pride Goeth Before the Fall."

9. WHEN IN ROME

THE WEEK WENT PAINFULLY SLOW, but finally it was Friday. Normally I'd be excited to hit the routine pub crawl in my neighborhood, but that day I just didn't have the energy. For me, it was day for going straight home to a cold brew and the couch. I needed some major relaxation to shut out the world.

Once the Martini Shot—which is Hollywood slang for the last shot setup of the day—was in the can, the crew couldn't pack up fast enough. I found myself smiling as I saw everyone clapping and rejoicing for their Friday. But suddenly, the cheering had come to an abrupt halt. I looked over the mic-boom stand and saw Lync standing on a chair. Apparently, he was using the Martini Shot as his chance to get the crew's attention. I rolled my eyes, folding my arms in disdain, wondering, *What does this prick want now?*

"Attention! Attention! Everyone, listen up!" Lync said.

He paused, waiting for everyone to quiet down. "Paul and I want to thank you all so much for the fabulous job you've been doing these last couple of weeks." He turned and cheekily smiled at Paul for dramatic effect. "I'm sure it hasn't been easy dealing with us celebrities"—he stuck his finger down his throat to mimic throwing up, as everyone laughed perfunctorily—"so we decided to throw a little par-tay tonight at The Nest!" He shimmied in celebration.

The crew whistled and applauded, happy that they didn't have to settle for a hole in the wall bar for tonight's entertainment. "The Nest" was the name of the new garish mansion Paul and Lync owned in the Hollywood Hills. In the past, they'd mentioned how they wanted to name their home after a theme in nature. I guess "The Nest" was the best those two dodo birds could come up with.

"And...you can bring a plus one!" Lync added, gleefully clapping his hands together. More cheering erupted. "But listen, we have one rule: absolutely no cameras." The crowd groaned. "Come on, no pouting! Don't you remember what happened the last time we threw a party?"

The crowd hooted and hollered like a bunch of banshees in the wild. He was referring to the St. Patrick's Day bash Paul and Lync had hosted some months ago. Most of the night's drunken debauchery ended up on every social media platform you could think of. The night had gotten so wild there were not one, but two, visits from the Hollywood Hills police due to excessive noise and general misbehaving. The network big shots and their advertising partners were decidedly *not* amused after the fiasco went viral.

"So...Caterina, our charming assistant, will be collecting phones at the door, and will return them when you leave. Fair enough?" There was scattered, unenthused applause. "That's more like it. Okay, gates open at 7pm. Ciao!" Lync waved, jumping from the chair.

The crowd began to disperse, and everyone chatted in their respective groups, excited for the evening. It was clear that Lync and Paul had something up their sleeves with this party invite, but for the life of me, I couldn't figure out what. But it didn't bother me, because I had absolutely no intention of going.

I shrugged and proceeded to put the equipment away when I heard someone shout my name in a forcefully excited way. *"Marc!"*

I almost jumped out of my skin at the sound of Lync's voice. I swear he could star in a horror film. "Don't sneak up on me like that!" I snapped, trying not show how nervous I was.

He raised his hands, slowly backing up. "Oh hey, sorry bud! I didn't mean to spook you," he said, poking me jokingly in the arm. "I just wanted to be sure that there were no hard feelings from the other day." He winked. "We're cool, right? I hope you can come tonight so we can put this whole thing behind us. Everyone deserves a little R&R after the dreadfully long week we just had."

He purposely waited, as if he wanted me to reflect on the week. But before I had a chance to form a reply, he chirped, "What do you say?"

Lync's smile had all the charm of a used car salesman. I took another pause as I set the mic-boom stand on the floor. "Look," I said matter-of-factly, "I can't make it tonight. I kind of have plans."

I was hoping he'd take the hint and move on, but no such luck. His face lit up. "Ohhh. Big date, huh?" He waved, snapping his fingers and waving his arm in a big circle like it was the gay code for "Oh look! This lame has got some game!"

"No worries, Mark. Bring her along. She'll have a blast!"

If only he'd known that my "big date" was with my neighbor, lounging on the back deck with a pizza and beer. I nearly smiled as I thought It *would* be interesting to see her cut loose with all "the youngsters" as she liked to call us. I thought about how long I'd have to do this back-and-forth with Lync before I gave in and agreed to go, as we both knew I eventually would. *Oh, what the hell*, I thought, throwing in my white flag.

"Sure, why not? If she's okay with it, we'll stop by," I said.

"Great! I knew you wouldn't hold a grudge," he said, smiling.

He was definitely challenging me with those words and the look in his eyes. Whatever surprise he and Paul were planning, I decided to play along and find out. "*In for a penny, in for a pound,*" my mom had always said. Besides, with Mrs. Fox as my escort she'd keep me away from any trouble they'd cause.

After Lync walked away, I took out my phone and called Audry. I called her for two reasons: one, I wanted to give her a loophole just in case she didn't feel up to such a big event; and two, knowing she was a hardcore party animal back in the day, I knew she'd want some time to "get all dolled up" as she liked to call it.

I ended up giving her the run-down on the invitation, to which she demurely accepted with a "hell, yes!" She quickly inquired if I was comfortable with going. Audrey was one sharp lady, and she remembered how much I groaned and complained about the situation with Lync and Paul during one of our back patio happy hours. She was probably curious as to why I would dare bother spending time with those losers. I tried making up a story about how I wanted to turn the other cheek. But, being the "no bullshit" woman she was, she told me to cut the crap and not to worry, as she would be my bodyguard. I happily exclaimed she had more *cogliones* than both of them put together. She let out a very non-ladylike snort. After agreeing to meet at 6:30pm, we hung up. All I could do was stand there, wondering how the night's festivities would end up with my new bodyguard by my side.

Mrs. Fox and Daisy, her hyper, yappy white bichon, greeted me at her front door at 6:30pm sharp. As the door opened, I nearly dropped my jaw at the sight of Mrs. Fox. I was used to her wearing her usual neon Juicy Couture tracksuit with red Converse sneakers. I wasn't prepared to see the dolled-up Aud. She was rocking a pair of dark designer jeans with a sharp crease down the front, four-inch gold strappy sandals that could be considered lethal weapons in some states, a leopard print blouse cut modestly low (well, modest for her standards), and taste-ful, expensive-looking gold jewelry adorning her neck, wrist, and ears. Not to mention the lilac highlights in her gelled and spiky, cropped hair.

"Gorgeous, right?" she said, running her hands down her still-in-great-shape-at-any-age body, giving me a sly wink. Subtlety was not Mrs. Fox's forte. I gave a low whistle and nod in response as I bent down to pet Daisy, who promptly rolled on her back for a tummy rub, her tongue sticking out in anticipated ecstasy. Audrey gave a hearty laugh that made her earrings jangle. "You think some rich young stud will think I'm a hot cougar?"

All I could do was shake my head and laugh. "You'll have to beat the poor bastards off with a stick." I assured her.

Aud clapped her hands and ordered, "Okay, then—let's get this show on the road!"

I felt my shoulders tense while driving up the mountainous terrain of one of the most luxurious neighborhoods in California, Hollywood Hills. It should've taken thirty minutes for us to arrive at The Nest, but with the crippling L.A. traffic, it took nearly an hour.

We turned up the winding Drive of Mulholland. She recounted to me how she once worked on the film with the same name. She had lived in the hustle and bustle of L.A. for years and knew everything there was to know about this area. After all, she'd spent most of her adult life in the industry. She told me that with its scenic beauty and atmosphere, Mulholland Drive was one of the most traveled roads in the United States. I had to agree that it had earned its reputation, dripping with the rich history of Hollywood.

"The rich and famous in *those* days..." Mrs. Fox detailed, "I'm talking Cary Grant, Marilyn Monroe, Steve McQueen—or, if you need me to make it relatable for you young Folk," she said, smiling, "imagine Denzel Washington, Paris Hilton, or Mark Wahlberg building their palatial homes here, lined up one by one. Each home was more glamorous than the next, AND the parties were outrageous!"

Mrs. Fox adjusted in her seat, gazing out the window. You could tell she was experiencing a wave of nostalgia, recalling happy memories of her youth. She snapped back into reality when I turned into a driveway framed by sixteen-foot iron gates. "Wow," she said.

Mr. and Mr. Prime's humble abode did not disappoint. Their "love nest" was sculpted like no other. Their house was, well, *marble*-ous. Literally. Everything was marble. The columns supporting the iron front gates were marble, the grand arched entryway with its fluted pink columns were marble, the floors, stairs, statues—it was entirely made of marble.

As we made our way up the long and winding driveway, we could see the blazing lights from the party already in full swing. It was no surprise that half the crew already looked like they were three sheets to the wind, even though the sun had just begun to set. And of course, it couldn't be a Hollywood party without a drug deal taking place right in the front yard. I glanced at Mrs. Fox to see her reaction at the sight of the illegal activity, but instead of shock, she wore a big unwavering grin on her face.

Pinching my side, she whispered, "You kids didn't invent drugs you know."

I gripped the steering wheel tighter, feeling a wave of angst build in my chest. After we found somewhere to park, we walked to the front door and waited to be greeted. I peeked through the windows, scanning the crowd for our hosts. My plan was to let Mrs. Fox mingle and have some fun, while I tried to figure out what the hell Frick and Frack were up to. I couldn't believe I was actually in this crazy place. It was like a bad dream.

A couple crew members came out the front door to

join the drug deal, and we took the opportunity to head inside. My nerves were beginning to show, so I decided some liquid courage was in order and looked for the nearest bar. Then a beautiful waitress, who could have doubled for Miss America, came gliding up to me with several glasses of champagne and shrimp cocktail. I nodded to her nonchalantly, and grabbed a flute of champagne in one hand and a shrimp cocktail in the other. If I had come alone, I probably would've stalked her most of the night—which would've been a welcomed distraction from the current chaos known as my life.

My daydream ended when I heard Mrs. Fox offer up a "Salut!" while she clinked her glass against mine. We both took a sip of the Moet et Chandon; it had a slightly dry taste, but it was crisp enough to relish and savor the flavor. The ice-cold shrimp was delicious and just enough to satisfy my hunger. Paul and Lync were no doubt a couple of sleaze balls, but they always spent big on quality product.

"Oh boy, this is the good stuff," Audrey chimed, raising her glass in the air as if it should be put on a pedestal. "Maybe you should be nicer to these boys," she added with a knowing wink, then let out a throaty laugh, making a scene for all those around her to witness.

She swiveled and flashed a thousand-watt smile to an admirer who was 30 years her junior. She finished what was left of her champagne and shoved the empty glass in my hand. It was nice to see her having a good time. "I am getting a real drink," she said, side-eyeing me before disappearing into the crowd. I took Mrs. Fox's stroll as a cue to sneak around for hard, cold evidence.

The Nest was a mix of tacky and outlandishly decorated rooms with an emphasis on pseudo-African safari themes. It was like I'd lost myself in the Jungle Book story, and I'd become Mowgli trying to survive in the wild. The mansion was packed with life-sized stuffed animals courtesy of FAO Schwartz. It must've taken years to collect all this crap. It'd make a perfect venue for a Kardashian baby shower. All in all, this place was incredible.

I found my way out of the den and wandered into the tricked-out kitchen. There were multiple high-end appliances—my eye hit on a Viking stove easily worth twenty grand—and a slew of various cutlery and cookware. There were foreign cooking gadgets I'd never seen before, and had no idea what they were supposed to do. And to top it all off, marbled pink flamingos gracing the countertops.

Next up was the living room, where everything was swathed in velvet, with furniture that looked straight out of *The Bird Cage*. Go figure. It was total sensory overload. How could anyone relax in this place? I could see why Paul and Lync drove each other crazy.

I eventually found myself back where I started in the Alice in Wonderland maze. I zoomed past the "his-and-hers" bathrooms, which paid homage to Marilyn Monroe and Clark Gable. What did they *not* have in here?

The noise coming from the backyard interrupted my self-guided tour enough for me to stop and see what was going on. I stepped out onto the back patio to find people skinny-dipping in the pool, splashing and dancing ferociously to George Michael's *I Want Your Sex*. There was also an impressive conga line led by—surprise, surprise —Aud, snaking its way through the naked and semi-naked partygoers.

My eyes roamed to the tiki bar where I saw one of our hosts downing the last of a bottle of Glenfiddich 12 to the chants of *"Lync, drink! Lync, drink!"* I knew better than to keep looking once I spotted him, but our eyes locked for an instant, and there was no way out now.

"My man, Marc!" Lync yelled, skirting his way through the crowd to get to me. "I wasn't sure you were going to make it," he said, out of breath from his short rush up the stairs. "I know what a long drive it can be from Canoga Park."

How Did Lync know where I lived? Coming here had been a huge mistake. *When will I learn?*

Inexplicably excited to see me, Lync snatched a glass of champagne and offered it to me—an offer I firmly denied. "Pretty, pretty good par-tay, am I right?" he exclaimed, spilling champagne on my all-too-worn pair of Converses. He was already three sheets to the wind, and I was desperate to find a way out of this conversation. I just needed the right person to latch onto, but all I saw was Paul coming straight towards us.

"Marc! So, good to see you!" Paul said, raising his voice to make sure I heard him coming. "You look great, but a little tired," Paul said, shaking his head with a fake look of concern and one hand on his hip. "We must remedy that!"

I guess his definition of remedy came in a bullet-shaped glass vile of white powder, which he pulled from his very snug Nautica shorts. It was a bit unnerving that Paul was being so outwardly gracious to me. If I hadn't know better, I would've sworn he was hitting on me.

Lync looked at me with an intensely jealous death glare, confirming my suspicions. *Yikes.* Lync made no attempt at trying to hide his disdain from the patrons; he was probably trying to embarrass me in front of the entire crew again. Luckily, they didn't notice because they were all too high and occupied with their own eating, drinking, snorting, and sniffing of anything that came their way.

Lync stormed off to the bar—you could see the fury in his eyes. Meanwhile, Paul continued his attempt at a flirtatious rendezvous. So much so that he kept asking me where I bought my clothes and noted that I had nailed the "slacker" look perfectly. Really? Gee, I didn't think Target was popular among Hollywood Hill's elite.

I tried to convince Paul that I was on thin ice with Lync, and that he was playing a dangerous game, but he kept ignoring me.

"Marc!" he interrupted. "You *must* see the new entertainment lounge we installed upstairs. It's been completely renovated. Of course, Moi, naturally oversaw the redo with just a smidge of help from our loyal decorators from Pierpoint. It's just wonderful if I do say so myself. Come see, it's totally to die for."

He whisked me inside the house while I desperately searched for somebody—anybody—to rescue me. Mrs. Fox wasn't anywhere to be seen. *Dammit. Just what I need on my Friday night.*

Once inside, he gripped my arm a little tighter. Who would've thought Paul had such a strong grip? He must've been working out with his steroid-abusing hubby. He dragged me up the *Gone with the Wind* staircase, with all its pink marble grandeur. He wasn't even winded as he raced to the top of the stairs, while I needed to slow down and catch my breath. *Better start hitting the gym again,* I thought.

We were on the second floor, and something seemed odd, as I noticed all the hallway lights were off and there was a sign on the door Paul was leading me towards that read: "Keep Out."

I noticed Paul looking around surreptitiously, which seemed even odder, seeing it was his house and all. We entered what I assumed was this had-to-see entertainment lounge. And as Paul turned on the light, I had to admit, it was definitely something to see. The room was painted in a deep cinnamon red with an entire wall filled with a collage of Andy Warhol reproductions. There was an enormous black leather couch and two matching chairs artfully arranged beside it, an 80" curved screen TV on the opposing wall, and a state-of-the-art sound system from B & D, a very high-end brand. There was even an ornate mahogany pool table in the corner to match the gleaming horseshoe-shaped bar. It was a bit psychedelic for my taste, but it was definitely a lot classier than the rest of The Nest.

When I turned to compliment Paul on his newly decorated room, he grabbed me by the collar and pinned me to the wall. "Marc! Forget the fucking room!" he pleaded, "I only asked you up here because I needed some time and privacy. Oh God! You have to help me!"

We'd all seen Paul do his hysterical routine before, but he'd never looked this scared or sincere before. He went on to explain how he was tired of Lync—that his steroid use was way out of control and his antics were frightening, not to mention, they could cost them their show. Paul was *afraid* of Lync! Well, no one could really blame him. Lync was paranoid, and always accusing Paul of flirting, though it was Lync who was the two-timing spouse.

On one hand, I was relieved that the "set up" I'd been so anxious about had nothing to do with me, but on the other hand, I felt kinda sorry for Paul. Even though he'd recently been a pain in the ass to me, when you see that naked fear in someone (and believe me, I know how that feels), it's hard to ignore.

Paul must've seen the bewilderment on my face, because he took it as his cue for tears. "Oh Marc, what can I do?" he continued hysterically, clasping my shirt tighter. "You must help! You've seen firsthand how crazy he can get...I can't take it much longer!" As if he'd been practicing in the mirror, he wrapped his arms around my shoulder and let out more tears. *There goes my one semi-decent shirt.*

It was in that moment that the door to the lounge banged open, with a wild-eyed Lync ferociously bursting into the room. Paul and I jumped away from one another, shouting in surprise. Lync looked like a homicidal maniac on a mission. "I thought so! You two-timing bitch!" he spat at Paul. "You put on a good show. All this time you said all you wanted was me, but you just want anyone who will pay you some attention—even this little shit of a grip from the show! Damn it, Paul! He's not even your type!"

Lync's forehead veins bulged and throbbed as he continued, "Maybe you don't have a type after all. Maybe you'll take any piece of ass you can get your grimy hands on!"

I found myself to be more concerned with Paul, who was shaking violently and ducking behind me, using me as his human shield. It didn't take long for Lync to attract some of the partygoers from downstairs who needed to see what the commotion was all about.

"Lync, you're crazy! Those steroids are killing you! They're killing *us!*" Paul protested.

"You're scaring me, and I just can't take it anymore!"

I tried to diffuse the situation, seeing that more people were crowding into the room.

"Lync, please listen to me! There is absolutely nothing —NOTHING!—happening between me and Paul," I argued. Realizing that I was starting to raise my voice, I dialed it back, trying to reassure Lync in the calmest, most non-threatening tone I could muster, "Shit, I'm straight!"

But in typical Lync fashion, he didn't buy it. "You little piece of crap!" he began shouting, pushing his finger in my chest. "You shut the fuck up, and stop defending him, you got it? I know how that little bitch works with his 'woe is me' show."

Lync maneuvered, trying to get a hold of Paul, who was conveniently shrunken behind me. "And to think I fell for that once. You lying piece of shit. I could kill you right now!" he screamed even louder.

As if on cue, the crowd gasped. I looked over and saw Mrs. Fox standing amongst them, visually upset and looking shocked. I tried to send her a reassuring look, but she remained terrified. Lync's ongoing use of steroids, now mixed with way too much alcohol, were finally pushing him past the point of no return.

Things were getting crazy, and you could sense

violence was in the air. It was déjà vu all over again. I'd
seen this before, and it was a no-win situation.

"Lync. I don't want to upset you or anyone else here," I
said, hoping to call attention to all the people watching
this ugly scene unfold. *Where are the TV cameras when you
need them? At least this footage would be good for something.*
"It's a great night...thank God it's Friday, right?" my voice
cracked. "Everyone here loves you, loves The Nest.
They're all having a fantastic time. Why don't I just leave
now, and then you and Paul can work things out privately,
after everyone has cooled off. Does that sound okay?" I
tried my best not to patronize him.

That's when Lync noticed everyone gathered around
in total disbelief. Some looked concerned, but most of
them were just excited by the shit show. Lync stepped
back and appeared to somewhat deflate, with his shoulders starting to sag. I took it as a good sign and tried to
extricate myself from Paul. I could see from the corner of
my eye that Mrs. Fox was sending a signal that she
wanted to get the hell out of here *now*.

Finally, the crowd began to disperse, assuming the spec-
tacle was over. But suddenly, I heard someone shout, "He's
got a gun!" I turned to see Lync pulling a gun from thin air,
waving it somewhere between me and the exiting crowd.

"No!" he commanded. Despite Paul trying to escape
with the rest of the crowd, Lync found his target, pointing
it straight at Paul.

Lync looked like a man possessed and at any second, he was going to pull that trigger. For some stupid reason, my mind went back to an old *60 Minutes* episode about how some teachers saved their students' lives during school shootings. I dove straight into Lync, hoping to grab him before he could pull the trigger and hurt anyone. We wrestled for the gun; not surprisingly, Lync was incredibly strong, thanks to those damn steroids. Time slowed and for a couple of very long seconds, nothing happened. Then it did.

The sound was deafening, and everyone froze. Lync and I fell to the ground, still wrestling for the gun. I wasn't sure if anyone was hit—it all was a blur. Then Paul screamed, "Lync! Please don't do this!"

The sound of his lover's voice broke through whatever trance Lync had been in, distracting him enough to pull away from me, but his grip on the gun shifted, causing it to fire again. This time, we both slackened our grip on each other and the gun. I felt like I had run a marathon. Experts say that shock affects you so that you may not be aware when you're physically harmed, at least in the immediate aftermath of a traumatic physical event. I didn't think I was shot—I just hoped nobody else took a bullet.

Then there was a general stampede for the door. I scrambled to push myself up and look for Mrs. Fox to assure myself she was okay and unharmed. She was standing across the room, looking unharmed but very sad and there were tears in her eyes. I looked back to see who she was looking at and spotted Lync, laying listless on the floor, with a blood stain on his shirt. I went to him and looked into his eyes and could see the life slowly draining out of him. Lync's color faded, and then, there was nothing but awful stillness. Mrs. Fox saw me carefully rising to my feet and rushed over to me, fulfilling her promise as my bodyguard. Everything suddenly went blurry. It was like I had tunnel vision, and the tunnel was getting smaller and smaller. I started to collapse with the sound of Paul screaming at the top of his lungs.

10. FLAVOR OF THE MONTH

I LOOKED up to see detectives writing things down in little note pads, and policemen moving about the room, everyone knowing what their job was and doing it. They observed the surroundings with minimal facial expressions. To them, it was just another crime scene.

I assumed one of the waiters must've called, but I couldn't be too sure. I didn't think one of the party-goers would call the cops, considering everyone had been on drugs for the majority of the night, but stranger things had happened. The crime scene investigators walked around the room and saw me slumped on the couch. Then they switched their focus to Lync; he was sprawled motionless on the mahogany floor with the gun resting in his hand. *Oh, god. And Paul.* He was exhausted, helplessly sitting on the floor, not responding to the crime scene techs who tried to get him to speak. They were treating him with kid gloves, as if they knew he would crumple at any given moment. I felt dizzy, and my eyes were burning and blurry. "At least Paul wouldn't have to worry about Lync anymore," I thought, as black swept over the room.

———

I started to get my head clear just in time to be whisked away by a local ambulance to the nearest trauma care hospital. I hated hospitals. Who didn't? Over the next couple of hours, I was subjected to being poked and prodded all over; eyes being checked, reflexes tested. It was all exhausting, even though I was sitting down.

"How do you feel Mr. Henderson?"

"Does this hurt?"

"Can you take a few deep breaths for me?"

They asked me a ton of routine questions that any adult should be able to answer like what today's date was, or who the current president was. Common sense stuff like that.

My head started to hurt like a son of a bitch. I'd taken a pretty hard hit. I was tired, but they wouldn't let me sleep. *Hospital staff should know by now that injured patients needed rest*, I thought. But good luck with that, a hospital was the last place a person could get any sleep.

Finally, as my eyelids started to droop, the ER doctor walked briskly into the room. He pulled up a wheeled stool to the side of my bed and started to read my patient chart. He told me I had a mild concussion and that I shouldn't worry about it, but not before casually rattling off a litany of life-threatening warning signs that I should be on the lookout for and monitor. Then he looked up at me with reassuring eyes and asked if I had any questions. I said I didn't.

He took a deep breath and hesitated. Then he asked me in a quiet, confidential tone if I needed to speak with anyone about what had happened. I stared at him, my eyes blank. "What I mean Mr. Henderson," he began, "is do you have any post-traumatic-stress symptoms?"

"Oh," I said, nodding solemnly, "I see." I assured him that I'd contact him or any of the hospital support staff if I did, but at the moment, I was doing ok. Honestly, I had no idea what "okay" was; my head was in the clouds and my brain was on vacation. Everything was blank.

He smiled kindly and went straight into protocol. "The police are going to have you transported to the police station for questioning, which is standard procedure in this type of situation."

Before leaving, he told me that he was going to make sure I had a prescription for pain relief, as well as contact information for a nurse practitioner on staff in case I needed any follow-up appointments or counseling. I thanked him genuinely, and he walked away.

It was happening. I was actually going to have to go the police station for questioning about someone's death. That explained why there were two uniforms stationed outside my exam room door. A series of the night's events flashed violently across my mind. *Oh God. Oh God. Lync is dead.* Another star was dead because I couldn't stay away. My body count was rapidly rising. What was going on with me? Was I losing my mind? Granted, those people were far from normal, and weren't even remotely nice. I mean shit, Lync had been mean as hell, but did that give me any reason to play God?

And Mrs. Fox—Aud! Where was she? All I could think of was the pitiful look on her face before Lync pulled the trigger. I hoped she was okay. How had she gotten home?

First thing's first. I needed to pee—badly. I got up on my own and felt woozy, stumbling for the door. It felt like I was on a merry-go-round. Luckily, the police officers on guard saw me struggling and steadied me before I hit the floor for the 2nd time. I thanked them as they helped me during my bathroom trip. I inquired about Mrs. Fox, and they told me they would do their best to find out. Then I was immediately ordered to sit still until I could keep my balance. I went to search my pockets for my phone, but realized I was in a hospital gown. I considered making another attempt to stand up, but my body voted against that. Besides, anything I'd had on me at the party had most likely been taken for evidence. But I felt anxiety prickle my heart. Was there anything incriminating on my phone? There was Petra, and then Andrea, oh yeah, and Lync, all in succession. I couldn't figure out what I felt, but it was a combination of fear, nervousness and helplessness.

Would the police try to pin a murder charge on me? There had to be enough witnesses to confirm that I'd only been trying to stop Lync from firing the gun. Lync was the culprit! He could've shot into the crowd and Mrs. Fox could've been one of the several people hit, or worse, *killed.*

My head was throbbing, and my nerves were shot. A few more hours passed before I was finally discharged from the ER and escorted by wheelchair out to a waiting, nondescript vehicle—a dark blue, older sedan with tinted windows that gave off the whole "unmarked police car" vibe. I appreciated that they didn't throw handcuffs on me like I'd been expecting. I asked someone to call my mom, knowing she'd have a heart attack if she saw me on the 11:00pm news. The one female officer told me that if her information was on my HPPA form, then she had probably already been notified, but that I would have to wait and get confirmation once we were at the station.

Unlike the boring monotony of the hospital on a Friday night, the police station was quite the opposite. Lights were strewn across every corner; several news vans were parked everywhere anxiously waiting for a story. Reporters were checking the frequency of their microphones, and the sea of curious onlookers were cheering and whistling. I could see smiles radiating, and fists pumping high in the air from the back of the police car.

Why are they here? My face wrinkled in confusion. A thought zipped through my mind, and my eyes lit up. *Holy shit, are they here for me?* Word must've traveled fast. The officer who had helped escort me out of the emergency room finally found a space to park, however, we weren't able to avoid the hyped-up crowd. Before the officer could open the car door for me, they swarmed like bees all over to us. Hands with blurred faces helped me out the car. There was so many of them. It was like stepping onto the red carpet at the Golden Globes or something. The cameras were ruthless with their flashes, blinding me with every step.

Countless mics were shoved in my face, and what seemed like thousands of reporters were shouting at me, asking me questions I tried hard to ignore. "We love you!" I heard one woman scream. Who would've thought this madness of hoopla and hysteria would be just for *me*? I kept thinking that Mrs. Fox would absolutely eat this up! But I sobered fast, shaking my head, thinking of her. I needed to find out how she and my mom were doing. I hoped they weren't too worried.

Applause swelled around me. A voice from the crowd shouted, "Thank you for saving all those innocent people —YOU ROCK!" It was impossible to take it all in. I decided to keep my mouth shut and my head down. I couldn't risk saying anything I wouldn't want anyone to hear.

As I squeezed through the station doors, it felt as if I

had entered another dimension. The decibel level was significantly lower inside the building, but there was still a palpable buzz throughout the station. The officers didn't skip a beat. They did their due process, which consisted of fingerprinting, snapping mugshots, and recording pertinent details. I noticed everyone was still treating me with kid gloves, like I had been the victim and not Lync. The officers were beyond courteous. They even went as far as putting me in some type of small room versus a cell. I thought only people with money got that type of privilege. Could it be due to all the recent political unrest, and the "sue-happy" mentality that had spread like wildfire across the country, that law enforcement agencies were actually exercising extreme caution in situations like mine? Whatever the reason, I was grateful for it.

I sat down in a battered wooden chair and waited for twenty minutes, give or take. Then I heard the echo of footsteps approaching. An officer appeared at the door and proceeded to escort me to another room with a sign that read "HOMICIDE INTERVIEWS" on the door. Before we stepped in, I imagined a squalid, dank, and dark room filled with a few chairs, a battered table with countless stains and marks, and a fluorescent light overhead. I imagined myself at the mercy of detectives as they tried to beat a confession out of me; me sitting helplessly across the table as beads of sweat trickled down my forehead.

Instead, the door opened to a small, clean, well-lit room. I had to stop watching so much *NCIS*. There was a peculiar-looking man in his late forties sitting in one of the chairs. He had short dark hair and wore a gray, rumpled suit and a dark blue tie with gray, triangular designs. He had to be Italian, or maybe Greek. The other man, who was my escort, was much younger. He was in his mid-thirties and had a very fair complexion. His background had to be Swedish or some country from the Scandinavian area. He was as tall as any basketball player I'd seen, and skinny as a rail. *Aud would kill for his cheekbones.*

"Marc. Detective Savino." He stood up and firmly shook my hand. He turned and introduced the younger guy as Detective Larsson, who gave me a curt nod. Detective Savino gestured with his eyes for me to sit. He and the bronze Swede followed suit. "You seem to be quite the celebrity," he said with a little smile, trying to put me at ease. "I'm going to put the audio/video recorder on, which is standard procedure during interviews. Do you understand?"

I answered yes and he continued, "The hospital says you should be up to an interview and questioning, but if at any time you feel tired or not up to continuing, we can stop. You also don't have to answer any questions you don't wish to, and request to have an attorney present. Understood?"

I answered yes again. Before they started in with

questions, they confirmed my mom and Mrs. Fox had been contacted and told that I had been taken to the hospital for observance but was fine and would be with the police for a bit to help answer questions about the shooting. Both women had seemed fine and relieved to hear I was okay. Detective Savino had even given them the station number, as well as his own cell number, if they needed anything.

He smiled when Mrs. Fox's name came up. "Your neighbor is quite a gal," he remarked. I smiled in agreement. Mrs. Fox got that a lot.

They began the questioning. I did my best to answer as honestly as possible, without going into too much detail. There was no telling what Paul, or Mrs. Fox, or any of the other partygoers had said. There was only one thing that I knew to be true: I *was* definitely innocent. I had acted instinctively, terrified that Lync would shoot at everyone in the room, especially Mrs. Fox. Lync *was* fucking crazy. I still couldn't believe what had happened. I *had* put myself on the line for other people. I honestly hadn't known I had it in me.

Finally, after a couple of hours and a lot of repetitive questions, I felt my body start to shut down as the adrenaline that had kept me going all this time finally crashed. Now I knew why people say they "hit a wall," because that's exactly how it felt. My head was pounding and I couldn't focus on the questions. The detectives gave up, because I guess there was nothing left to gain. After thanking me, they informed me that a statement would be prepared for me to sign before I left, but that they would appreciate me hanging around for a bit longer, in case any more questions came up. By this time, it was already early Saturday morning.

The female officer I had spoken to earlier escorted me back to the holding room. There was only that uncomfortable chair to sit on—no couch or cot—but since my legs felt like jelly at this point, it was better than nothing. I tried closing my eyes to rest, but my mind couldn't help but review the facts.

First, my head, brain, and body were hurting all over. But until I grabbed some Tylenol, there wasn't much I could do about that. Second, regardless of what the police had told me, I was still worried about my mom. I would make sure to call her as soon as they'd let me. Knowing her, she'd do anything to get to me, including breaking sound and speed barriers in the process. At this very moment, she and Mrs. Fox were probably already concocting an exit plan for me. That image allowed me the first real smile and sense of happiness I'd had since before this whole nightmare with Lync and Paul had begun. And third, well, there was no third, because the next thing I knew, I was nudged awake by another officer, with my head lolled forward on my chest, with a little drool on my mouth, which I quickly wiped away.

I was brought back into the interview room to sign my statement. Someone had kindly provided me with a sandwich, chips, and a bottle of water. At that moment, I realized how ravenous I was and started in. Detectives Savino and Larsson were sitting across the table with cups of coffee in their hands, watching me. I thought I was the one who'd had a bad night, but they looked like shit. *A detective's job is never done, I guess.*

I read through the statement, signed at all the 'X's' and was told I was free to go. Detective Savino smiled, mentioning "my ride" was there. That had to mean Mrs. Fox had come to get me. I followed a police officer into the main lobby and there she was, adorned in a Juicy Couture cotton candy-colored velour tracksuit. I could tell from her body language that she was flirting with the officer at the front desk. He was young enough to be her nephew's age, but why the heck would she care? The poor fellow was turning beet red, as she must've been telling him one racy joke after another. The cops were getting a huge kick out of her and treating her like a celebrity. Of course, Aud *loved* the attention.

I was glad to see her happy, considering the circumstances. I felt ashamed. If I hadn't brought her to that stupid party, none of this would've happened. I came around the corner and her face lit up when she saw me. As she rushed over to hug me, I saw a few tears spring from her eyes. "Thank God, you're okay!" she exclaimed. I made sure to emphasize that I had been treated extremely well by everyone and told her how much I appreciated her coming to pick me up.

She eyed me up and down, probably not liking what she saw. She tugged at my sleeve and began walking towards the door. "Let's blow this popsicle joint, kid," she ordered. Arm in arm, we walked out the exit doors.

Even the next day, there was a crowd milling about outside, but it was much smaller and quieter than it had been the night before. I stuck to my routine, keeping my head down and my mouth shut until, at last, we were safely ensconced in Mrs. Fox's silver Toyota Camry, with its bumper sticker that read: "Good Girls Go to Heaven, Bad Girls Go Everywhere." Seriously, how could you *not* love this woman?

I'd only been at the police station for a night, but even that was enough to make me appreciate the space and real freedom of the outside world. The morning sun was peachy and bright, the blue sky beautiful. On the drive back home, we made a stop at my favorite coffee house and bought a few cups to go. The aroma and taste of my favorite pumpkin spice coffee soothed me to no end. The French Crullers we'd bought on an impulse melted in my mouth. *Heaven.*

As we headed to our apartments, Mrs. Fox decided to share what she'd received from the officers at the station. Apparently, there was enough visual evidence from the hidden surveillance equipment at The Nest to back up my recollection of events. And my fellow crew members had come to my defense too. They had not only signed affidavits that Lync was the obvious aggressor who threatened Paul and me with a gun, but they also painted a very ugly picture of Lync's character in general, exposing his steroid abuse, hostile behavior, and paranoia.

"Enough of that slimy pig," she dismissed with a wave. Her expression changed in an instant as she went on to tell me that in just a few short hours, I had become the "talk of the town." Like it or not, I was smack-dab in the middle of yet another—third, to be exact—reality TV star's death. It hurled me straight into the spotlight. "You're a star now," she glowed. "Do you know how many calls your mom and I have gotten asking all of us to do interviews?"

She tried to sound offended, but as always, she ate it up. *Mom!* I had to call her right then or facing a jail sentence would be the least of my worries. Mrs. Fox noticed my sudden alarm at the talk of my mom. "Don't stress, sweetie. Your mom and I have been in constant touch. She's okay. Worried, but okay. She's flying in to see you. She'll be here later today or tomorrow, as soon as she can ditch that stubborn press. I let her know you'd call as soon as I got you home."

At that, I let out an audible sigh. As I approached the top of the stairs, two thoughts came to me. One, I was a free man again, and hopefully for the rest of my life. And two, was it true? Had I become a reality star of sorts? *Great. Just great.*

11. SWIMMING WITH THE SHARKS

BOY, oh boy. I couldn't believe it. What the hell was going on in the world? I started getting emails and calls from what seemed like every major talk show in the game. From Fallon and Kimmel to Ellen DeGeneres, you name it. They wanted *me*—if you could believe it—to be their special guest.

As flattered as I was, I politely turned down all their requests. Honestly, I just wanted them to leave me the hell alone. I didn't want any spotlight on me. I tried to rationalize everything that had happened to me in those last few hectic months. I couldn't wrap my head around what I might have become. My now very vocal entourage, which included my mom and Mrs. Fox, had a different opinion. They were thrilled by all this commotion in my life. But if they'd actually known the whole story, I knew they'd be ashamed and hope I'd crawl behind a rock and hide. But, as much as I tried to shun away from all the hoopla, if I hid too long, people might wonder why.

I expressed this concern to Aud, and she was adamant that I needed to do at least one interview so people could hear from me. That way, I could tell the masses that I have absolutely no interest in being any kind of hero, and most importantly, I would like to be left alone. As Aud put it, "You know, just to get your side of the story out there. It will pacify the press and you'll be done with it. In five minutes, they'll move on to the next big thing." I shrugged at the thought. It made sense, so why not?

I carefully mulled over the numerous offers, but since I refused to appear on TV, that knocked out about seventy-five percent of the offers. As I looked over the remaining offers, one in particular jumped out.

The major radio personality and self-dubbed "King of all Media" Howard Stern had reached out, asking me to be on his show! How had I missed that one? I couldn't believe it. Howard Stern's show had grown to over 20 million listeners. Not to mention, he was a major player in the game, and I'd be an absolute fool not to take him up on his offer. When I was growing up, me and some of my high school buddies would sneak over the hill behind the school just about every day and smoke cigarettes while listening to his show. Boy, those had been good times.

But, being that his studio was in New York City, and I was bound by release limitations to stay in L.A. until the police told me otherwise. I obviously couldn't do a sit-down interview. So, Howard's "people" proposed a phone interview instead. There was no way I'd turn this offer down. I was ecstatic that I was about to be interviewed by my hero, Howard Stern. If only my high school buds could've seen me now.

———

"Marc! Hey man," Howard started off, "I'm glad you could come on the show."

I took a deep breath, "Thanks Howard. I appreciate the invite. It's great to be speaking with you."

Howard let out a small laugh and continued, "I don't think you guys need any intro for the man of the hour, but for those who've been living in a dark cave over these past couple of days, Marc Henderson's face has been plastered all over the media. He's been described as an everyday guy who courageously took out that pill-popping, steroid-abusing, reality asshole, Lync Prime."

Howard let out an overwhelming sigh. "The first thing I want to say Marc is, thank you, man! Okay? I mean, if you were here in this studio, I'd kiss you."

I could hear Howard's co-host Robin laughing at his joke. "Think about it man. You did what all of us with no balls couldn't—you killed that lowlife!"

"Howard, what are you talking about? You killed in

'Nam, remember?" Robin chimed in, letting out another chuckle.

There was a short pause as I heard Howard take a sip of his coffee. Since the interview had been set up so quickly, I wasn't really prepared for how this whole shtick was to play out. What should I say? What *shouldn't* I say? *Crap, I wish I'd taken Aud up on her offer to set me up with her former PR person.* This kind of thinking would get me nowhere fast, so before I got too nervous, I shrugged it off and figured, what the hell? I'd come this far. I was pretty sure I could handle anything that came along with it.

"Ok, Marc, take us through it. In your own words," Howard prodded me.

"Well Howard," I said matter-of-factly, "unfortunately, Lync had a lot of serious problems. Most of us on the crew of *Getting Primed* tried our best to avoid him whenever possible. But as time went on, he became more and more...what's the word? Aggressive. Confrontational. Paranoid. We were fed up, Howard." I spoke honestly. "Of course, I still did everything I could to avoid a confrontation with him. It was tragic what happened, you know? But Lync was a walking time bomb. And it was total self-defense on my part. I'm just grateful and relieved that the surveillance cameras got the incident on tape. Plus, the other crew-members backed me up."

"That's the truth, man," Stern said. "Believe me. I've met so many so-called 'celebrities.' It pisses me off. I mean, I worked my ass off for thirty years just to get to where I am, and these slime balls do nothing and expect to be rich and famous!" His voice suddenly shifted, "So tell me, Marc. How many times have you gotten laid since you've been out of jail?"

Robin giggled as they cut to an abrupt commercial. I couldn't remember much else from after we came back on the air, it was mostly a blur. I was just so thrilled to be talking to one of my childhood idols. Plus, I didn't think I did that bad.

After the interview, I barely stepped foot out of my apartment. The high I felt from being on *The Howard Stern Show* didn't last long. I crashed—hard. I started to get depressed, and it felt like I couldn't get out of my own way. The troubles I had caused started to weigh heavily on my mind.

That fateful night when I'd killed Petra felt like it had been years ago. And Andrea's death felt like a hallucinogenic dream. It was all too surreal. My mind was swirling non-stop. I was having nightmares and images that wouldn't get out of my head. When I would finally fall asleep, it was like pressing "REPLAY" on a DVD player, with a reenactment of Lync's death. But each time it played out, it would end differently. Was I on the verge of a nervous breakdown? How much more could I handle without losing it completely?

And to make matters worse, whoever *Primed Minister* had hired as their PR reps were working overtime to squeeze every bit of publicity they could out of the situation before Lync's death fell off the public's radar. It had gotten so bad that the press was literally camping out on the sidewalk in front of my apartment building. They reminded me of a pack of wild animals, just skulking around, waiting for their prey to show.

What really bothered me were the onlookers taking countless selfies in front of my complex. *Really? Get a life, people.* I shook off my depression long enough to realize I had another problem: I was running out of food. I didn't know what to do so I called on one of the most reliable people I knew, Aud. Like a ninja, she snuck through my back patio door, triumphantly holding a plastic bag filled with what she excitedly called, "the goods."

Aud looked like a kid on Christmas morning—she was loving this. She had on her disguise, consisting of her oversized, black Jackie O sunglasses, and a white and gold 70s vintage tracksuit, with big gold hoop earrings, and a pair of vintage Converse sneakers. She'd make even the biggest stars jealous. I couldn't help but smile and be grateful for everything she did.

Aud laid everything she had out on my coffee table. She sat me down and began formulating my disguise. I could tell she was getting a kick out of this whole thing. She went to work—basically turning me into a preppy, conservative up-and-comer. She cut my hair and demanded I shave. She then dug through her bag some more and shoved a man's white oxford shirt and a navy blue sports jacket into my chest and told me to change "pronto." When I came out of my room, she finished my disguise off with a designer pair of aviator sunglasses and said, "Let the adventure begin!"

We quietly snuck out my back door like a set of rebellious teens trying to break their curfew and slipped into her place. It was a mighty convenient hideaway. She graciously loaned me her car, and I escaped through her attached garage.

I was relieved to finally be out of the house, even if it was only to go to the market. I was nervous the entire time. I couldn't help but think someone was going to recognize me and blow my cover. I hated living like this. Sneaking around. Sweaty palms. It wasn't for me.

I didn't want to, but I knew I'd have to lay low for a few more days. At least until the media got disinterested, which I prayed wouldn't take too long. Thankfully, my prayer was answered. Lara Beckett, the star of TV's top-rated soap opera, *Manor House,* was apparently found unconscious after too many tokes on the crack pipe. Lara's frantic maid had called the medics after finding Lara sprawled out on the bedroom floor. Lines of cocaine were still on her vanity table. Lara's stomach was pumped at the ER, and she was quickly released the next day. As I pulled into Aud's driveway, I noticed my front yard was now almost vacant where all the paparazzi had been camping out. It also looked like the onlookers had closed up shop and moved on to their next prey. At last, things were a little normal again.

12. IN IT NOW

I KEPT HOPING that the media frenzy was over for good, but after the 100th message left on my new cell phone—the majority of them by one very persistent James Spitz—I knew I wasn't out of the woods just yet. Anyone who worked in the TV industry knew Spitz—or rather, about him. What a colossal nut job. He was the producer and "brains" behind *Being Stronge*. As if I didn't have enough nightmares about that show as it was, Spitz had been sending me voicemail after voicemail requesting to meet me. How the hell had he even gotten my new number? He wasn't very specific about what he wanted, just that I had to call him back "ASAP" and it was "important." Whatever the reason, I needed him to stop.

I picked up my phone with more than a little trepidation and dialed the number he had left. Spitz had always treated those of us who worked behind the scenes like crap. If you said "hello" to him or tried to make small talk, he'd look right through you like you didn't exist. The only time he'd spoken to us was when he was barking out orders or telling us that we'd done something wrong. A real sweetheart.

So, I was surprised when his voice sounded polite, even friendly, on the phone. He wanted to meet and discuss a proposition he had for me. I thanked him but said I wasn't interested and asked if he would please lose my number. But like all men with oversized egos, he said he wouldn't stop until I heard what he had to say. Apparently, that was all he wanted. If I wasn't interested after hearing it, he'd leave me alone. No doubt about it, the man was tenacious as hell. It was probably one of the main reasons he was so successful. I caved and said we could meet at La Gondola, a quaint but pricey restaurant on Wilshire Boulevard. One of my friends, an actor who made ends meet by bartending at La Gondola between gigs, said the place was pretentious, as were the people who went there, but the tips he made from there were phenomenal.

As I drove to the dreaded Spitz meeting, I couldn't help but feel anxious. Stuck in the perpetual I-10 traffic, I had the feeling that I was playing with fire. *Being Stronge* had been Spitz's first love, his baby. It'd be the end of Marc Henderson if Spitz ever found out that I was the one who'd killed his golden goose, Petra. He wouldn't give a shit if it was in self-defense. My peripheral vision started to darken, and I felt myself spiraling into panic mode. Did Spitz know something about that night? Was this meeting just a ruse to confront me? Why else would he call me out of the blue like that? It's not like he cared about anyone who couldn't help make him richer than he already was.

My mind was going a mile a minute, and my palms were sweaty, gripping the wheel. I had to calm down or I'd soon find myself wrecked in a ditch. I pulled over on the shoulder and did a few deep breathing exercises that Aud had showed me. She'd told me she'd learned the techniques in one of her Sassy Seniors yoga classes. It did the trick. I regained my composure and returned to the highway, eventually making it to the restaurant in one piece. As I pulled up to the valet parking stand, I felt immediately out of place. La Gondola was upscale; through the windows, I could see crystal chandeliers, buttery leather seats, and a grand piano in the corner. *Whoa.* Not only was I in a battered Ford Focus, but my attire was hardly GQ. I searched my back pocket to see if I had at least a five dollar bill to tip the valet. I found only one measly five, which I knew I needed for the way out. Damn.

The valet gave me and the Focus an unimpressed look as I handed over the keys to the car. I buttoned my top collar and fussed with my hair as I entered through the foyer, which was decorated with expensive floral arrangements and oversized bottles of champagne. I scanned the crowd and spotted a guy who looked like Spitz in a corner booth, taking a small bite of a delicious and expensive-looking shrimp appetizer. Yep, it was him. He had finally changed hairstyles from a comb over to a sleek bald look. He was wearing a navy blue Armani suit, with his cell-phone glued to his ear. He was talking a mile a minute, probably to someone important. He had gained a few pounds since the last time I'd seen him. His face was a little fuller, with jowls beginning to show. Not hard to guess how he had put the extra weight on, given he probably spent too many meal times gorging on rich food in places like this.

I felt the anxiety rushing back to me, but before I could turn and run away, Spitz saw me and waved me over. As I approached his table, he hung up his cell phone, stood up, and gave me a hearty handshake. "Hey Marc. I'm so glad you could join me," he said, greeting me with a pat on the back. "You know, I was beginning to get worried you wouldn't show, being so famous and all." He nudged his elbow in my side. "You're getting more press than the Kardashians!"

Spitz laughed at his own joke, as I cringed and made my way to my side of the table. He continued, "Because I didn't know when, or if, you were actually going to show up, I decided to order already. I hope you don't mind," he said. "This place is famous for steak and seafood. So, I ordered their finest prime rib and blackened mahi-mahi. You've got to try it!"

He signaled the closest waitress and ordered two

extra-dry martinis. I wasn't particularly a martini drinker, but when in Rome....

Mistaking the look on my face for an aversion to drinking during the lunch hour, he went on, "I know, I know. It's a little early in the day for a few drinks, but after this meal is over, you're going to want to celebrate. Trust me," he said with a mysterious smile.

Spitz started off by expressing how shocked he was about Lync's death and the craziness that had led up to it. He said he thought I was very courageous for doing what I did to save other people's lives. He said he had a new-found admiration for me, because "you can never know who a person truly is until they face a hard life-or-death situation. Am I right?" he asked me rhetorically. Clearly, he was on a roll and didn't need me to add anything to the conversation.

He was really trying to butter me up, even adding that I "intrigued" him. He stopped to gauge my expression. Honestly, I didn't have a stinkin' clue as to where he was going with this or how I was supposed to respond to all this lavish praise. So, I just sat there, taking large gulps of my martini, and waited.

He laughed. I take it he was used to getting similar responses from other people. He sat back and took out a thin piece of paper from the inside of his jacket and slid it across the table. I peeked over my martini and saw that it was a check—written out to me. I set the martini down to make sure I was seeing correctly. Maybe the martini was hitting me hard on an empty stomach. But no. It was a big fat check signed by Spitz for what looked like six figures. I couldn't stop staring at it. Then I looked at Spitz. He seemed very pleased with himself, with a cat-that-ate-the-canary grin on his face. I took another swig of my drink, choked, and my eyes started to water. Spitz thought that was hilarious.

"Pretty cool, right?" Spitz said chuckling. "Believe me when I tell you that you and I are about to create something very special." He paused for effect. "HUGE! Let me explain—"

But that was as far as he got. A beautiful young blonde woman, who could pass as a model for Victoria's Secret, appeared at the table to ask if I could autograph her menu. I looked at Spitz with a "what the heck?" expression on my face. I was embarrassed beyond belief, and I didn't know what else to do. I snapped out of it, took the pen from her, and signed her menu. She thanked me and sauntered away.

I turned back to the table and saw that the check was still there. Whew. I picked it up to take a closer look. I hadn't been hallucinating. It read: "Pay to the Order of: Mark Henderson."

But I was wrong about one thing: the amount wasn't six figures. It was seven.

13. HOW TO BE A MILLIONAIRE

I FELT blood rush to my head as all of those zeros came into focus. The room began to spin, and I felt light-headed. I glanced up at Spitz only to realize he'd been calling my name with concern. Did he think I was going into cardiac arrest? Before Spitz could do anything about it, I gathered myself and blurted out the first thing that came to mind, "C, my first name is spelled with a C, not K."

Spitz stared at me, holding the check and looking perplexed. Then he roared with laughter, drawing other diners' attention to our booth. "You're priceless! You really had me going there for a minute. I thought for sure you were having a heart attack!"

Spitz's jowls jiggled from laughing. He snatched the check from my hands, took out a platinum Cross pen, and changed the K to a C, then scrawled his initials next to the change for added verification. Leaning back in his chair, he said, "You can cash it if you want but be sure not to spend it all in one place." He winked and handed the check back to me.

We were silent for a moment. "Now, don't you want to know what the check is for?" he asked.

"Oh yeah, sorry. Of course. Of course, I'm interested. But I'm in a little bit of an unsettled situation right now, and I don't want to do anything that might make it worse."

"Unsettled. You're funny, Marc. You're going to love what I'm going to tell you..."

Spitz paused, leaned in, and lowered his voice. He explained that he wanted me to be the star of a new reality show created and produced by Spitz Productions. I didn't know what to say. I had so many thoughts rushing at once, you could've knocked me over with a feather. Spitz's offer was a complete surprise. Never in a million years would I have thought I'd be offered a deal like this. It would've been easier if he'd asked me to knock off every producer competing against him for airtime than to offer me a reality show. His offer was like asking a vegetarian to work in a slaughterhouse. I felt the color rise in my cheeks and looked at the check once more.

"I mean no disrespect, Mr. Spitz, but why do you want to give me a show? I'm just a grip who's, to be honest, fed up with the entire concept of reality TV."

Spitz ordered another round of drinks before he answered. It was time for business. "Hear me out." He unbuttoned his jacket. "This is a freakin goldmine, my friend. It's an opportunity that only comes once in a lifetime. Given recent events, you're one of the most well-known names in the tabloids right now. And you could have thousands, if not tens of thousands, of Twitter followers by now. That practically makes you a rock star!"

Spitz put his hands to his head as if to grab hair that wasn't there. "You're like...damn! What's that character's name all the kids love nowadays ? Aha!" He snapped his fingers. "Dead Pool! That's it. What I'm trying to say here is that there has never been a regular guy who's become a community hero overnight by taking out some doped-up, crazed celebrity. Can you think of a single person who's done what you've done and become a hero? It wasn't OJ. That's for damn sure."

I had to take a quick reality check before I got carried away with everything Spitz was saying. This couldn't be right. There had to be some catch. What if this was a setup, and I was being *Punk'd*? For all I knew, Spitz could be pulling my leg for more TV ratings. But he did look pretty serious—you could almost see the dollar signs in his eyes.

"It'd be called *Get a Grip*. Catchy, right? It's fucking brilliant! Here's what I'm thinking in a nutshell." He was on a roll now. "We film you doing your job in a behind-the-scenes of a behind-the-scenes type show. Get it? We both know what crazy shit goes down behind the scenes of filming a reality show. Let me put together a production crew that follows you, and a few other crew members, as you all work together to make top-rated television shows happen. The reality of working on a reality show."

His hands mimed a headline in the air. "You know firsthand how uppity, and flat-out crazy these sons of bitches can be. I can't think of a better person to capture the craziness. It's obvious you know how to handle yourself when it comes to these whack jobs. Let the viewers see what really goes on. Let them into your world. It will give the audience a completely different side of reality television than that scripted crap they're used to seeing."

Spitz took a deep breath. "Come on, Marc. You know you love it, right? The audience will love it too. What do you say?"

I waited to see if he was finally finished talking. I looked down at the check, back at Spitz, and back at the check. "It sounds interesting, but I don't think I'd be the right guy."

"Marc, you are the right guy. In fact, you are the only guy! I am never wrong when it comes to making television stars. Trust me, I don't give my money to just anyone. We can iron out the details once you've had a chance to meet with the writers and project development team. We want to bring you on board as soon as possible to help us put this whole thing together."

Spitz waved for the check and looked at his gleaming Phillipe Patek watch that probably cost more than a year's worth of my rent. I considered reminding him that my only "qualification" was that I was in the very wrong place at the very wrong time. Truth was, I was no reality star. But I decided to let him think what he wanted. I stole a glance back down at the check—all those zeros did have a hypnotic effect.

"So, what do you think? Just say the word and I'll have the paperwork started. Then we can lay out the foundation for the show. This could very well be the first reality show to get an Emmy! Well, maybe I'm thinking too fast, but it won't be too far off. *Get A Grip* will be a monster hit —but only with you in it."

He tossed his black American Express card at the bill and buttoned his jacket. I had to admit it; the idea was sounding more and more interesting the more Spitz ran his mouth off about it. There was a peculiar appeal to all of this. I had always wanted to "make it" in LA, and this could be the stepping stone to a better career. And I'd make my mom proud in the process.

I took a deep breath and looked up at Spitz. "Okay, Mr. Spitz. You convinced me—let's do this."

I smiled and Spitz looked shocked but in a good way. "Marc, you just made me a happy man! Oh boy, you won't be sorry. We're going to make history with a capital H, my friend. And that check is only the beginning. Call it a signing bonus. We'll work out your paycheck for each episode. I'm thinking $150k per?"

He smiled at my obvious shock. "Okay Marc, I've got

business to take care of. More meetings, you know? I'll have my assistant Mary call you, and we can talk legalities and paperwork by Friday. Any questions, concerns, whatever—you just let me know. Everyone's dying to meet you. Get yourself some new threads. You're a TV star now—you gotta look the part, am I right?" Spitz winked and gave me a hearty pat on the shoulder. "And one more thing, kiddo—get yourself a fucking Twitter account!" And just like that, he was gone. I sat there dumbfounded, with a check for a million dollars.

14. MONEY TALKS

I HANDED the valet the wrinkled five dollar bill after he pulled my car off to the side of the front door. I drove away, replaying the day's events to the loud sputter of my dying muffler. Everything in my life had become way too surreal, and it was all coming at me way too fast.

I held my newly gifted check in front of me while I stayed steady on the road. I wanted to feel it. Smell it. I needed to make sure I wasn't dreaming. I wouldn't put it past myself. And, if you think texting and driving is bad, try staring at a check for a million dollars.

The palm trees aligned perfectly as I made my way down Wilshire to the California Bank and Trust to deposit that bad boy. I was slowly adjusting to the fact that I indeed held a million-dollar check in my hand. I was beyond ecstatic—so much so that I found myself smiling, looking into my rearview mirror. I couldn't help it. So many thoughts. So many decisions. I now had the freedom to do whatever I wanted. And hopefully, today was the last day I'd ever have to drive this piece of crap car anywhere.

I stood in line at the bank, thinking, *I'm a millionaire!* Just hours before, I'd had no idea how I was going to pay my electricity bill, let alone my school loans. My fear of being in public eased with the thought of being a millionaire. I mean, who'd judge me now? I could look like money, talk like money, and most importantly, actually have the money.

I began looking over my shoulder to see if anyone was watching. I noticed people from all walks of life coming in to deposit their hard-earned paychecks, only to have next to nothing left once their bills were paid. I saw defeated-looking mothers and fathers who were probably just scraping by. Then there were the wannabe's who were paying high mortgage loans and credit card debt they'd foolishly acquired.

I snapped to attention as I heard the bank teller bark in my direction, "Next in line!" I walked cautiously up to the counter. I casually slid the check under the glass pane. The teller looked down at the check, "I'm sorry, sir, but you need to sign the back of the check and fill out a deposit slip," the older, dark-haired teller informed me.

My insides sank. I felt like an idiot. For God's sake, what was I—an amateur? I snatched the check back, mumbled an apology, and hurried to get a deposit slip. It wasn't easy cramming six whole zeros into those tiny blue boxes on the slip, minus the $150.00 I decided to cash for gas and groceries—and maybe to take Aud out for a celebratory dinner later on.

I returned to the teller and slid the check and slip to her. After watching her examine the check more closely, I began to get nervous. She showed the check to the teller next to her. There was a brief, whispered discussion. The teller next to her nodded and scurried off to the back, probably to find the manager.

"Uh, I'm sorry sir," the teller said, looking down at the check. "But this size of a transaction requires an upper management authorization. Would you mind taking a seat while we notify the branch manager?" she asked, once again sliding the check back to me.

In less than a minute, a man wearing a charcoal grey suit approached me. He looked quite dapper. I think he was in his mid-fifties, but it was hard to tell because his face had that tight, plastic look to it that was the result of at least a few cosmetic surgeries. He had very black (read: dyed) hair without a streak of grey, and a very small nose that was turned up, making it practically impossible to look at him without seeing the insides of his nostrils. *Ew.*

"Can I help you, sir? I'm Jeff Edwards, the branch manager." As courteous as his words were, his face was telling me that he thought I was a forger or some kind of fraud. I froze, staring back at him, unsure of what to do. *Should I just take the check back and leave?* After all, I didn't have an account here but Spitz had said it would be alright.

Luckily, I didn't have to make that decision. After examining me a few seconds longer, the branch manager's face lit up in recognition. "Well, I'll be darned—I know you! You're Marc Henderson. You're the young man all over the news! Please accept my apology, there's absolutely *no* problem with the check, Mr. Henderson!" He continued, "We thank you for deciding to be a California Trust valued client. Mr. Spitz is also a valued customer here, so you're both good as gold."

He patted me on the shoulder. "I will *personally* take care of this." Before he walked away, he turned to look back at me. "And let me just say that it's about time we had some positive role models for our children."

He returned in no time with my deposit receipt and cash. He then looked at me sheepishly as he searched for something in his pocket. "Could I bother you for your autograph? My daughters will be ecstatic I had you as a client today."

He was positively giddy. The teller who was originally helping me stared blankly at the manager, who was now making quite the scene by asking me for my autograph. I couldn't lie. I was getting a little embarrassed by all the attention I was getting. But what the hell? My million-dollar check was getting deposited with my newly formed account and I had some extra cash in hand for the first time in a long time.

Once everyone caught on to who I was, I had to stay a little while longer, making small talk and signing autographs for the bank staff and customers. Then, I said my goodbyes and started to leave. I stopped in my tracks when I realized this doesn't happen every day and asked the teller for one last request: a picture of me with the check, so I could frame it. Things were looking up indeed.

15. THAT 'NEW CAR' SMELL

THREE DAYS LATER, I was pulling off the lot as a proud owner of a brand new cherry red BMW 630i convertible, decked out with a white leather interior. I finally felt like *the man.* I raised my new aviators to my face and turned up the Pretenders on my Boss sound system. It was freaking insane.

I revved the engine as I anxiously waited at each red light to turn green. After fooling around on the streets, I decided to swing by the *Primed* set to catch up on the crew. *Yeah, right.* I wanted to show off. Nothing more, nothing less.

I pulled around to the back lot where most of the crew was having lunch. I circled slowly to get a good glimpse of everyone's faces as they oohed and aahed; it was like music to my ears. Some of them looked jealous, but I knew most would be happy for me. Why wouldn't they be?

The next couple of days were crazy as hell. I was busy moving out of my apartment and into a new place at the snooty Windsor Lofts in Downtown Hollywood. The time had finally come for me to say bye to Aud. Daisy could tell something was up. She kept yapping, and I knew she wanted me to take her for a walk. Instead, I bent down, and gave her a good scratching behind the ears. She thanked me profusely by licking me all over my face and new sunglasses. I had to laugh. As I said my goodbyes, I promised Aud I'd visit soon and told her to set a date for us to have dinner next week at the restaurant of her choice.

Her eyes lit up, delighted at my suggestion. Then she pointed her finger at me. "I may be easy, Marc Henderson, but I'm not cheap!" We both burst out laughing, easing the sadness.

Aud waved as I pulled away, and I saw her wiping away tears. I felt a pain in my chest that I tried hard to ignore. Here I was, driving my dream car to my new luxury apartment, but I couldn't help but feel like I had just lost my best friend.

"Buck up," I said out loud, shaking the feelings of sadness off of me. I needed to remember that I was on my way to a new life. A life I hoped to be better and more fulfilling.

It was imperative for this new life to start out right, so I gave all of my old apartment furniture to the local Goodwill. Aud had hooked me up with a friend of hers,

Charis, from Restoration Hardware, the upscale home store at Hollywood Mall. I'd seen the store a thousand times before, but I'd never dared to go in, let alone buy anything from it.

I had promised Charis that I wouldn't interfere with her apartment design, so I had stayed at my old place while she'd prepared my new home. After much contemplation and anxiety, I was excited to see the finished product. Then I could finally begin my new life.

An hour of driving through traffic later, I finally made it to my new home. I was kindly welcomed by a bellman in a burgundy uniform. He had an extraordinary handlebar mustache straight out of the 1920s and a flawless smile. He directed me to an etched glass elevator that took me to the 8th floor. The doors dinged open, and I stepped out and walked five doors down to apartment 826. I held the card to the electric keypad, not sure if I liked the technology or not. Once the keypad's light turned green, I opened the door and stepped in.

I immediately caught a whiff of some type of pine fragrance. *Ahh, so far so good.* I walked down the narrow hall into an open living room and kitchen. The place was beautiful. There were floor-to-ceiling windows, marble countertops, and a leather couch that looked so soft and inviting that I nearly cried. My last couch had been a hand-me-down from my mom, which had more stains and smells on it than I cared to remember. I wanted to take it all in, but I had more pressing matters at hand that needed to be taken care of immediately. I threw my shoes off and plopped down on my new black and tan Fidarsi chair and pivoted to take in the view of Downtown Hollywood.

After the craziness of the past few weeks, and with the first day of shooting coming up, all I wanted to do was lounge around on my new leather couch and zone out to whatever crap television show was on. And that's exactly what I did.

16. DÉJÀ VU ALL OVER AGAIN

BECAUSE OF MY PRE-FIRST-DAY JITTERS, I had barely slept all night. I waited as long as I could, then jumped out of bed and opened the curtains to see the sun's rays piercing through the window. I had to squint my eyes to look out. It almost felt like I had a mild hangover. There was no amount of coffee or espresso that would help how I felt. I continued on with my morning routine, trying over and over to get myself together by smacking my face with cold water in the shower—to no avail. I just hoped I would come alive on the drive to work.

Forty-five minutes later, I pulled up to a gigantic building that someone must've called home at one time. It was impressive, to say the least. I rechecked my email just to make sure I was at the correct address. I saw a lot of cars parked on the nicely manicured lawn, so I pulled into an empty spot. I checked myself in the visor mirror; I didn't like what I saw, but there was nothing I could do to remedy it now, so I took a deep breath and got out of the car.

As soon as I walked in the front door, I was taken aback by the cavernous foyer. This was definitely a much nicer and classier place than the *Primed* and *Stronge* locations. Crystal chandeliers, marble floors, 20-foot ceilings, you name it. I walked around the corner into a kitchen that would make a professional chef weep. The gold-flecked marble counters were decorated with dozens of cups of Starbucks Coffee, stacked boxes of Krispy Kreme donuts, and little pink boxes filled with pastries from a local upscale bakery that specialized in gluten-free, dairy-free, and even vegan alternatives. I decided to play it safe and headed straight for a Krispy Kreme. *Heaven.*

It felt good to be surrounded by all this *luxury.* I needed to check the place out, so I started to wander around and take everything in. Spitz spotted me lurking around like a lost puppy and decided it was time to get the show started. He gave a quick whistle. "Okay everyone, quiet," he said. "Let's get situated, shall we? Take a seat, and let's begin."

We took our seats at a massive oak table in the corner of the large great room. "Please grab a packet, and familiarize yourself with its contents," Spitz said, pointing to a pile of stuffed manila folders on the table. "Today is the day we make history," he said triumphantly to a sea of confused faces. He motioned to a tall, lanky man who looked like he'd time-warped from the 70s. He wore bell-bottom jeans, a plaid shirt with the sleeves rolled up, and a pukka shell necklace.

"This is Rich Masters," Spitz said. "Think of him as the *other* Spitz! Rich is the head of our development team and what he says, goes. What do you say, Rich? Why don't we all move this meeting to the pool?"

Rich shrugged and said, "Sure thing, Spitz."

Pool? Did he just say pool? Now he had my full attention.

Rich led us down a long-tiled hallway with walls that were painted up like jungle scenes. Halfway down the hall, there was the sound of running water. When we came to the end, I couldn't believe my eyes. This was no ordinary pool. No, this was a freakin' *lake*. But it didn't stop there—the entire area was decorated with lounge chairs, a tiki bar, and a massive jacuzzi that looked like it could fit twenty people. And to top it all off, there was a dramatic two-story waterfall at the far end of the pool. The whole setup looked like it was straight out of *Insane Pools* magazine.

We all gathered in front of the bar where Rich stood. "Okay," he yelled, looking impatient. "You can turn the fucking water off now. I can't hear a damn thing!"

As if on cue, the waterfall abruptly shut off. Everything was quiet, except for the tropical bird noises projecting from the surround sound speakers. Rich added, "And shut off those goddamned birds, too!"

Those stopped immediately as well. His face

morphed back into a calm state and he smiled. "Let's begin, shall we? Now I'm only going to say this once; on behalf of myself, Mr. Spitz here, and the entire executive staff, we're sorry." He shook his head, looked down, and raised his hand in dramatic surrender. Silence filled the air.

"Sorry for what, Rich?" a young twenty-something girl (who I later learned was Jenny, the site manager) asked.

BANG! The doors of an upper balcony that looked down onto the pool area crashed open, and an all-too-familiar voice yelled, "I can't sleep without the sound of water! I told you that, damn it! Turn it back on!"

We all turned and looked upward. Jenny's face froze in horror. She turned angrily back around at Rich. He closed his eyes and nodded slowly. "Yep."

The atmosphere instantly changed. There was an electricity in the air that hadn't been there before. Spitz addressed the crowd. "Please don't antagonize her. It will only get worse." He broke out in an evil grin and said with a flourish, "*She's baaaaack!*"

I was dumbstruck. No, it couldn't be. But before I had time to process what was going on, Rich commanded everyone to follow him back into the hallway to a door with a sign that read "NO CAMERAS." We walked into an enormous library. Rich casually positioned himself next to the ornate fireplace. "Everyone get comfortable. Okay. So. You've probably been wondering what's been going on. Some of you may have guessed it already, but the Strong family is back—I mean Sandy and the boys are back, with a new show called, *Only the Strong Survive*."

Blake, Rich's assistant, jumped in, "Here's the synopsis: Sandy needs to get back out into the world now that her loving husband is no longer with her. She's moved into this new house in hopes of starting the next chapter of her life. She must also deal with being the new head of the family. Between those two major roles, she's learning how to manage a household with three practically grown sons all on her own. Well, not all on her own. She has an assistant, Shana, who is constantly running through hoops for Sandy sun up to sun down. Well, more like 24/7, but I digress. There's also, Betty Tauscher, or "Mrs. T," as the boys call her. Her official title is "Home Office Manager," however, she's mainly in charge of keeping the boys out of trouble, and on occasion, out of jail. Thankfully, she's got the most sense out of everyone on the show. If you haven't seen her before, she's tall, lifts weights, and practices judo. She's a physically imposing woman, so the boys take her and her no bull shit attitude seriously—and I strongly suggest you all do the same."

"There you have it, folks!" Rich interjected. "Oh! There's also a full-time housekeeper and landscaping staff managed by a fellow named Milo. He was a jack-of-all-trades guy at one time, but he has since 'graduated' into more of a financial planner role, I guess you could say. He advises Sandy on financial matters now and acts as her agent 'when necessary,'" he said, making air quotations with his hands.

Blake chimed in again. "Let's just try to get some good dirt on him," he said conspiratorially. "I don't like the son of a bitch, and who knows how long this parasite will be around. Oh! And this monstrous house and pool with the waterfall? Yeah, that was all Milo. Need I say more?" Everyone laughed politely.

As Rich was about to conclude the meeting, a loud crash sounded in the hallway. This triggered Spitz to jump up and make a run for the door. Looking apprehensive, Spitz cracked open the door to see what caused all the noise. After a quick look, he shut the door and turned back to us, smiling. "Okay, boys and girls! It's time to get to work." He scanned the crowd. "Peter, get the camera. We need to start rolling *now*."

No one moved. Everyone stood around looking confused. "Don't just stand there!" Spitz said, flailing his arms. "Showtime, people!"

We all sprang into action, running around like chickens without heads. We filed out of the library and back into the massive foyer. The first thing I noticed was a guy standing in a bathrobe looking down from the open second-floor hallway leading to the stairs. Boy, did he look pissed. The second thing I saw was dirt, water, flowers, and the remnants of a huge broken vase scattered over the foyer floor.

"Fuck you, Measles!" came a voice from behind the front door of the house.

The front door opened slightly, and there appeared Army, using the front door like a shield. "It wasn't me!" Army shouted.

"Yes, it was!" Navy shouted from outside, gleefully throwing his brother under the bus.

The man in the bathrobe, who I assumed to be the aforementioned "Measles," ripped off his bathrobe and was standing naked in all his glory. "Beat it, you little fuckers! I'm busy with your mom!"

Then he turned and went back into what must have been Sandy's bedroom. I knew I wasn't the only one wondering what the hell was going on. I spotted Greg, my grip buddy, across the room. He just nodded in my direction as if to say, "Here we go again."

Then I heard Army's whiny, soprano-like voice. "Hey! It's Henderson. *Fuckin'* Marc Henderson."

His voice made me wince. I looked at the front door and saw Army stomping towards me with his dimwit brothers, Navy and Ranger, in tow. "What's up, Killer?" Navy said hitting me on my shoulder. *Whoa. If they only knew.*

"Hey, Marc," Ranger said, advancing towards me like a lion circling its prey.

He held out his hand like he wanted me to shake it. Ranger was always the nicest of the bunch, which wasn't really saying much, because as soon as I shook his hand, he yelled, "Rosa! There's a mess in here!"

"Hey guys. Good to see you again," I tried my best to say warmly.

I could tell by the way the boys were looking over the new crew that they were trying to figure out who was going to be their next victim. They couldn't help but assert their dominance. One of the biggest lessons I'd learned from these sadists was that if you can't figure out who their next victim is, then it's probably you.

"The fucking hero is here! Welcome to our humble abode, *Mr. Reality Killer*," Army said with a smirk, invading my personal space. He backed up, scanned the crew, and zeroed in on Rich.

"Hey man, what's up with this shit?" he said, throwing his arms up in the air. "This is our show, remember that! You fuckers are just temporary."

Proud of their dramatic entrance, the boys decided they'd had enough and headed for the kitchen.

"Hi, all!" Ranger said, then followed his brothers.

As soon as they were out of earshot, Rich looked at Peter, who was holding his mini-camera.

Peter nodded and whispered, "Got it."

"This is going to be *great*!" Spitz said with a sigh of relief.

Greg, who had sidled up to me, leaned in and whispered, "Yeah, it'll be real great from where he's standing."

17. A SLIGHT CHANGE

GREG and I spent the rest of the day fine-tuning all of the stationary cameras so we could get acquainted with the new location, which was a nightmare considering the size of the place. Walking around the place made me really nervous, knowing that I was personally responsible for the entire show. I was happy to be working with Greg again; it made me feel better knowing someone had my back. We were discussing how much a house like this must've cost. He looked it up online and found an old listing, and the price almost blew us away. "Man, reality TV is definitely where it's at," Greg said, poking me in my side. I winched.

As the day began to wrap up, I heard some buzz that the crew were going out for a few beers after work to discuss the new adventure. Happy that I finally had the opportunity to hang out with them again, I asked if I could come along, but their reply really threw me off. They said, "Sorry, crew only."

It felt like a slap in the face. Greg, being the good friend he was, jumped in and reminded them that I *was* a part of the crew. That was always my favorite part about being a grip—we'd all go out once or twice a week and talk trash about the cast. I told everyone I was looking forward to catching up, and that seemed to do the trick, because they relaxed and agreed that I could come along.

On the way over to the bar, I got stuck in a bit of traffic. Usually it would bother me, but I was still basking in the glory of my new car. As I dropped the top down, I saw a faint glimpse of something very disturbing on the corner of West Sunset Blvd and Vine. I pulled my sunglasses down, and squinted harder, but no luck. I had to be sure of what I was seeing, so I made a U-turn, causing a few disgruntled honkers to flip me off as I pulled over to the side as they sped past. I eagerly got out of the car, looking up in awe and confusion.

What. The. Hell? I couldn't believe my eyes. It was an advertisement for *Get a Grip*. Apparently, Spitz's team had cropped a photo from one of the most recent tabloids and had put me smack dab on this giant billboard. And get this, Sandy Stronge and her stupid sons were on it with me. They were making immature, weird faces at me. Behind Sandy and her sons were some big, menacing, old school gangsters who were pointing a gun at a Danny DeVito look alike. And behind them, were four women, in so much makeup they looked like cartoon characters.

I couldn't believe it, but I had to give Spitz and his team props. They worked fast. The entire thing was bizarre. Don't get me wrong, it was thrilling to see myself on a giant billboard for the world to see, but I couldn't help but feel unsettled. It was just *strange.*

I got back in the car and met up with the crew at The Young Turks, a hipster pub that served all kinds of designer coffees and craft beers. I prayed no one had seen the billboard on their way over, but had no such luck. The second I walked into the bar, they all started in with the jabs. To ease the tension, I bought everyone their first round. I asked the bartender where was a good place for us to gather and he pointed to a table in the back that fit our party of eight.

My generosity didn't have the effect I was looking for, because it didn't take long for some of the newer crew members to start dogging me on how I was just trying to show off my new salary. It made me nervous that they felt that way. Apparently, they looked at me as nothing more than a pathetic cast member who was tagging along, which in turn, made me some kind of an enemy. They didn't have much confidence in me, and they had no problem telling me that it was only a matter of time before the Reality Bug would bite me in the ass, just like it did every other reality show "star."

Ouch. I tried my best to reassure them that besides

the hideously massive billboard on Sunset Boulevard, which I'd had absolutely no clue about, none of this was going to change me. "In fact," I said, "I totally understand where you're coming from. We've all seen firsthand what happens to these people, if you can call them that." That elicited some laughs, so I relaxed a bit. "I mean, look at Andrea Milk, or that steroid-happy Army Stronge. Jeez, is that guy a walking nightmare or—?"

I stopped mid-sentence; the group had shifted their focus to something at my immediate left. I turned to see what or who it was. This gorgeous girl in a crop top had approached our table and was standing there, looking at me. She politely asked if she and her girlfriends could take a quick selfie with me. The whole table immediately burst out laughing. My face sank.

"Fuck 'em," Greg said reassuringly to me, then turned to the girl. "Let's go take some selfies with these lovely ladies."

We both stood and Greg, blessed with an easy-going charm, put his arm around the girl. As he sauntered away, he glanced back at our table and winked, which effectively shut them right up.

We walked over to the girl's table, where three of her equally gorgeous friends sat. They all appeared enthusiastic and a bit buzzed. "Hello girls! Are we ready for some tequila?" Greg asked. He was met with giggly approval. He sat down, putting his arm around two of the other girls, while he gave the middle finger to the crew behind the girls' backs.

We ordered a couple rounds of Cabo Wabo tequila shots from the bartender who looked bored with our little party. It was fun, I guess. We all talked and flirted shamelessly back and forth. It had been a while since I'd had a good time, plain and simple. In a way, It felt good and it definitely stroked my ego. I was happy to have Greg by my side. After a while, I decided to look over to see how the crew was doing, but the table was empty. They'd made their point by not saying goodbye.

An hour later I felt pretty buzzed and told Greg I wanted to leave. I snuck out the back and called for an Uber to take me home. I stumbled into the car and gave the driver my new address. As I let my head fall back onto the head rest, I reflected on the day's events. The street lights were turning into blurred lines as the driver coasted through downtown. I was excited about my new gig. It was the first job I actually felt happy about. I had a sudden urge to call Aud and invite myself over for a night cap. I really wanted to share with her all that was going on. And, if I were to be totally honest with myself, I could use her reassurance and the straight-from-the-bottle advice.

I fumbled as I pulled my phone out of my pocket and scrolled until I found "Audrey." She answered on the second ring. "Talk dirty to me," she said.

"I bet you say that to all the boys," I replied, playing

along. I asked if I could come over and tell her about my first crazy day on the job.

"Would love it, toots! But Daisy and I have company right now," she chimed.

"Oh, okay" I said, taken aback. "No worries. Another time."

"Okay, bye now!" she said quickly, hanging up.

Huh, that had been pretty vague, even for Aud. Normally, she'd suggest meeting up later that same day or the next day, but she didn't follow up with anything. How weird was that? She'd *always* had time for me before.

18. TOO LATE TO TURN BACK

THE NEXT DAY, I arrived early to our next filming location, feeling pretty certain today was going to be just as crazy as yesterday. I immediately knew something was off. I mean, this place was nowhere near as nice as the Stronge mansion. As a matter of fact, I didn't see any luxury at all. The roof was—let's just say this place could use a new roof. And the yard looked like a war zone.

I walked up to what looked like a new set of concrete stairs, which the insurance company must have made them install just to be able to use this place. As I opened the front door and stepped through the threshold, I was happy to see a tableful of assorted goodies. The spread looked to be from the same caterer as yesterday's. While I was busy stuffing myself with tiny lemon cream pastries, I looked through the window and saw the group of guys Greg and I had gone out with the night before congregating outside, sipping their coffees.

I waved to say hi, but they looked through me as if I wasn't there. I could practically feel the cold coming off them in waves. "Screw 'em," Greg said over my shoulder, seeing me standing at the window hurt and confused, like a kid who wasn't asked to play in the neighborhood football game. I immediately felt better and shrugged off their diss. God knew I didn't deserve a best bud like Greg, but I was grateful as hell for him. My reverie was broken, however, after a whiff of his morning-after breath that could knock over King Kong. I could smell traces of several different liquors, which made for a very unpleasant experience. My eyes watered and I backed away, keeping my donut away from the boozy stench.

"Whoa, dude, your breath smells like shit! Did you even brush your teeth at all?" *Yikes.* Greg laughed, and we both proceeded to get a cup of coffee.

A few moments later, the door swung open, and Spitz appeared with a manic energy about him. "Let's go, people!" he said, shoving his way to the coffee table.

Taking that as his cue, Rich decided to get things started. "TO THE POOL!" he yelled. Everyone looked confused. "Oh wait! Never mind. There is no pool in this Godforsaken place. Ha! Let's go to the conference room," he deviously snickered.

The "conference room" was really a dining room located off the kitchen. There was nothing impressive about it. We opened up the folding chairs that were propped up against the wall and sat down. By the look on everyone's faces, it was clear we were all bracing ourselves for who knew what.

"Yesterday was fun," Rich said, slapping his hands on the table. "But today is a new day, and we're onto bigger and better, right? Today's show takes us behind the scenes of a new reality show James Spitz and I have created called...wait for it....*Proven Killers!*"

He flashed a smile that seemed even brighter against his deeply tanned face than it did yesterday—maybe he had hit the tanning booth last night. We all looked like deer caught in the headlights again. "So, here's what's happening with this freak show. This place is a halfway house for criminals on parole." Rich paused for the effect, apparently liking what he saw on our stunned faces. "Now, if I didn't have your attention before, I'm sure I have it now. Don't worry, we've carefully cherry-picked a few inmates who've recently become eligible for parole thanks to their good behavior records, which we thought would make for good television." He paused for effect again. "Of course, we did all this with the blessings from the state and the approval of the CDCR. These inmates have been approved to appear on our new show while still satisfying their parole requirements."

You could hear a pin drop in the room. I looked over at Greg and shook my head in disapproval. "Reality television will stop at nothing," Greg whispered just a little too loudly, because a few chuckles sprinkled throughout the room.

"Excuse me, what is the CDCR?" Jenny interjected.

Rich answered, "The California Department of Corrections and Rehabilitation."

Rich looked quite pleased with himself. He went on, "Everyone at this table was also cherry-picked as the crew who will be following these people around as they try to adjust to the outside world. We will hear their stories in their own words as we find out how they've changed since being incarcerated." Rich waited for nods of agreement. "So, I'm sure you can all see why getting their unique perspectives, experiences, and struggles will make for 'must-see TV,'"

Rich waited for more nods of agreement. Seeing none, he continued, "Oh, one little note. Every parolee chosen for this groundbreaking series has spent extensive time in prison for one or more homicides, hence, we titled the show, *Proven Killers,*" he said with a big smile.

We all groaned in unison. "Lighten up, people!" he laughed, clearly enjoying our unease. He turned to look at Spitz who just shrugged.

"Anyway. It's the crew's task to get the real stories from each cast member. Now, listen carefully! There has never been anything done like this before in television. Sure, there have been some documentaries, and that *First 48 Hours* series. But trust me, nothing like this has ever been tried. And with ratings for true crime dramas on the rise, this show is going to be off the charts!"

My stomach churned at the thought of their concept.

Maybe my guilty conscious was starting to get the best of me, just thinking about working with these people. But I had to get it together and distance myself from my personal harrowing experiences with death and this job, before I found myself on the wrong side of the *Proven Killers* show. Spitz caught my uneasiness and came to pat me on my shoulder. He leaned down and whispered, "I know what you might be thinking, but don't worry about it. You're new to this side of the biz, you're just nervous, right?"

He stood up and said louder, addressing the group, "People, we've all been in the biz awhile. We know what it takes. But being on the opposite side of the camera lens can be intimidating. Marc here may be feeling a bit nervous, which is totally understandable, right?"

He looked among the sea of faces around the table. He turned to me, placing a reassuring hand on my shoulder. My cheeks were burning in embarrassment. "You're a natural, Marc. Just know that we have complete faith in you, and we're totally behind you! Right, people?" Not waiting for a response, he powered on, "We all need to remember how unique this opportunity is. Is everybody with me?"

His audience decided to play along and clapped half-heartedly. He addressed me again. "I mean, Marc, you've experienced exactly what these people have...well, without the jail time, of course!" he joked, to some laughter around the table. "Seriously, what I'm trying to say is... you have credibility. You can relate to these people, certainly more than anyone else in this room," he said dramatically, pretending he was firing a gun at someone. "Who else can say that? Nobody gets to kill someone and then gets to star in a television show relating to others who have killed someone, or *two*," he added for more comedic relief. "You'll be the *one guy* who'll be able to gain their trust and get them to open up on what goes on inside of their heads. That'll be *your* job, and nobody else's," he confirmed triumphantly.

He was really trying to convince me—and the entire room—that this was a good idea. "Now, the only downside I see is," he began to crescendo his voice, "well, you're not exactly Zac Efron, but we can't have everything!"

He laughed along with the rest of the conference room. Greg reached over and started mussing up my hair. "So," Rich nonchalantly eased in, "while you two are busy in wardrobe, I'll be taking care of getting all the liability release forms that the CDRC requires signed."

"Liability releases?" I asked, to anyone willing to answer. Spitz unfolded his arms seeing my look of alarm and winked at me. "It's all standard. All we're doing is making sure you're not going to sue us if someone tries to take you hostage," he said casually.

The entire table roared. "Now, now," Spitz lowered his hands. "Brad, here, is our liaison between everything *and* everybody for this show."

He motioned to a nerdy-looking guy who had snuck into the room during the speech. Brad was tall, lanky with blonde hair and black thick-rimmed glasses. Think of a 7th grade science teacher and you've nailed it. All Brad needed was a pocket protector and he was set.

Spitz went on, "Basically, he's the one responsible for smoothing the path for our new residents to get them used to being in front of our cameras, and most importantly, making sure we've got all the required permits."

"Sarah," he said, pointing at a pleasant-looking woman about my age who was wearing glasses and a green, ribbed turtleneck, "she's the absolute best at research and will be prepping everyone with the background and history on each of the criminals—I mean, residents," he said, quickly correcting himself. "Sarah, love, stand up so everyone knows who you are."

Sarah didn't stand but instead waved shyly to our group. I tried to smile, but I could feel my uneasiness starting to rise. I felt like I was drowning. When did I ever think this show was a good idea? Oh yeah. I rolled my eyes. That's right. When I saw all those damn zeros on that check.

The meeting carried on for what seemed like forever, but I was already checking out. I could feel the lump of regret in my throat, and my mouth was parched. I didn't want to accept it, but I was screwed. I mentally kicked myself and told myself to man up, because—like it or hate it—I was now reality TV's new poster boy. Yup, royally screwed.

Looking back, I couldn't believe I'd ended up spending a lot my signing bonus on a new car and a luxury apartment overlooking the city of Hollywood. But those decisions seemed to make sense at the time and hindsight was 20/20, right? I wanted to crawl into a hole and never come out. *Can I get my money back for the car? Or my new place?* I'd screwed up, and I didn't know if there was a way to undo any or all of it. I closed my eyes and prayed hard. Harder than I'd done in a while.

If I didn't before, I *really* hated reality TV now.

19. SHOWTIME

AFTER STAYING UP ALL NIGHT, binge-watching every true crime show I could find, I couldn't sleep. The stories were horrid, but I couldn't turn away. I was glued to my brand new, crystal clear, 80" curved, high-def Sony television. I was a researching maniac—if anything had to do with crime, I was all over it. I surfed the web, hunting down eye-catching headlines from the past several years. I was trying to memorize, and hopefully emulate, what other crime show hosts and reporters did. I had to know what I was getting myself into. I wished I had more time to prepare—maybe talk to some people, take some notes, follow a few professionals around—but it was probably way too late for that.

———

It was 9 am when I woke up, still laying in the same place

as last night. I had morning breath and my hair was beyond scruffy. I felt like I had a hangover, which was sadly becoming a part of my normal morning routine. With so little sleep, I could barely wrap my head around all the things I'd watched last night. After shows like *Locked Up* and *The First 48 Hours* , I was even more scared of all the possible kinds of criminals that were going to appear on the show, and I was seriously starting to doubt if I could pull this off. My armpits were sweaty, my muscles were twitching, and my mouth was dry. I smacked myself in the face and splashed it with cold water and told myself to get my act together. This "pep talk" was also becoming a new morning ritual. I needed to be prepared for whatever might happen today. It was time to man up, take control, and put on my game face. Since I didn't need to show up till after lunch, I decided to at least do something about my hair, and hoped a change in my appearance would do some good and psych me up a little. I searched for a nearby hair salon that I had seen advertised a few weeks prior; they looked like they might take walk-ins. Since it was still fairly early in the morning, I was able to get a seat quickly.

Casey, my hairdresser, was a slim young girl probably fresh out of cosmetology school. She looked no more than 18 or 19 years old. She seemed thrilled to help me with a new look. She suggested a few natural-looking highlights to go along and I agreed. That seemed to make her happy, and she said, "Excellent! You're not going to believe how great you'll look!"

Jeez, I hadn't thought I looked *that* bad. She gave me a complimentary coffee and donut, then got to work. After she worked her magic, I was blown away by the man I was looking at in the mirror. Casey must've noticed how stunned I looked, because she was clapping her hands and laughing at my expression. I gave her a generous tip and headed out. I felt like a new Marc—well, maybe not new, but definitely an improved Marc.

I drove to the set wearing my new Ray Bans, a shirt that cost more than a week's pay back when I was just a grip, and of course, my new "fresh" spiky haircut complete with the highlights, feeling a lot more confident than I did hours before.

At the parking lot, I hopped out of the car, tossed the keys to the parking assistant, and headed for the front door where a few crew members were standing around, smoking cigarettes before the set got rolling.

"Excuse me," I said, trying to act nonchalant, as if I belonged there. The crowd stepped back, but there were a few sneers as I walked by. I couldn't help feeling a little foolish with my new look and all—I mean, it had only been a few weeks ago that I was one of them.

I spotted Spitz and approached him from behind. He was in full executive mode, directing his harried-looking assistant with multiple simultaneous orders, all of which apparently needed to be done "ASAP!" That poor girl. Spitz dismissed her, then turned and saw me.

He immediately poured on the charm. He put his arms around my shoulders and guided me towards the kitchen, where a few people were gathered around the food table happily stuffing themselves with donuts, muffins, and coffee again.

"Marc! I love the new look." He then turned his attention to the table. "I want you to meet one of our first house guests you'll be interviewing today for the pilot episode."

He smiled and gestured towards a very pale, thin, twitchy young guy with a bad haircut. He looked sixteen but was probably in his early twenties.

"Owen! How's it going, buddy?" Spitz said over-enthusiastically, which alarmed the boy, making him spill his coffee. *Boy, and I thought I looked nervous.* This kid looked like he'd eaten a plate of static electricity for breakfast.

"Marc, Owen will be one of our guests on the first show. He survived an incredibly tumultuous and tragic family situation a few years ago. He tried to stop his father from physically beating his younger brother, and as the situation escalated, he ended up having to defend his own life. Since then, Owen has been fighting a tough uphill battle with the court system. For now, he's spending his time in the NA Chanderjian Youth Correctional Facility."

Spitz exhaled, acting deeply distressed by Owen's situation. But I had the feeling he didn't care at all.

"Hi Owen, it's great to meet you. I'm sorry about what happened," I said sincerely, moving to shake his hand. I picked the wrong time to greet him, because he had a donut in one hand and coffee in the other. We both smiled at the awkwardness. He shoved the donut in his mouth to shake my hand. Afterwards, I felt a little sticky jelly in my hand, but I pretended not to notice. I definitely didn't want to scare him anymore than he'd already been.

"Oh, great!" Spitz exclaimed, as if all the magic pieces were gloriously falling into place. "Marc," he said placing his hands on my shoulders, looking into my eyes, "I'm going to send you off to the producers and segment coordinators. It's important that you have all the notes, info, and background, so you can do right by..." Spitz snapped his fingers, straining his mind to remember.

"Owen," I interjected.

"Right! Right," he slapped his leg. "Yes, sorry, Owen. It's a big day, and we're all a little nervous." He shook his head and went about his executive duties.

It took about two and half hours to go over notes, cues, numerous walkthroughs, lighting tests, makeup and wardrobe, and of course, the final "dry run." Thankfully, my initial bundle of nerves were beginning to wear off. I was given step-by-step instructions, and as a former grip, I was excellent at following orders. As I hit more of my marks, repeated endless uninteresting dialogue for sound checks, sat for lighting tests, and changed my outfit a slew of times, I felt a little more comfortable and at ease.

It was finally show time. As soon as they brought Owen out, it looked like he was going to faint. I really felt for the guy. While the cameras rolled, we started talking about his unbelievably difficult childhood. His mother had died when he was seven, and his dad was an abusive alcoholic. Owen wasn't a big guy at all, so he wasn't able to defend himself too well. He was also selfless, taking the beatings his father had inflicted so his younger brother Charlie didn't have to.

But as Charlie got older and bigger, his father started ramping up his abusiveness, and smacking him across the face, pushing and shoving him. His father had tried to justify his actions, claiming he was trying to make a man out of poor Charlie. But Owen knew it was just a matter of time before it escalated into something even worse.

On the night in question, Owen's dad was in a drunken rage over some imagined injustice that he'd had to endure. His father's way of handling injustices was to create injustice himself, so he decided to go after Charlie, who was hiding under one of the beds in the room he shared with Owen. From the onset, it looked like this wasn't the ordinary fury that their father was always in, so Owen instinctively intervened to protect his younger brother.

Owen watched a lot of television in those days and

especially loved the UFC and MMA fights, imaging that he himself would one day be able to defend himself like the fighters he idolized. One of the moves he tried to master on his younger brother was the sleeper hold. Owen practiced all the time and for some reason, thought this would be a good time to test it out for real on his father. Well, that didn't go as planned, because he was easily overpowered. His father threw him against the wall, where Owen fell limp on the floor. His dad turned his rage back to Charlie, visibly more angry. He aggressively pulled Charlie from under the bed and in doing so, lifted the mattress and box spring off the ground with him. He started to viciously pummel Charlie, who was curled up into a ball. Seeing his father hurt his younger brother, Owen mustered up the strength to stagger to his feet and grab one of the metal bed slats that had fallen in the midst of the chaos. He swung like a bat out of hell and hit his father on the back of the head, immediately causing his father to stumble and fall heavily to the floor. Horrified by what he'd done, Owen stopped in his tracks, fear plastered across his face, backing up as he stared down at his father.

Dazed and wobbly, his father scrambled for balance, and pulled a gun out from the back of his jeans. He cocked the trigger and aimed it right at Owen's heart. Owen, looking from the gun to his father, froze. He didn't know what state his father was in, or what he would be capable of doing with a gun. His father's face curled up into a sinister grin, and the boys knew from experience that when that grin appeared, something very bad was about to happen.

Being young, petrified, and scarred from years of abuse, Owen screamed when he noticed his father's gun had moved off of him and was now pointing straight at his younger brother. Knowing he had to do something fast, Owen charged with everything he had. Before his father could react, Owen drove the metal slat straight through his father's chest. His father's eyes went blank and he slumped over.

Owen said he remembered breathing so hard that he could barely stand. He didn't dare let go of the metal slat. But that's when he noticed blood dripping from where he'd penetrated his Dad's chest. Blood was pooling every-where, and Charlie and Owen both knew their father was gone. Kneeling down, Owen dropped his weapon and picked up Charlie from the floor, telling him that it'd be okay, that no one would hurt them again and they were free now. Together, they fled from their horror movie of a life and never looked back. I felt a wave of sympathy as we wrapped up the interview, and thanked Owen, and told him he'd done a great job.

From there, I made my way to the editing room, which was set up in what looked to be the old laundry room to see if they needed to do any retakes. All they said was that this was going to be a great show, and nothing needed improving. The crew was satisfied, and I was able to take a break. What a day, and what a story! I couldn't believe this was my job now.

I was hyped up on adrenaline and called Aud to see if she was busy. She said she wasn't, but commanded that, "If you are coming over here, you better not show up empty-handed."

I hung up and immediately headed to her favorite Southwestern restaurant for takeout, and then to the liquor store. I bought everything I needed to make her favorite margaritas. I was sure we'd both need a drink—or two—while I told her Owen's story.

I took a minute to examine my old digs as I pulled up to the apartment complex and made my way toward Mrs. Fox's front door, stopping to peak in the window of my old place. It looked empty. It probably hadn't been rented out yet.

Mrs. Fox greeted me at her front door. Of course, I had to give Daisy her standard amount of puppy love before Mrs. Fox and I could get to happy hour. Aud gave me a big kiss on the cheek and a fierce hug, which I returned. Man, I'd really missed her. Maybe I was just imaging things before when I'd called her the last time?

In a few minutes, she whipped up our drinks like a pro, and I laid the takeout on the table. It was like I'd never left. We slid right back into our comfortable routine of shooting the breeze. We took the time to update each other about our lives. Sadly, one of her "peeps," Joanie, had had a stroke and wasn't doing well. I got a rare glimpse of Aud's vulnerable side, something I hadn't expected.

"I don't think she's going to come out of this too good..."she said. "Her doctors think she didn't get to the hospital quick enough, and there may be some serious, permanent damage. No one was with her," she looked down, clasping her hands together.

I leaned in towards her, "You always tell me that it's not over until it's over, right?" She slowly nodded. "So, give Joanie all the love, support, and encouragement that you can. She probably needs you right now."

I hugged her and she clasped on to me, hard. It dawned on me that Aud was contemplating her own immortality. Suddenly, she straightened up and said, "Enough of this bullshit. How was your day?" She was acting like her old self again. "If you came over here to bring me down like this, next time I will be busy when you ask to come over!"

She threw her head back and let out a throaty laugh. I told her about Owen's story and what was happening on set. Hours quickly passed, and the food and margaritas looked to be finished as well. There was a calm in the air, and then we said our goodnights. I confirmed that I'd be back tomorrow with even better stories than today. I gave Aud and Daisy good night pecks and walked out the door.

20. THE BIG DEBUT

WHEN I GOT home from Aud's, I checked my email, quickly scanning my inbox for anything that looked important. Spitz had sent over some of the footage they had pieced together from that bizarre first day on the Stronge set. I was always amazed at the talent some of the behind-the-scenes people had. With only a little footage, they could arrange and switch things around like a puzzle. My initial reaction was, *not bad.*

It was really weird seeing myself in the footage. I knew better than to get too excited about what to expect. I sent back a reply telling Spitz I thought it was good and I was really excited to see what they were going to do with Owen's story. I emphasized that I thought his story was going to be the hit. I figured, what the hell, I'd try to do anything I could to get the Stronge's show out of our lineup. Who wouldn't love to be rid of those guys for good?

Thursday came around quickly, and I found myself struggling to get out of bed again at 4 am. Spending the last few days with Mrs. Fox had really lightened my spirits, but I still wasn't fully prepared to tackle a new day on set.

This time, I decided to park the car myself. As I turned the corner for the parking area, I noticed a different group of guys standing around smoking cigarettes. I hustled up the stairs and as I tried to squeeze my way through the small crowd and into the building, I couldn't help but hope that I didn't literally rub any of them the wrong way. It was not the day to find yourself splattered on the floor chewing broken concrete. As I got to the front door, one of the younger guys stepped in front of me, blocking the entrance.

"Yeah, you that Marc Henderson guy, right?" he said as he side-eyed me. "Hey, Benny, this here is our *boss man,* Marc Henderson," he said smirking at me.

The guy who spoke looked awfully familiar, and then it dawned on me. This was the guy from that crazy billboard. The guy who resembled a younger, but more obnoxious Joe Pesci, and he couldn't have been more than seventeen. He seemed more or less harmless in real life, except for the nasty-looking skull tattooed on the front and side of his neck. His buddy Benny was a different story. Benny looked mean and menacing— exactly like he did on the billboard. Benny looked over at me and stomped his cigarette under his black work boot and shouldered his way to where we were standing. He measured me up and down, as if to decide if he should show respect or not—a process that he probably went through with everyone he met.

He was huge, hairy, and tall, much like Sasquatch. He had sleeves of tattoos, and yellow teeth that needed help from the dental gods. The way everyone moved out of his way, I assumed he was the ringleader of this group, or at the least, its enforcer.

"Yeah, hey, I'm Marc," I said, turning to address the group. "Good to meet you guys. Look forward to working with you, but I'm sorry, I'm not the boss. That would be Mr. Spitz."

I tried to smile, but it came out more like a grimace. Benny spit at the ground and proceeded to squeeze my hand until it was numb. "Well, I was told," Benny pumped up, "to take my orders from you and my money from Spitz."

Did I mention Benny looked like he weighed as much as a school bus? He was now literally blocking the sun, and it strained my neck just to look up at him. Unknowingly coming to my rescue, David the line producer popped his head out the door. "You guys need to be in makeup. You're supposed to be ready in twenty."

Benny looked horrified, almost like he'd just seen his own reflection. It was nice to know that something at least scared the beejeezus out of Benny. I'd file that away for future reference. "We don't do makeup," he objected, pointing to the gang.

David gave them a look and said forcefully, "No makeup, no money!"

Ah, the universal language of greed. Still not happy, they complied and pushed past David into the building.

"Are you sure this was a good idea?" I asked, looking at David as I was sitting in wardrobe.

Benny and his gang were a huge distraction; they were trying their hardest to give the makeup artists a hard time. It was like watching a train wreck, and it was clear that my criminal status couldn't hold a candle to these guys.

Then it was my turn in the makeup chair. The artists looked frazzled beyond belief, but also relieved their part was over. I wouldn't be so lucky. As the finishing touches were being applied to my face, Spitz popped in to give an unsolicited and wholly insincere "we're all a team" pep talk, but he knew these guys didn't give a rat's ass about any of it.

"Okay!" Spitz clapped his hands together. "Are we ready to make some history? I'm talking about some cutting-edge, hardcore shit! Something that's never been done before!"

Then he looked sternly, pointing at each of us, "But for this to work properly, and if you guys want your fifteen minutes of fame, not to mention your moolah, there are a few unbendable rules you must abide by."

Spitz inhaled, closing his eyes as if these were the most important words he'd ever have to say. "The first and most important rule is that there are absolutely NO FUCKING WEAPONS. No exceptions."

He spoke slowly and forcefully, as if he was in front of a kindergarten class and not hardened ex-criminals. It was kind of funny watching Spitz stand there, hands gesturing wildly like some mad conductor, and speaking in that loud, all-in-caps type of way he did when trying to shove a point home. He paused, waiting for Benny and the boys to give some type of nod or indication that they heard and agreed. It was pretty ridiculous telling gang members that they couldn't carry weapons of any kind. If the cameras had been rolling, they would've zoomed in on bulging vests filled with only God knew what, and that was what you *could* see. I wouldn't be surprised if they'd had some other hardware tucked neatly away for "special occasions."

Spitz carefully ticked off the remaining rules, followed by numerous threats to fire everyone before their checks even cleared payroll if they didn't play right. It was pretty clear that Spitz was serious about these non-negotiable standards. He even said that everyone would be subject to frisking at any time should management deemed it necessary, just to make sure everyone was living up to their end of the bargain. After a few stern looks, the group reluctantly agreed. *What the heck, I thought, these guys have been living locked up for who knows how long now. They're probably used to taking orders.* These guys knew how to get around orders and within hours, I knew there would be all sorts of weapons hidden away in this place. And even if they couldn't have their weapons close by, they'd find a way to protect themselves if the shit started hitting the fan. It wasn't exactly a warm and fuzzy introduction to our new show.

It was finally time to prep for the next taping. I looked over the notes that I'd been given about our next guest, who went by the name of "Armando." After quickly reading about this guy's past, I was immediately impressed with his story and looking forward to meeting him. In prison, Armando stood out, but in a good way. He'd found a passion for helping the lives of some of the other gang members, who initially were told they were lost causes. Because of his work with gang members, for the first time in years, the statistics of prison fights and gang-related killings in the Union City Maximum Security Correctional facility had decreased by 20%. This was huge, especially when you learn that violence in prisons never goes down—just up. Soon after, other correctional facilities were coming to Union City to learn their secret. I was looking forward to interviewing him and hearing what he had to say, especially what had made him decide to turn his life around.

Spitz approached as I was finishing up my preparation for the Armando segment later this week. He was ecstatic and remarked about how good the pilot for *Proven Killers* looked. He was expecting "pretty big numbers." *Let's pray these numbers are as big as he hopes,* I thought. He congratulated me and patted me on the back, then quickly took off searching for his overworked assistant. *If she was smart, she'd be hiding in a closet somewhere right about now.*

As the day of filming some of the background footage wore down, the anxiety of the crew heightened, as we were all nervous about hearing the world's reaction to our first episode. After taping, Spitz invited me to watch the test pilot with him and his executive team in his office. It was tempting, as it would be exciting to see everyone's hard work come together, but I decided it would be best for me to go home, just in case things didn't go so well.

As I headed out the door, Brian, one of Spitz's team members, stopped and asked me if I was going to join them in Spitz's office. "Thanks very much, but no. I'm just really nervous about it and honestly, I'd just rather be alone—just in case things don't go as planned," I said politely.

"No problem, man. I totally get it," he said, waving it off. "Opening night jitters can be a bitch."

"Yeah, something like that," I said with a half-smile. "Talk to you later."

But he was no longer paying any attention to me. He was already leaving, on his way to the next "to do" item on his list.

After getting home, I laid down to take a nap, but it was no use. I couldn't turn my mind off for a single second. Mrs. Fox had invited me over, but my stomach was so tight with knots that I couldn't bear the thought of being around anyone until I heard the reviews from the show. To top it all off, my mother called. She was excited for me, correctly assuming I could use some maternal support. We talked for about 15 minutes and I started to relax. She teased me about how everyone thought they now had a bona fide TV star in the family. It was just what I needed.

But then she started going into the whole family rundown. Cousin Bernadette was getting married *again* and everyone was hoping the third time was a charm. Uncle Stan's dementia was getting worse. Blah, blah, blah. I cut her short, knowing this could go on for another thirty minutes and I'd miss the show.

Spitz set up a Google Portal conversation so he, his executive team, and I could watch the show more or less together. I guess even though we all weren't in the same room, Spitz wanted all of us close by. I was okay with that, but I was still just as nervous.

I grabbed a beer out of the fridge and settled in on the couch for the big debut. I waited anxiously for a few minutes. Then, after a few preemptory commercials, the show finally came on. The knot in my stomach was getting bigger and bigger. It took everything I had not to cringe when the beginning credits started to roll. I thought listening to a recording of yourself was weird, but seeing yourself on a TV screen was worse, and pretty humbling in a strange way.

My eyes were glued to the TV for the next hour. The more I watched, the more I felt the need to critique everyone's performance, especially mine. There were so many things we could've done differently. But as the show continued, my nerves settled. Once the second interview came on, I felt a little more relaxed, like I could enjoy it for what it was. It definitely flowed more naturally than the choppiness of the first interview. As the final credits rolled, I was relieved. I turned off the TV and sighed. *Thank God it's over.*

Ping! It was Spitz texting me. *Ack! Should I respond?* But before I had the chance to, my phone pinged again. This time it was Greg. And then another one from Sarah, an assistant producer. I closed my eyes. How bad was it? I didn't think it had been *that* horrible, had it?

Okay, get a grip, Marc. I took a deep breath and read the first message.

James: *Don't have numbers yet, but the team seems to like what they saw! Not bad for a first run, Marc, eh? See you in the AM!*

Ok, that was pretty encouraging. There was no mention of being fired, so that was definitely a good thing. *Not too shabby, Henderson. Maybe this wouldn't so bad after all.*

21. HURRICANE SANDY

I SAW Greg talking intently to Sandy's assistant, Shana, after I arrived at the Stronge mansion for day two of shooting. I walked around the long way, so I wouldn't have to approach them and get caught in the crossfire. I tried my best to stay incognito, as I wasn't ready for the day's unnecessary shenanigans. However, I was curious as to what Greg and Shana were discussing. From my angle in the kitchen, it appeared that they were in the middle of a heated argument.

Veins were bulging, faces were red, and arms were flailing around, accentuating frustrations and proving points. I was hoping to stay hidden and snatch some peace and quiet before taping, so I quickly grabbed a hot cup of dark roast coffee and a chocolate donut before heading to the pool.

As soon as I walked to the end of the long jungle-themed hallway, I saw Rich and Spitz talking privately behind the waterfall. I wasn't paying attention to where I was walking and accidentally bumped into a large, standing bronze vase holding some type of green leafy plant. I tried to right myself but couldn't avoid making some noise. Their necks snapped and immediately turned to what caused the noise. Crap—there went my cover. It was too late to turn back now.

Surprisingly, they didn't dismiss me. Instead, they motioned me over like two kids with a secret they couldn't wait to tell. James grabbed me on the shoulder and excitedly whispered, "Sandy and Milo are having a huge fight. This is going to be great. We've already sent a camera guy over to their room to catch the whole thing. Hurry," he pushed, "Move!"

I had to leave my coffee and donut next to the decorative rocks surrounding the waterfall. We weren't due on set for another twenty minutes. No peace, no quiet, and no donut. Damn. It was time to work, and I needed to do as I was told, so I sprang into action. Spitz handed me one of the lightweight portable cameras, and I headed toward the action.

As I was getting closer to the room, I could hear Sandy screeching, "You lying son of a bitch! How dare you come into MY house stinking of her!" She punctuated her accusation by throwing a vase at the wall.

I could hear the desperation in Milo's pleading response. "Sandy! Honey. *Baby.* You've got it ALL wrong! Margot is *not* my girlfriend. She only works for me as a consultant. That's all! It's not what you think," he said, dodging more hardware.

At the rate things were flying in the air, the set designers would have more job security than they needed, dealing with these two. Sandy was no push-over, nor was she a stranger to borderline abusing her latest boy toy. Sadly, Sandy was a twelve-year-old bratty tween trapped in an adult woman's body.

I braced myself and slowed my steps as I approached the door. I peeked inside, looking left and right for the other camera guy, but he was nowhere to be seen. He was probably hunkered down somewhere, trying to protect himself from flying objects while trying to get all this craziness on video.

Crash! "One, two, three," I counted. I took a deep breath and slipped quietly inside, covering my head. Fortunately, I came in to the left, behind Sandy, who was in such a rage, she wouldn't have heard a herd of elephants stampeding into the room. Her face was contorted in rage, and I could feel the heat a mile away.

I looked up and saw Milo at the end of the room, where there was debris and broken glass scattered all around. Luckily for him, he was far enough away that Sandy's aim kept missing him.

If Milo noticed me or the other guy, who I eventually spotted tucked behind an overstuffed chair in the other corner, he gave no notice or warning. He looked terrified, and I was an up-close witness. The scene playing out right before my eyes was reality TV ratings gold. Unable to afford missing a second of footage, I setup the camera and hit Record.

"You vile snake! How could you slither into my bed reeking of that slut's perfume! You two-timing piece of crap! You thought you had it made, didn't you? You thought sleeping in MY bed, wearing MY husband's pajamas, eating MY food, and spending MY money was going to allow you to do whatever you wanted! She's young enough to be your daughter, you pervert—I could just kill you! I know people who would slit your throat right now —just to be in your position!"

For Sandy's finale, she hoisted a ceramic lamp in the air, yanked its cord out of the outlet, and hurled it straight at Milo's head.

Reflexively, Milo ducked behind the liquor cabinet just before the lamp crashed into the wall behind him. Damn. That could've been the money shot.

But Milo's luck was running out.

Sandy charged a little closer, grunting and grabbing a small Grecian statue off the coffee table. Crouched like a scared rabbit, Milo pleaded, "Sandy! Please! You've got to believe me! Margot is nothing. She's nothing to me. She's just a poor stupid young girl with a crush. That's all. I swear to you! Why would I want her when I have you?!"

Without warning, the door flung open with a bang. It was Margot, and by the royally pissed off look on her face and her defiant stance, she must have heard the whole thing. I stole a quick look at the other cameraman who had popped his head out from his hiding place. He gave me a thumbs up sign and disappeared again.

"You dirty old man! *'A young girl with a crush'?*" she shrieked, storming towards Milo. "Are you kidding me?" she screamed at the top of her lungs. "You and your baby-sized dick were rubbing up against me every chance you got! The only reason I slept with you is because you promised me a spot on the show. And let me tell you, that twenty seconds of torture definitely wasn't worth it. Everything and everyone about this place is horrid. I'm out of here!"

And with that, Margot turned and left as quickly as she had entered.

Milo timidly popped up briefly behind the cabinet to see if Margot was gone for good. Sandy took advantage of the moment and hit her target right on the money. There was a thud, and Milo crumpled like a rag doll. Just perfect.

"Oh my God! Boys!" Sandy screamed in a panic. *"Boys!"*

I heard voices coming from the hallway. Thankfully, it was a female's voice and not one of Sandy's offspring. I turned to find Shana and Greg entering the room, their eyes taking in the room and assessing the damage. After spotting Sandy, Shana made a beeline and did her best to calm her down. Greg ran over to Milo to see if he was still breathing. "Milo!" he shouted.

Greg gently shook Milo to get him to come around. Greg then slowly helped him to a sitting position against the wall. "Ugh," Milo groaned. He looked dumbstruck, eyes widening as he saw blood—first on his fingers from where he rubbed his head, then on the floor, where a small amount had smeared. His features quickly switched to rage.

Shaking Greg off, he staggered to his feet, determined to confront Sandy, who, seeing the murderous look on his face, started to scream. Before anything could escalate, Spitz appeared.

"Knock it the fuck off! I've had enough of you two!" Spitz roared. "Milo—get the fuck out of here! You are off this show!" Spitz's authority sure came in handy when you needed it.

"Oh yeah?" Milo growled. "You think so? I'm suing *you* and *that bitch*!" He pointed to Sandy, who was now using Shana as a human shield.

"Peter? Marc? Please tell me you got all this shit," Spitz asked, looking for confirmation.

"Got it," Peter confirmed, looking spent.

I stood up, straightened my shirt, and nodded in agreement.

"Go ahead," Spitz challenged Milo. "See how far you get. Now get the fuck out of here before I call the cops, or better yet, before I get Sandy's boys to kick your ass!" Spitz said, daring Milo to give a rebuttal.

Milo pushed Greg out of the way and stormed out the

door. "Bastard!" Sandy shouted, hurling one last insult at Milo. She was more courageous now that she had reinforcements.

What a day. Shana, Greg, and I shook our heads at each other, knowing this was turning into just another "normal" day on this crazy job.

22. LIFE IS A DRAG

AFTER MILO (AKA "MEASLES") and Sandy's meltdowns the other day, Sandy demanded that the cameras be shut off for a while so she could figure things out. But since reality television must go on, Spitz came up with a plan for Greg and me. He sent us over to meet a few new cast members from the third show that he was involved in called *Reality Is A Drag*. I had to hand it to him—Spitz definitely knew how to scour the landscape for all his off-the-wall TV show ideas.

Apparently, this new show was about some L.A. drag queens who had developed a cabaret act that became a huge hit, with waiting lines for every performance. Now they wanted their shot at the "big time" (didn't they all). Spitz claimed he had found them by accident, but nobody believed him. There were always rumors going around about his penchant for kinky things like this, but since he was the man paying the bills, no one had the courage to rock the boat. The way Spitz told it, what really intrigued him about this idea was not their well-produced and professional show, but all the conversations that took place behind the scenes, and between the acts and afterwards, when the cast chilled out in the bar and let their hair down, so to speak.

Being the self-proclaimed reality TV genius he was, Spitz thought it'd be perfect to follow them around with a film crew to record their performances, their back stories, day-to-day lives, and anything else that would grab the audience's attention.

With that in mind, we drove to a club downtown off of Hollywood Boulevard. There was a neon sign that read, "The Venetian Blind," which reminded me of that great Robin Williams flick from some years ago, *The Birdcage.* Greg and I looked at each other, both with the same unsaid question, *Are we actually going to do this?*

Walking into a darkened foyer, I could vaguely make out some tables and chairs which were randomly arranged throughout the cavernous room. There was also a good-sized stage along the back wall, with a catwalk jutting out into the seating area. There were pink and purple lights twinkling all over the place.

"Hi, sweeties!" said a voice from the front of the room. The club was pitch black coming in from the outside, and our eyes hadn't quite adjusted to the sudden change in light.

"Oh, cut it out," another voice popped up.

Greg elbowed me in the ribs. Apparently, his eyes adjusted quicker than mine, and he was considering making a run for it. "Last chance to turn around," he whispered.

As we walked further into the main room, we noticed a small round table right in front of the stage where four women dressed in their finest were sitting and drinking. The closer we got, the more I noticed that each lady had very high hair and dramatic makeup just like the woman I'd seen on the billboard that promoted our show.

"Hello, gorgeous!" said one of the women. She patted the vacant chair next to her. "Come sit down here."

She could've passed as Tina Turner's identical twin. Greg—always the braver of us two—sat first, and I went around to the other side and sat next to an Adele look-alike. "Well, look at you," the woman next to Greg said, smiling. She struggled to wiggle her chair closer to him. She was twice the size of Greg and had on a skintight leather outfit.

"Be nice, Stella," the Adele clone said. Then she turned to me, introducing herself. "Hi, my name is Cherish," she offered, giving me her hand. "That big brutish one is Stella. This is Sam," she said, pointing to a Cher doppelganger, "and this is the beautiful Daphne."

Daphne was the fourth in the group, who indeed was gorgeous and was a dead ringer for Christina Aguilera."Uh, nice to meet you all," I said, "This is Greg and I'm..."

"Oh, we know who you are, honey," Stella chimed in, batting her eyelashes flirtatiously. "*Spitzy* already told us you were coming."

I looked at Greg, who was mouthing the word *Spitzy?* at me.

"Everyone knows you, Marc. You're the kind, handsome man who had the tragic confrontation with that vicious Lync Prime. Listen. We all knew Lync, if you know what I mean, and let's just say," she said in a conspiratorial whisper, "the community won't miss him at all."

"Stella, Marc doesn't want to hear that," Daphne snapped.

Stella frowned, but quickly got over it as she began snuggling up to Greg, who looked a little uncomfortable. And I, well I was getting a kick out of watching Greg all squirmy. Mr. Never Gets Flustered getting nervous? Priceless.

Apparently, Daphne was the leader of the pack. So, I focused in on her. She was delighted to give us her background story, which would hopefully motivate the other three to open up as well.

But I shouldn't have worried about that. These girls were all talkers. It became apparent that this was going to be a reality gold mine, just as Spitz had envisioned. Each drag queen had an interesting, if a bit peculiar, background. And they were all very eager to share their stories of hardships, growth, and eventual success.

Sam was a happily married heterosexual man with

two kids who unfortunately got laid off from his corporate job at AT&T. Finding meaningful work that could provide the same income for him was tough, especially as the days dragged on into months. He was one of thousands of white-collar workers who'd been downsized, all in the name of corporate greed. Then one lucky day, Sam ran into Cherish at the grocery store. He'd known Cherish from high school, but back then, Cherish had been known as "Charlie." Both had spent a lot of time in the school's drama & music departments, performing in concerts and plays together. After that bump-in, they quickly became friends again, always grabbing a coffee or a beer to catch up.

Charlie was thankful that Sam had never judged his lifestyle and that their friendship remained solid. When Cherish heard Sam explaining his job situation, she told him there was a job opening at the club where she worked. And that with his terrific voice, Sam should audition for it. The pay was not only good, but it could be a stepping stone to new opportunities. After many failed attempts at landing "normal" 9-to-5 jobs, Sam was open to any and all suggestions.

So, Sam went home and discussed this new opportunity with his wife. To Sam's surprise, she not only gave him her blessing and support, but she was more than happy to be his makeup and wardrobe stylist. Before he knew it, Sam had become one of the "girls." His only caveat, however, was that he wouldn't change his name.

He thought it'd be too confusing to answer to anything else. Besides, Sam could easily be used as a man or woman's name.

After getting everyone's background stories, Greg and I talked about what was expected from them and the rules they would have to follow during the filming of the show. It felt pretty cool to stand in as a liaison between Spitz and his clients. I could see how all this could become a little addictive.

Once we finished, we gave the ladies a chance to ask questions of their own, answering what we could and ironing out any potential issues they raised. Greg asked them if they were ready for television, which was answered with delighted squeals and shrieks from all four. I had to smile. I was reminded of the time I'd taken Audrey to see Bruno Mars in concert for her birthday, and all the females, including her, were screaming as loud as they could.

As Greg and I said our goodbyes and started heading out, Stella grabbed me by my back pocket and spun me around with ease like a ballerina and said with a wink, "So, how long until we're famous, cupcake?"

23. INTRODUCING: ARMANDO

I SPENT the whole night dreaming of different scenarios where we could best use the cast from *Reality is a Drag*. My mind was taking me places I wasn't sure I wanted to go, as I found myself thinking of one bizarre situation after another.

I was startled out of sleep by my cell phone beeping. It was Greg, asking if he could get a ride to work with me, because apparently, he had decided to hang out with our new "girlfriends" and watch them perform their entire show at The Venetian Blind. He said he'd had so much fun and that he'd gotten smashed drunk. He had wisely taken an Uber home, but now needed to pick up his car in the club parking lot. I told him I was glad he'd done the right thing and that I would swing by and pick him up.

"Man, you look terrible," I said, watching him

gingerly ease himself into the car. "Please don't tell me you did an all-nighter."

Greg winced, closed his eyes, and said, "Not so loud. Just drive and don't ask questions."

When we pulled up to the *Proven Killers* set, we saw Benny and the rest of the crew sitting on the front porch, smoking cigarettes and drinking something that looked like Kool-Aid out of red plastic cups.

After helping Greg stumble out of the car, we slowly made our way to the building's entrance. "Man, you guys have any idea who's here?" Benny asked, slapping me on the stomach. "This place just got real, "I heard from the Joe Pesci look-alike.

"Yo Arms, come here and meet the new warden!" Benny said enthusiastically. "Arms, this is Marc." He gestured towards a good-looking Hispanic guy who looked to be dressed a couple of notches up from the rest of the crew.

"Hi, nice to meet you" Armando said, staring at the ground.

"Hello, Armando—or uh, Arms—whichever you prefer. I'm Marc and this sick-looking puppy is Greg," I said, extending my hand for a shake.

Greg muttered, waved, and continued on his way to find the coffee station.

"I saw you on the news," Armando offered, finally looking me in the eye as he shook my hand with a powerful grip.

We had a brief, pleasant conversation while I proceeded to show him his bunk and outlined the rules of the set. From just meeting him, I could tell that he was a little different than what I had imagined from hearing his story.

When Armando was only a few days away from turning sixteen, he made a bad choice. He felt like a man at that point and decided to take fate into his own hands by seeking vengeance for his brother's murder. When Armando was only fourteen years old, his older brother Carlo had been caught in the crossfire of a shoot-out between rival gangs. Carlo hadn't been a gang member, just an innocent bystander who was in the wrong place at the wrong time. It took Armando a long time, but he finally learned the identity of the gang member whose bullet had killed his brother, and he paid him back in kind. Unfortunately for Armando, he was caught and tried as an adult, which resulted in him receiving a prison sentence of 22 years.

After serving 14 years in prison, the system decided it was time to cut him a break due to good behavior. They gave Armando a choice: stay in the halfway house and appear on the show for one season, with his parole time being served while on the show, or stay in prison for another year, until he would officially be eligible for parole.

While incarcerated, Armando had been a model prisoner and became very passionate about helping others;

more specifically, he decided to dedicate his life to helping young gang members turn their lives around in honor of his late brother. He expressed to me just how much he was looking forward to helping others avoid getting caught up in the violent gang-banger life.

As we were talking, I could hear Spitz yelling for me. I excused myself and walked out of the conference room to see Spitz looking a bit disheveled and fired up, which was odd, as he always prided himself on staying calm and in control.

"We are done with the Stronge show!" he erupted. "I have had it with those ungrateful motherfuckers." Spitz proceeded to explain how the boys wanted revenge on Milo for how he allegedly mistreated their mother.

"I had half a mind to let those punks teach that piece of shit Milo a lesson, until they said they wanted to do it on one of our shows," he said, visibly shaking.

"Those Stronge bastards are insane, Marc!" He paused and I could see him force himself into a calmer demeanor. "Driving over here, I gave this some thought. We're going to have to make this show our focal point. We need *Killing Reality* to be our main show! The drag girls can fill in some extra time until we can manage to come up with something else. I know they won't mind more air time."

"I'm no lawyer," I said, "but don't we have a legal obligation to continue?"

He put his hand on my shoulder, "Kid, this is reality

television. We can do whatever the fuck we want." I stared at him blankly.

"Okay, I need you to ramp up the schedule on the shooting of this show, now!" he said, clearly back in boss mode. "All the focus is going to be on you and *Proven Killers*. I want Greg to start taking more of a leadership role on the filming of the *Reality Is a Drag crew*, since from what I've been hearing, he's been doing great work with that sort of stuff. Plus, it'll free up time, so you can stay focused here."

Before I could say anything, he marched out the front door. He was a man with a plan. The Stronge boys must've made one hell of an impression. I smiled.

Finally. Good riddance to the Stronge family.

24. BY THE NUMBERS

THE REST of the week was spent doing some behind-the-scenes filming for *Proven Killers*. After the debut of the pilot episode, I was eager for the show to be a hit, and although reality television seemed like a cash cow, it all depended on the numbers, which we were still waiting for. The more viewers we had, the better our future looked.

I felt the makeup brush tickle my nose as I heard an overstimulated Spitz call for me from the hallway. "Marc? Marc, there you are! Feedback from the *Proven Killers* pilot came back from the brass today and it looks like we brought in a pretty decent review." I could see it in his face that he had more to say. "But not exactly what we had hoped for with all the hyping we did."

He must've seen the disappointment adorn my face, because he added, "Hey, I'm not telling you this so you worry. Marketing has already gotten a few focus groups together to screen the pilot and take a look at some of the other footage we've put together. Depending on what they like, we can see what works and what doesn't. Then we'll just do a little tweaking and we'll be as good as gold. Cheer up, pal," he said, patting me on the back as he turned to leave.

We ended the day early, because all that was left to do was to take a few candid shots and get some filler coverage for the transitions. The exec team didn't want to invest much more into the new episodes until they had heard back from the focus groups.

Spitz called me early Saturday morning to tell me he had some news and that he was sending someone over to my house that afternoon to review data from the focus groups. My doorbell rang a little after one, and as I opened it, my mouth dropped to the floor. One of Spitz's marketing "Mactor Girls" (model/actor) from his office was standing at my door. Her name was Laura, but at her insistence everyone called her "Laurey." She was around 5'7" and had long, sleek brown hair. She spoke very quickly, as if she'd rather be anywhere but my house on a Saturday afternoon. It took a little bit to catch what she was saying. I was sure I heard "terrific news" in there somewhere.

I asked her to slow down a bit so I could better understand. Apparently, one of the focus groups scored us through the roof. The group consisted of females between ages 18 and 49.

"They LOVED the segment you did with Armanda and have been asking to see more!" Laurey said.

"You mean, they really liked what I did with Armando's interview and want a follow up?" I asked, trying not to stumble over my words. *Hmm, this didn't sound that bad, and the ladies liked me too? Not bad, Marc. Not bad at all, I thought.*

"Well, kind of," she said. "You see, they *loved* Armando! And of course, your work, also." She hastened to assure me. "Don't get me wrong. It seems like this Armando character in particular is quite appealing to the ladies. Here, take a look at this."

She pulled out her phone and scrolled through some of the focus group reviews: "'Sexy,' 'Dangerous,' 'He can save me *anytime.*' The list goes on and on, Marc!" she said, waving her arms and laughing as if this was the funniest thing she'd heard in a long time.

I got a huge pit in my stomach, and I had the funny feeling that she wasn't here just to give me the news about the focus group.

She continued, "So, this is what the team is thinking. We either scrap the other segments and make this interview with Armando longer so it runs the entire episode, *or* at the end of it, we bring in Armando as your...as your right-hand man, your number two. What do you think? It's pretty fresh, right?"

It wasn't pretty 'fresh' at all. What it was, was pretty fucked up. I had to put the brakes on this fast. "Laurey, I agree that it's *fresh* and all, especially with the ladies as part of the audience, but this concept is way too different. What will Benny and the other guys think? What would I be doing? It's my show, right? That is why Spitz gave me the big bucks, right?" I said, thinking I sounded like a whiny little brat.

She shifted her feet and went into full Spitz mode. "Listen up, Marc. You didn't score that well on your own as a solo lead. You didn't do as well as we had hoped. So, we're giving the audience, and our shareholders, what they want. And what they want is a little more Armando. Your ass is lucky they didn't pull the plug on this show, so you need to get on board. Got it?"

Now I could see why Spitz had sent Laurey over—she was a mini Spitz. What choice did I have? If I didn't go along with the plan, I could get kicked off the show altogether.

"Fine," I said. "Got it."

"And one more thing," she said, smirking. "We need to find out some more information on this Armando character. Spitz isn't going to waste a big check on someone who isn't going to deliver. And seeing as you'd be his new cohost, we think *you* should be the one to do the digging."

She really *was* the mini Spitz. The two together were a scary combination. Had there been this much conniving before *I* was brought onto the team? I pushed the thought away. "And how do you suggest I do that?" I asked.

She shrugged with a devious grin. "I'm sure you can figure it out, Marc. Let's just hope everyone's following the no weapons rule when you start asking questions."

My heart raced. *Crap.* What did criminals hate more than an outsider asking too many questions? "Yeah," I said, my mouth going dry. "Let's hope."

25. BROTHERS IN ARMS

THE NEXT DAY, I still couldn't believe Spitz was sending *me* to snoop on Armando. After asking around—while trying to be inconspicuous—I came across Claudio and Felix, two of the younger resident gang members from East LA, who were outside playing a dice game called "Dudo."

"Hey, what's up guys?" I asked, walking confidently through the backyard, careful not to surprise them. "I need a little help. I'm hoping you could tell me a little more about Armando, seeing how tight you all are with him."

Felix and Claudio looked at me like I was speaking Chinese. My request had obviously put them on alert. "What do *you* want to know about him for?" Felix asked, sneering at me, rolling the small dice between his stubby, tattooed fingers.

I was completely out of my element trying to be "one

of the guys" amongst these two. But I couldn't go back to my old life, living paycheck to paycheck, so I wasn't going to give up so easily. I reached out and gave Claudio what I intended to be a friendly clap on the back. But before I knew it, Claudio had pulled out a kitchen knife from inside his sock and had pinned me against the patio door.

Holy shit. These guys had clearly violated the no weapons rule. I had to be careful with what I said here.

"Guys! Seriously, there's no problem here. I just wanted to learn more about him. Spitz wants to have Armando take on a bigger role on the show, and I just want to see if he would be a good fit. I swear, that's all."

Honesty was sometimes the best policy, right?

Claudio cautiously backed off. I adjusted my shirt, still trying to recover and gather my composure. Not wanting to be left out of the fun, Felix got in my face. "Why do you think we know anything about Armando? We ain't no snitches!"

"I heard he came from the same gang as you, so I figured you all were friends," I said. "You know, stick-together-type stuff. That's why I'm asking you about him."

Felix answered, "Come on, man! What did you think? Armando ain't one of us, Homes. He ain't no gang banger. Watchu talkin' about?"

"I...I'm not sure I understand," I stuttered in confusion.

"Armando just checks in with us, 'cause he knows we ain't too popular with the other boys in the hood no more. Thanks to this fuckin' show. They think we sold out —that we got legit coin and they don't. He looks out for us, you know? He keeps preaching and saying what we're doin' ain't good for our community, that *P Killers* is making the gang life look all cool and shit. You all ain't keepin' it real."

Claudio nodded and added, "That's right. He hates this show, and if he had it his way, we'd all walk off. Boom. Gone." They began to laugh, "Yeah, like we got a choice."

Felix further explained, "I'm telling you Homes, he only let you boys give him a small part so he could stick around and do his thang."

"Okay. What's his story?" I asked, trying to get to the point. "I mean, where's he from and how did he decide to turn his life around?"

Claudio answered, "I know what you want, man," he shrugged. "He's your show's Brad Pitt and Enrique-fuckin'-Iglesias all wrapped in one. And the chicas love him!" Claudio Laughed, punching me in the arm.

Felix rolled his eyes and pushed Claudio to the side. "Man, here's a small warning. Armando's a heavy dude. You just don't go around asking questions about him, and you *definitely* don't fuck with him. He's pretty good friends with some of the big boys in the game. You know, the real big boys." he winked.

Claudio nodded, "That's right. Armando only came on the show because he's only biding his time. He doesn't want to be a part of this system, but I guess he figured if you can't beat 'em, join 'em."

"So all this time, he's wanted the show to fail? Why's he against you guys earning legitimate money? Isn't that a good thing?" I asked.

"He knows the dudes on the streets are mad jealous. When they got out there, nobody was offering them no show for some dough. Jealousy in a gang is *no Bueno*. Somebody has to pay," Claudio said, looking pleased with himself.

Felix interrupted, "The jelly on the stick is that his parents had been running some kind of meth lab out of Compton. They weren't too bright and got their asses blown up cooking up a big-ass batch. Armando was just a kid, so the Church took him in. I guess they was good to him, 'cause all he wanted was to be some kinda street preacher, like a reformer or some shit. Just watch. He'll tell anyone who'll listen how drugs fucked up his parents' lives and shit like that."

I tried to wrap my head around what they were telling me. "Let me get this straight. Armando wants to put an end to all the paychecks you guys are earning legally on the show? Is that what you're telling me? And no one holds that against him?"

Spitz would be dumbfounded by this news; he definitely didn't have any inkling that this was happening under his watch. I knew Spitz would want to keep Armando right where he was, so Spitz could keep those ratings up and that demographic of 43% females would be glued to their seats. The real question was, how could we not only make Armando stay and fulfill his contract, but also ensure he'd be willing to step into a starring role on the show?

Claudio's voice jerked me back into the conversation. "Yeah, that's right. But you gotta understand, dude. He has some major street cred. Everybody gives him wide space."

"Yeah, and he can also kick some serious ass!" Felix interrupted with the kitchen knife still dangling from his left hand, "and that's the ultimate street respect."

"Kick ass?" I asked, keeping an eye on the blade.

"Hell yeah! He's some kind of martial arts guru. You know, that Flying Tiger shit? Oh, and he does that UFC fighting too. He's got big ups in the hood. He was undefeated in the house. They was beggin' him to go pro when he got out, but he just kept refusing. It's like he chose the big man upstairs over big bucks. *Mucho loco!* But everybody, gang or no gang, looks up to him. He's a protector. *Our* protector," Felix finished.

"I don't think Armando's gonna like you wanting him to show his face more, Homes. He hates *P Killers*, so good luck with that." Claudio laughed.

I knew Felix and Claudio's stories wouldn't stop Spitz from pursuing Armando to star on his show. Where money was concerned, Spitz was like a pit bull, and not unlike Felix and Claudio, he was part of his own kind of gang. You could call it a "white-collar gang." Armando was in Spitz' wheelhouse now.

"Well guys, I know the bosses would really like Armando to have a bigger role on the show. From hearing your stories, I think he deserves the respect, so it's time he stops taking a back seat and gets in front of the camera. That's all." I went to leave, then turned back to the guys. "Think of all the people he could reach with his message, if only he had a spotlight. Enjoy your game."

26. MADE OF STEEL

THE MYSTERIOUS AND elusive Armando stood roughly six feet tall, and dark brown hair with a stray lock that often fell between his eyes, a la Brad Pitt in his debut role in *Thelma and Louise*. The eyes were a piercing blue, and habitually hidden behind a pair of pitch-black sunglasses. He sported gray-flecked stubble and had the tan of someone who spent a lot of time outside in the sun. Last but not least, he had a build the ladies loved. In short, Armando was a stark contrast to Benny. Hell, he was a stark contrast to everybody that was even remotely associated to the show, for that matter. Armando was a sleek Lamborghini in a sea of Chevy Malibu's.

For all the physical gifts God had bestowed upon him, Armando Quesada (full name) didn't like the spotlight, and for good reason. First and foremost, he did prison time. *Hard* time. There were still people out there who did not like Armando or his message, so it was important to stay under the radar. Secondly, he didn't want his looks to supersede his message about the pitfalls of gang life. The message was the star, not him. And Armando would stop whatever he was doing to have a heart-to-heart with anyone who was willing to listen—especially gang members—about the evils of drugs, gangs and street violence. The message was clear: that way of life was a dead-end.

———

After I left Claudio and Felix, I needed to get rid of the four cups of coffee I'd had that morning—quickly—before my eyeballs popped out. After sprinting to the nearest restroom on set, I settled myself on the throne and got busy in the cramped stall, conjuring up a potential anti-drug campaign that would bring this Armando character into the fold. My concentration was snapped when I heard two men come in and enter the stalls adjacent to mine.

"We got about an hour before the next shoot. Then, you get to drive with Benny and three others over to East LA. Your home turf, right?" the first voice asked, with a laugh. It was a voice I recognized but couldn't immediately identify.

"Well, I wouldn't call it home," answered a low, smooth Latino voice. I finished my business, exited the stall, and went to the sink to wash my hands. Looking in the mirror, I saw a heavyset man with red hair and a beard to match coming out of the adjacent stall. It was Carl, the props man, and owner of the voice I'd recognized.

"Hey," Carl said.

"Hey. How are you, Carl?" I responded. I was hurrying, as I hated having conversations in small, confined areas, let alone next to urinals. Then the last stall opened, and Armando exited like a slow-motion Adonis.

I seized the opportunity and said, "Armando, since you have an hour before you're needed, could I see you in the makeup room, in say, fifteen minutes?" I tossed my used paper towel into the garbage can.

"Sure," Armando replied agreeably.

"Great!" I said, then exited the bathroom without so much as a backwards glance to either Armando or Carl.

Fifteen minutes later on the dot, Armando appeared in the doorway of the makeup room, which doubled as an on-location meeting room, when needed. It was anything but posh, but it got the job done.

"Come in, have a seat," I waved.

Armando glanced at me, grabbed a chair, and sat down. I sat in the other chair, adjusting it so I could face Armando directly. I hadn't had much time to notice his face in the men's room, so now I was able to really see what Armando looked like without his trademark sunglasses. His good looks more than lived up to the hype that was going around the set.

I wasn't sure how to start, so I decided to just put it out there. "I need to get something out there." I said, looking up at the ceiling tiles. "I know you want the show to fail. I know you're not a fan of *Proven Killers,* and you *especially* don't like gangs being portrayed as glamorized criminals on this show."

I leaned in closer and whispered, "But between me and you, I don't like it either. The way I see it, it's like this. We can do each other a favor; together we have the opportunity to turn lemons into lemonade, if you know what I mean. The more you appear on the show, the more you can spread the good word, and the greater the chances we both have in saving a few lost human beings from going down the dark path."

Armando just stared, listening intently but not giving his emotions away. I continued on, "The good thing about reality TV is that we have the power to showcase the realities and tragedies of gang life to thousands—no millions! —of viewers. We can help people realize that they have a choice in what happens in their lives. But to do that, I need your help in steering this ship in the right direction. This partnership will not only help keep us on air, but it will also help keep these young men from continuing down the wrong path. I think it's a win-win situation."

Armando kept my gaze as he got up slowly and stood.

I tensed in my seat. He leaned over me and looked directly into my eyes, "I hear what you're saying. I'm happy to do whatever it will take to advance both of our goals."

Armando quickly flashed his thousand-watt white smile and winked one of his sea blue eyes. I realized at that moment why the ladies loved him. Armando Quesada was 100% TV ratings gold. Think of a Latino Paul Newman in his prime and there you had it.

I stood and said, "Good. What do you think about doing a backstory on your past? You know, how you tragically lost your parents at a young age and how they turned you—" I stopped talking when I noticed that Armando's dazzling bright smile had vanished. "What? Not a good idea?" I asked, puzzled.

"My past life, and everything about it, is none of your business," Armando said in a no-nonsense, discussion-closed voice. "If you want me to help you with this show, then you'll make certain whatever you know—or you think you know—about me and my past, has nothing to do with whatever plans you or Spitz have up your sleeves. *Comprende?*"

Armando waited for a response. I held a breath for a moment, then clasped my hands together, playing it cool. I wasn't sure how Spitz would react to this, but I wasn't about to piss of this guy.

"Absolutely! Your past is your past—off limits. Gotcha."

Armando relaxed a bit but gave me one more good, long look before he was satisfied with what he saw.

"I'll pass on the good news to Spitz," I said.

We shook hands, and I waved goodbye as Armando turned to leave. *Like taking candy from a baby*, I thought, feeling like the new mini Spitz.

27. THE GIRLS

The sun was pouring into my windshield, partially blinding me as I drove down the A-10 on my way to The Venetian Blind. I was busy keeping my thoughts calm when I heard my phone buzzing on the passenger seat; it was Greg.

"Yo, where you at? These girls are ecstatic and can't wait for their big day."

"*Ladies! We are ladies!* " I heard them yell, giggling in the background.

"Okaaay, ladies," Greg amended, then turned his attention back to me. "Just hurry."

Click. Had Greg just hang up on me? That wasn't like him. Poor guy must've had his hands full. It wasn't only a big day for the official cast of *Reality Is a Drag*, but for everyone involved, including the crew and production teams. With the Stronge show finally out of the picture, it was imperative for the remaining shows to succeed. The initial concept of *Killing Reality* was to get behind-the-scenes looks at three completely different shows, not just the two we now had left.

I walked through The Venetian Blind's rusty back door, hoping to avoid a big entrance. As my eyes adjusted from the harsh L.A. sun to the darkened atmosphere inside, I noticed that Stella, Sam, Daphne, and Cherish were already in wardrobe and makeup, putting on a full-blown show on the small stage. I squinted my eyes to focus, and sure enough, in the middle of the stage, poor Greg was tightly tied to a chair with his t-shirt pulled over his head. The ladies were tickling him with long, pink, glittery feathers.

The club was packed like a can of sardines. Almost every drag queen in L.A. was in attendance and having the time of their lives. When the girls ended their torture, I noticed there was a vacant chair right next to Greg, and I had a bad feeling that one was being saved for someone else.

I carefully approached the stage side stairs and peeked out from behind the red velvet curtain, intrigued by the outrageous antics on stage and the noise level of the crowd. I felt like I was at a Justin Bieber concert. Just then, Daphne saw me and slowly moved in my direction. The audience got in on the action, raving and yelling. As if on cue, the other three performers excitedly began cheering and clapping. "Please pull his shirt down," I commanded in my nicest tone, as Daphne still headed in my direction. I obviously hadn't been authoritative enough, because Daphne took that as a dare of sorts and bull-rushed me like an NFL lineman. She scooped me up and over her shoulder, and not so gently plopped me into the empty chair next to Greg's. The only thing I could see were the pink ruffles from her puffy dress. I could hear the crowd roar, loving the scene: two unwilling, completely embarrassed straight guys being tied up and toyed with.

"Ladies! Ladies!" Daphne exclaimed, trying to calm the audience. I took that as a chance to help Greg out and pull his shirt down. I had figured he was miserable, but when I pulled the shirt and revealed his face, he was grinning from ear to ear! He turned to me, laughing. "Welcome to the show, bro!"

"We are the stars of this magnificent show," Daphne said confidently to the audience, "but none of this would've been possible without these two hunky young specimens here."

She threw her arms in the air like a circus ringleader. The place erupted in more waves of whistles and screams. Each girl took turns and triumphantly graced the stage with a bow and unexpected burst of fast dancing and twerking before thanking us in front of the audience for turning them into big stars.

I thought, *Stars?* I wished I'd had the same confidence as these ladies; they hadn't even watched the pilot yet. The whole reason we were there wasn't to be show toys, but to have a small pilot screening for a very select audience of fellow drag queens to support the girls, as well as a small focus group, who were probably lost in the wild audience.

Confused, I pulled Sam aside, knowing he was the more level-headed one of the group. "Sam, what's going on? I think it'd be best if we started watching the pilot," I stressed, letting him know it was time to speed things up.

He batted his eyes in full drag mode, smiled, and then gave me a quick wink to let me know all was okay and that I should relax, which I did. *Whew, she had a plan.* He turned and whispered to Daphne. She gathered the other girls like a mother hen and directed them to take their seats and get ready to watch the pilot.

A huge projector screen scrolled down in the middle of the stage. Whispers were hushed as everyone braced themselves to witness the first TV version of *Reality Is a Drag.*

"Is everyone ready? Action!" Daphne squealed, clapping her hands.

BOOM! Crack! A collective gasp of surprise rippled throughout the audience. A small cap gun had been shot, signaling the release of a massive wave of balloons and confetti from the stage ceiling.

I peered at Sam, who was laughing. "That was supposed to happen *after* the screening."

"Oh, boogers to Betsy," Daphne said, clearly disappointed. But being the trouper she was, she rallied. "Oh well, on with the show!"

28. TEMPER TANTRUM

ALTHOUGH EVERYONE LOVED the *Reality Is a Drag* pilot, the same still couldn't be said for the *Proven Killers* group. After my chat with Armando, it was official that he'd be given more of the spotlight. One day, during our break, Spitz decided it was a good time to reveal the TV exec's new ideas for the alternate direction of the show. Some "genius" on the team had come up with the bright idea of scouting local gangs for a few members who were dissatisfied with some of their *compadres* being on the show. If willing, these members would appear on the show and room with some of the parolees for a while. The goal was for the experienced ex-cons to try and help these guys get out of the gang life before it was too late. In Spitz's words, to "scare them straight."

I hated the idea, but I didn't have much say in the matter. I also desperately needed the show to be a hit, so I was willing to do whatever it took to be prepared and be a team player. I tried reaching out to some of the so-called future house guests, but most were reluctant to talk to me. As far as they were concerned, they were taught to always keep their mouths shut, and to let nothing trap them against their will.

If I was ever going to stay on top of the show, I knew I needed to get some respect from these guys. I really needed to toughen up, even if it was just a little bit. Yet, I wasn't quite sure what "toughening up" actually meant or how I could go about it. I figured if I acted more like one of them and stopped trying to play nice all the time, maybe I could make a statement. I needed to let them know I wasn't going to take any shit. But that was a lot to ask of someone who never went to the gym and always wore long sleeves to the beach. *Screw it,* I thought. If I wasn't a bad ass, I'd have to start acting like one.

I decided to pattern my new persona after some of the sickest, weirdest dudes I could think of, so I started acting like one of the Stronge boys. Brilliant idea, right? I threw tantrums, wrecked props, and made demands on everyone around me. I criticized other people's work, nitpicked things that went wrong on set, and in general, I made other people's lives miserable. And the truth was, I was making my own life miserable as well. It didn't take long for me to realize that my bullying and loud-mouthing didn't do anything except get me into trouble. In fact, it worked *against* me, not for me. It worked against me so badly, that I earned a new nickname behind my back: "Killer Bitch."

———

I needed this to end—fast. I figured Spitz would hear me out, but all he said was, "Well, Marc, what can I tell you? They'll stop calling you a bitch when you stop acting like one."

Who was I kidding? It was apparent that I didn't know how to act tough or reverse people's poor perceptions of me. I wracked my brain for a new strategy, hoping it wasn't too late to salvage my reputation on the show. After a long, arduous week, I plopped myself in front of the TV with a bottle of Jack Daniels and a Valium that one of the new on-set roomies had given me. I did my best to think, but alcohol and a depressant weren't the best combo when searching for clarity. I barely made it through one show before I passed out cold.

———

My entire weekend was a haze. Monday came around way too fast. The very moment I arrived on set, I decided to ask Benny directly if we could speak in private. I led him outside to a balcony where I knew there weren't any cameras; I needed to confide in someone who could keep their mouth shut.

I put on my best Ray Donovan face and explained to him that I could be a big help in his career going forward. I told him we could make a really good team; as long as he had my back, I would have his. I waited. Benny didn't say anything at first, just gave me a good, hard look.

He seemed to make up his mind. "Look, Marc, I don't want to mess up the good deal I have. And I don't need a 'partner,' especially not one like you," he said He chuckled. "I ain't even sure why you're here. Anybody can see you ain't cut out for none of this shit. That whack self-defense you did on TV? That ain't gonna get you no respect with my boys. And even that whole prima donna thing you tried? Shit, that was probably the most *worst* thing you coulda done."

He laughed a little more, shaking his head. I needed to step up my game; I was losing him. As he turned around to leave, I knew I had to impress him with something. "Benny!" I called, pulling out my gun from my jeans. "This is my CZ 75 out of the Czech Republic. It's a semi-automatic with selective five variants You do understand this, right?"

Benny turned and gave me a look in return. He was assessing me, really looking at me for the first time. I could see something shift in his eyes. He looked down at me and smiled a slow, creepy laugh. "Well, alright man! That's what I'm talking about! There may be a little gangsta in you after all!"

Benny laughed, then abruptly looked around to make

sure no one was lurking close by. He inched closer to me, bent his head and said quietly, "Okay, I hear ya. I'll have your back. We're good, man. You go be Mr. Reality Star or whatever."

Benny laughed again, thumping me in the chest. He must've seen how relieved I felt, because he turned serious and warned, "But listen here, Marc, don't ever think of pulling that piece on me. I'll stick that thing so far down your fuckin' throat, you'll choke on it. You feel me?"

He didn't wait for my answer. I watched him walk away, shaking his head. I turned, leaned over the balcony, and promptly threw up my breakfast.

———

With Benny now on my side, I could now focus on the other cast and crew members who still had a grudge against me. Granted, I wasn't always going to have Benny with me for protection, but I had to get my point across if I was ever going to survive on the show. So, I mustered my best Tony Soprano impersonation and declared to anyone in earshot as I walked back into the living room set, "Hey! I'm giving fair warning to anyone who calls me a bitch one more fucking time, that I'm gonna hang you up by your balls and let you bleed dry."

Hm. Good job, Marc. I like the sound of that. You could

have heard a pin drop. The entire floor was quiet, if only for a moment. Then laughter erupted.

"Did you write that line yourself, Henderson?" one of the grips shouted, followed by more laughter.

"Come on, Henderson. Give us a break and shut the hell up."

I looked for Benny, who was supposed to have my back, but he was nowhere to be found. I'd been expecting him to step up. Suddenly I felt the familiar heat of rage well up inside. I was mad and humiliated at the same time. Then I had another stupid idea and before I could stop myself, I took out my concealed pistol and fired a shot right out the window and into the backyard. In the cavernous room, the noise was amplified, echoing through the entire building. Everyone froze with mouths wide open.

"I'll only say this once. You all have your jobs because of *me*. I'm not your little bitch, and if anyone wants to argue that, you can come see me and my partner here." I nodded to the gun, which I still had in my hand and out in full view. "Do we understand each other?"

I scanned the crowd, trying to make eye contact with as many people as I could. I met Benny's gaze, who must have heard the shot and had come running in. His eyes first looked at me, with a *WTF?* look, then to one of the cameras that had been rolling through the whole episode.

Everyone hurried back to their tasks, studiously

avoiding me. Anybody who wasn't working, ran to the nearest hiding place. All except for Eddie (the Danny DeVito look-alike), who stood his ground like a pit bull. Then he got right up in my face and my feelings of power evaporated as fast as they'd come.

"You *ever* pull a gun like that again around me, I promise you'll be the one who disappears," Eddie whispered harshly in my ear.

Then he thumped me on the forehead with the open palm of his hand and strutted away. Everyone who was trying to pretend they weren't watching, resumed their tasks at hand with a renewed focus. My plan had *not* gone as planned.

29. THE SQUEEZE

NEWS of my hissy fit circled back to Spitz very quickly. He seemed to be disinterested until he found out there had been a gun fired on the premises. Spitz wasted no time hunting me down. I was in the makeup room, getting my dark circles covered for the next shot. The door flew open and I saw Spitz standing there, just staring at me in the mirror with that pissed off look on his face. He then politely asked the makeup artist to take a ten-minute break in a very calm, steady and low-pitched tone. In other words, he was about to blow.

Sensing Spitz's mood, she bolted from the room, leaving me wrapped in a black plastic cape they used to protect the wardrobe from getting stained. Spitz approached me from the back and jerked the chair around so I could face him. I felt totally exposed and vulnerable, not to mention ridiculous.

"Hey James..." I said in greeting, hoping he wasn't carrying any concealed weapons.

He sharply cut me off. "Is it true? Did you really fire a fucking gun on my set? Are you crazy!? On *my* fucking set?"

I tried to calm him down. "James, I'm so sorry! Things just started unraveling so fast. I was constantly being berated by the cast and the crew. I figured I needed to handle this the only way I thought they would understand. It was just a little scare tactic to make them back off. It was wrong, I know. I realize how wrong now, but I just wasn't getting the respect I deserve as the star of this show. But look, I purposefully aimed it out of the window, so no one would get hurt. It was totally, totally wrong, but you understand where I was coming from, right?" I asked, hoping I was flashing my most disarming smile.

"You idiot—you fuckin' moron! What do you think you're doing, you ungrateful little shit? You'd still be a pathetic, unemployed grip if I hadn't made you a somebody, and this is how you thank me?"

His face was turning red and spittle was coming out with every other word. I was praying for him to finish already. "And for your information, Mr. Big Shot, your timing couldn't be more perfect. We just finished our focus group testing and you ain't the guy, pal! That's right. The viewers could give a crap about you," he scoffed. "They said you simply don't have that 'star quality' that's needed to carry this show. Hell, you can't even follow one simple rule. So you know what, Marc? You're fired! You have fifteen minutes to pack your shit and get off my set. Turn in your ID and get the hell out of here."

Spitz turned to walk away, not even waiting to enjoy my stunned, horrified reaction. I could hear him saying under his breath, "First it's those Stronge kids, now this asshole."

Not knowing what to do, I ripped off the salon cape and ran after him. "James, wait! I'll do whatever it takes. I —I'll take a back seat, I won't cause any more trouble. I need this job—I'm in debt, I've got bills! I just can't lose everything!" I sounded like a whiny little twerp.

Spitz stopped and turned to look at me as if I were a piece of dog crap he'd stepped in. "You broke your contract, Henderson! Read the fucking print. You *can* read, can't you? You did this to yourself. You're no better than those Stronge kids. We're done, and the show doesn't need you anymore."

He turned to go, and then stopped one last time. Some of the anger seemed to drain away, and he looked more disappointed than disgusted. "Marc, listen to me. You had a good thing—hell, a *great* thing—and you could've carved out a nice little career for yourself. But you didn't focus on the show, you focused on you, and only you. I've seen this a million times in my career. You were all wrapped up in *you* and how *you* needed respect. Your insecurity basically sucked the life out of your scenes. The camera never lies, Marc. And while this may be 'show business,' it's still a business. I'll be using your remaining salary, which will end as of this moment, to cut my losses with you. We don't need you anymore. Good luck and goodbye," Spitz said in parting, as he began to power-walk away.

I stood there, devastated and frozen, like a deer in the headlights. Everything was crashing down around me. Without thinking, I took off running and saw Spitz crossing the street towards his waiting stretch limo. He was already ensconced in the back seat when I finally caught up to him. "Please!" I begged, trying to see through the tinted window. "Give me a chance. Just one more! I swear I can do this."

I had no pride left and was begging like a man for his life. Spitz lowered the window down a few inches. "Really, there's nothing I can do for you. It's out of my hands. Policy is policy—especially involving guns and security. So, get a hold of yourself, man. Show a little pride. It might be the end of the show, but it's not the end of the world."

Spitz rolled up the window, looking forward as the car sped off, leaving me standing alone in the parking lot. I fell to my knees, drained and broken.

30. NOT BAD ENOUGH

IF BEING FIRED HADN'T BEEN bad enough, more problems kept piling up. Once the show started airing, I became increasingly depressed and needed a way to suppress my feelings, so I started to dabble in the elite Hollywood's favorite vice: cocaine. I began experimenting, but it quickly spiraled into spending a large portion of my remaining funds on my new "hobby."

———

After a particularly bad day, when another new episode aired without me, I locked myself in my apartment and went on a three-day binge, hoping I could either come up with a way to save my ass on the show or at least figure out a way to make some money before what was left of mine ran out for good. On the third day, I rose. Unfortunately, I wasn't reborn or anything. Instead, I was hit with

a back-to-reality headache and, to top it all off, I was out
of my entire stash of drugs and booze. I rolled over in bed
and took a deep breath. I braced myself for the day and
decided to get out of my stupor. I was completely out of
everything: food, water, beer. I ran my head under cold
water trying to knock myself into some kind of sense. No
groceries? Fine. But I needed a cup of coffee—a *strong*
cup. I put on some sunglasses and stepped out of my
door.

When I got in the elevator, I examined my reflection
in the mirrored walls. I looked like hell. I felt the movement of the elevator pulling itself down to the lobby. I
tried fixing my uncombed hair before the elevator made
it to the lobby. No such luck. The doors silently opened to
an ambush of hyperactive reporters. Shocked, I hurriedly
pushed the close button several times, but of course, the
doors didn't close fast enough. A brown-haired reporter
stuck his arm in the door, prying it open.

The cameras were flashing, and they were all yelling,
"Marc, did you try to kill someone?"

Another yelled, "Were you attacked again?"

I had no idea what to do. I was trapped. There was no
way to easily or safely exit without force, so I screamed
the first idiotic thing that came to my mind, "I have a
gun!"

It worked. The reporters buzzed away, and even the
bellman dove behind his desk station for cover. I
hurriedly pushed every button on the elevator just to get

out of there and make my way back to my apartment. Just as the doors were closing, someone threw in an *LA Times* newspaper and, lo and behold, there was a picture of me from a previous interview smack dab on the front cover. By now, my head was spinning like a top from my hangover—not to mention all the rabid reporters—so it was hard for me to focus. But what *did* come into focus was the headline: "Reality Killer Losing His Grip."

I snatched the paper up and ran back into my apartment, dove onto the couch, and read the article as fast as I could. *Whew.* The article wasn't as bad as I'd been expecting. All it claimed was that the show was most likely causing too much stress, and the most important part: no charges would be filed. *Thank you, God.*

But there was one thing that I didn't like, and it was a statement from Spitz: "It just goes to show that being a reality television star isn't as easy as everyone thinks. You need someone who has self-awareness, who can lead others, and especially crucial, someone who can handle the stress of being in the spotlight."

What the—? My eyes grew wide and I threw the paper across the room. Before I'd been scared, but now I was just mad.

31. WHEN OPPORTUNITY KNOCKS

AFTER GETTING BACK to my apartment and finally settling down, I called the doorman and apologized. I made sure to let him know that I'd panicked and hadn't known what else to do, and that the last thing I needed was the paparazzi hanging around again.

He laughed and said "Well, it sure did work."

I asked him if he would call me when the coast was clear, which he said he would. The article made my still partially hungover mind start to turn its wheels and think. If I had that many reporters for just firing a gun out of a window, imagine what would happen if they knew about what else I had done. Since both of my previous murderous encounters were in self-defense, I reasoned that this might be my chance to get back into real money again. The more I sat there, the more I thought of the debt that was piling up while I wasn't making any money. And with everyone in the business knowing by now that

I'd fired a real gun on a professional set, there was no way I was getting a grip job in this town again. I became overwhelmed with anguish and felt depression settling over me like a black cloud. The longer I sat there, the more negative scenarios came into my mind.

A good while later, reporters must've still been hanging around outside the apartment building, because I hadn't received a call yet and it was dark outside. All night, I pondered if I should come clean or not. I tried to play out every scenario in my head. I thought there was a good probability I'd get off on self-defense if I came forward. Was it too late, though? What were the repercussions for withholding evidence of a crime? And not just one crime, but two? There had to be a way for me to get out of this mess.

In my absence, Spitz and the writers would be busy trying to come up with an easy way to write me out of the show. Maybe I could help him with that and help myself out in the process. It was worth a try. I called Spitz's office an hour later with a pitch I was hoping he couldn't resist. As his secretary, Tracy, buzzed his private office, I heard Spitz answer her buzz with a short bark, "Not now, Tracy. I'm busy."

"I'm sorry Mr. Spitz, but Marc Henderson is on line three," she said, sounding like a whipped dog. "He said it was urgent." Tracy didn't realize she hadn't put me on hold as she'd dialed his inner sanctum, and I could hear their exchange.

"I'm sure he did, Tracy. *Everything* is urgent to Mr. Henderson." There was a pause. "Alright, go ahead and put him through."

I heard Spitz's voice come through my phone's speaker. "This better be good."

"I just want ten minutes of your time, James. I've got something that you'll find interesting. No, not interesting —unbelievable. And I guarantee it's money in the bank. But I need to tell you in person." I was trying not to hyperventilate, but it was nearly impossible not to sweat.

Spitz was silent. I plowed onward. "This isn't a trick, or a gimmick—nothing like that. What I have to tell you could push the show to a higher level, one you've been dying to get to since you started all these shows. Think Kardashian-level...and that's an understatement. I promise."

"Fine. Meet me at my office tomorrow morning at ten sharp. I'll give you ten minutes and no more." And with that, he hung up.

That night seemed like an eternity. I was up and out of the house in record time, arriving at the studio at ten sharp and was frisked by a security guard who seemed to enjoy his job a tad too much. I was ushered in to Spitz's office and sat in the leather wingback chair across from the ornate oversized desk that all but dwarfed anyone sitting opposite of Spitz.

"The clock is ticking. Ten minutes," Spitz said in a bored tone.

"Okay. First, I'd like to apologize again for what a horrible mistake I made bringing the gun to the set and I—"

Spitz cut me off. "Fuck your 'I'm sorry.' Now, get to the point—you've got eight and a half minutes left."

For a moment, I thought about what I was actually about to do. I wanted to turn back, but back to what—more ridicule and crippling debt? I knew I couldn't face either. I took a deep breath and then dropped the bombshell. "I need to tell you something, but I need your word you won't tell *anybody* until we agree that this information can safely be put out to the public. I'm serious. This has to be like 'attorney privilege' type of stuff."

I knew this was taking a big chance, because Spitz would only do what was best for Spitz. But I was out of options by now.

"I told you to stop wasting my time. Just spit it out—what the fuck do you want?!" He was quickly losing his patience.

I reiterated my condition. "I am dead serious. I need your word."

"Okay Marc, you have my word. Now," he said, glancing at his watch, "you have three minutes."

"Lync Prime wasn't my first brush with death, you could say," I began, pausing to see if the statement had registered.

Spitz stopped swiveling back and forth in his chair,

and while still looking pissed, he started looking a lot less bored. "Keep going," he said.

I took a deep breath. *Whew, here goes...* "When I was a grip working on the *Being Stronge* set, I saw Petra Stronge having sex with Andrea Milk in the electric closet. Petra saw me and later came to my apartment to make sure I wouldn't talk. He wasn't alone, either. Andrea was waiting in the car. He beat me up, tied me to a chair, and then tried to kill me, using Andrea as his getaway driver. I had no choice but to defend myself, so I hit him hard with my Louisville Slugger. He went down like a rock and never regained consciousness. I panicked and didn't know what to do. I figured the police would never believe a nobody like me and would take the side of the big television star, so I drove to the river and dumped the body in it, hoping no one would ever find him."

I stopped abruptly, my mouth dry and heart hammering in my chest. Spitz looked incredulous, like I'd just told him I was from Mars. Then he leaned across the desk, squinted his eyes at me, and asked, "Are you shittin' me, Henderson?"

He probably thought I was high as a kite on something. I couldn't really blame him. "No way in hell—it was totally self-defense. I panicked and never went to the police. I was scared shitless. Still am."

While part of me felt relief to have told someone— even a prick like Spitz—I also felt more than a little uneasy now that someone else knew my secret.

"Wait a sec—what happened to Andrea that night? Did she come inside or what? Did she just drive away, or did you have to kill her in self-defense too?" Spitz demanded.

I worried that Spitz didn't believe me—by now, he probably thought he had a whacked-out serial killer sitting across from him, so I lied and quickly assured him that I'd had nothing to do with Andrea's death. Confessing one self-defense killing was more than enough for now. Spitz didn't need any more ammunition. Plus, I might've needed to use that information later.

There was an awkward silence. I thought, *Oh shit, I really did it now. He's going to call the police and I'll be on* The First 48 Hours. But then, Spitz's face split open into the biggest smile, as if he'd just won the lottery. Twice.

He demanded details and I complied, giving him a play-by-play account of what had happened. Spitz was furiously scribbling notes as I talked. I could tell Spitz was over the moon—he couldn't stop smiling or giggling. If I knew anything about Spitz, he was already counting the money this news was going to make him. And he'd be laughing all the way to the bank. Relieved beyond measure, all I could think was, *God bless his greedy little soul.*

The wheels were turning so fast in Spitz's head, I was surprised smoke didn't start wafting from his ears. He didn't know what to do first. He did agree that the ratings would explode if the public found out that the star of *Get a Grip* had killed not one, but *two* reality stars. Spitz also realized he would get amazing publicity himself for being the one to not only convince his star to "do the right thing" and turn himself in, but also help the police close an open homicide case.

This could turn him into an even bigger power player in the TV industry. It was a slam-dunk. Spitz would play the Good Samaritan to obtain my confession, his picture would get plastered all over the papers and social media, and he would receive even more press by bailing me out of jail and following the self-defense case as part of his reality show.

Once again, I wondered if or when I was going to be arrested for murder. I really didn't know how Spitz would play this whole thing out. I felt a very sharp, deep pang of guilt and regret when I thought about my mom and Mrs. Fox finding out. I hadn't even returned any of their calls for the last couple days, but I deeply regretted that I hadn't told them all this first. Hearing about this would tear them apart. I thought of calling them the minute I left Spitz's office but realized I couldn't turn their lives inside out. The fallout from my actions had to be on my shoulders alone, and I'd protect them at all costs. I couldn't bear the thought of them getting sucked into the downward spiral I was heading in. They were wonderful, kind, and amazing women who loved me, in spite of the fact that I'd done nothing to deserve it. At least now I could protect them by keeping my distance for a while.

I told Spitz I couldn't go back to my apartment with all the paparazzi hanging around, so he decided to put me up in one of his many apartments around town until he could figure out the best course of action.

I asked him again, "Spitz, do I have your word that you will help me with this?"

"Kid," he said, standing up and putting out his hand. "When it comes to your well-being in this matter, I will do everything in my power to keep you safe. Now, you go and take it easy. I need to bring in some counsel on this."

He shook my hand as he practically pushed me out the door.

32. BACK IN BUSINESS

IT DIDN'T TAKE Spitz long to put his plan into motion, because the next morning I received a call from his secretary telling me to be on set at noon sharp that same day. So, at noon sharp I stepped through the familiar front door of the dilapidated house that was used as our set with new eyes—the eyes of a second chance. I noticed the people on set were acting a little nicer to me. Granted, the news of my little gun episode in my apartment lobby had probably helped promote this change, which was one positive thing that came out of that whole disaster. I noticed right away things felt a little different. I started getting more attention than the other cast members. It was definitely a good feeling. Maybe, just maybe, I was back on top. Or, at least moving in the right direction.

While Spitz was brainstorming how best to incorporate this new twist into the show, I was in wardrobe working on a new look that was a little less *slacker* and a little more *hipster*. While I did like my new look, I kept my mouth shut and kept my eye on the prize, a second chance at the brass ring. Claire from wardrobe was taking in the sides of my new shirt, pins sticking out from her lips, as I mused, "You know Claire, it's good for today's kids to see what really happens when you get instant fame and treat people badly."

Claire looked confused and alarmed, stopping in mid-tuck. She had obviously heard of my earlier meltdowns and was probably nervous to see what might be coming next.

"I mean—don't get me wrong, Claire, I don't believe that killing *anyone* is good, or that it should even be acceptable. But there are some circumstances where you don't have much of a choice."

Claire just looked more disturbed, so I shut up before she accidentally swallowed one of those pins—or worse. Inwardly, however, I knew I was right. Reality TV had a unique psychosis of its own. It should've come with its own definition in the psychology textbooks: *Reality TV Addiction: A potentially deadly illness in which a person is addicted to living in front of the TV night after night. Sufferers experience symptoms including, but not limited to: wishing they were a Kardashian, a Stronge, or whoever the flavor-of-the-month currently is. Prognosis: fatal. Chance of Recovery: slim to none.*

Twelve-step programs should be implemented for these wannabes who didn't have lives and were content watching vapid, self-centered "stars" acting badly in front of the camera. Maybe then, more young adults could see what happens to these whack-jobs in real life. They could see that they act badly—very badly—hurting other people, lying, and turning into greedy monsters. With treatment by experts and a little group therapy thrown in, they might realize that the stars they worship aren't role models at all; they aren't even borderline decent people. They are scum. And they're expendable. Then another thought popped into my head: *Am I becoming one of them? That means I'm expendable too.*

While Claire pinned the last hem on my pants, Spitz showed his face in the door in an uncharacteristically jovial manner. "Hey Marky Marc! Great to see you, kiddo —looking good!"

"Hey, James. Thanks. Again, I really appreciate you letting me stay on the show."

"Hey, I'm glad you're with us! This is going to be great —you just wait and see," Spitz said with that dopey grin still plastered across his face.

On the surface, I was trying hard to appear professional, courteous, and most of all, cool as a cucumber. I pretended to be keenly interested in the buttons of my shirt in the mirror. Spitz noticed and asked Claire to step out of the wardrobe room for a few minutes so he could talk to me in private, and then he shut the door.

"Listen, no need to be nervous, Marc. You're going to be fantastic. Listen, just between you and me—and you're the first person I'm telling this to, of course—we have some new twists in story ideas coming up that could push our ratings way, *way,* up. I'm talking 'move aside *Scandal, Game of Thrones,* and *Ray Donovan'* kind of changes. Think of it as an all-new, jacked-up, kick-ass *Proven Killers!* The details are a little sketchy at the moment, so I can't say anything more, but if the team can deliver on even half of what they're promising, we're all going to love it! Okay, talk to you soon—break a leg!" And with that, Spitz winked and disappeared out the door before I could form a reply.

If possible, I became even more nervous. What was Spitz up to? *"New twists...jacked-up show"?* What the hell did that mean? I prayed to God Spitz hadn't told anyone else what he was up to. I hadn't even been back at the set for a day and he was already going 100 miles per hour. So, Spitz was going to throw a new curve ball into the show, huh? *This had better be good.*

But deep down, I knew it wasn't going to be good at all.

33. QUICK SAND

LATER THAT SAME DAY, Spitz called and asked me to come by the office the following morning for a meeting. He arranged for a car to pick me up so I could go straight from the apartment to his office. He said he wanted to discuss the new ideas for the show he'd alluded to earlier. But I wasn't buying any of it. If Spitz was happy, I had a feeling I'd soon be unhappy. In the short time I had known him, Spitz was the proverbial "fair weather" friend, throwing something away (or more likely, some*one*) if anything better came along. When the weather turned ugly, so would he, and he'd kick you to the curb and not give it a second thought. TV stars were a dime a dozen, Spitz always said, and even with my whopper of a confession, he had no allegiance to me. I was starting to get a bad feeling about all of this.

———

As promised, the car service arrived early the next day and this time, when I showed up to his office, I wasn't frisked. Spitz's secretary escorted me into his personal office so I could wait for him there.

I sat in the guest chair, checking my phone messages and playing Words with Friends for a good twenty minutes. Glancing down at my watch, I wondered why Spitz was late for the meeting. It wasn't his style. I got up out of the chair to stretch my legs and walked around. I was bored and antsy by now, so I walked over to his desk and started snooping—wondering if any of the files laying on top of it had anything to do with the new so-called "twist," or if there was some information about me in them. Before I could take a peek, however, I noticed the tip of a shoe sticking out from behind the desk.

I slowly leaned forward to get a good look at what my mind could not yet process. There, crumpled up and stuffed like rubbish between his chair and under the desk was James Spitz—who looked deader than a doornail. I froze. My head swam, my mind reeled. I took what I hoped was a steadying breath and leaned down to touch Spitz's neck. No pulse. Having had some experience with this kind of thing before, I knew if I lingered any longer, I would be suspect, so I pressed the intercom button on the phone.

"Yes?" came the secretary's voice.

"I found him—Mr. Spitz, I mean. I mean, I found him

lying on the floor—I think he may be dead. Can you please call the police?"

There was a shriek from the outside office, followed closely by the secretary rushing in, the phone still in her hand. She came around the desk, confirmed with her eyes what her ears had just heard, looked at me, and shrieked again.

———

Forty-five minutes later, the crime scene unit was lifting fingerprints from Spitz's office. They also took a set from his secretary—just to rule her out, they assured her. There was no need to take prints from me, seeing how mine were already on file. Once again, I was riding in the backseat of a police cruiser. The officers couldn't have been nicer. After all, these guys and I had gotten to know each other over the past few months.

At the station, they brought me into a conference room where a bored-looking detective sat. I recognized him from one of my previous interrogations in the Prime case. He asked several questions, but it was as if he was just going through the motions—perhaps knowing I wasn't involved with this latest case and couldn't be bothered to care. Maybe he had teenaged daughters at home who watched *Proven Killers* and figured I'd be out before the ink was dry on the paperwork. When he was done, he asked me to sign my statement, which I did. Then two young officers standing guard near the door asked if they could get my autograph "for their girlfriends." I smiled and complied.

Just as I was about to get up to leave, an older, more senior detective came in who did *not* look happy. He looked like ex-military with a crew cut. He wasn't tall or short, but built like he could readily handle himself in any given situation. *Just like a bulldog,* I thought. He dismissed the other detective with a nod and sat down across from me.

He introduced himself as Artie Kramer. I had heard the name before. Kramer had a reputation around the station as being very tough, but fair. You didn't want to get on his bad side, and most of the younger guys were afraid of him, so I'd been told. Before I could say a word, Kramer jumped right into what would be the first of countless rapid-fire questions. Some had already been asked by the other detective, while others were more in-depth about Spitz and his background, who he associated with, and so on. There were even a few oddball questions I think he threw in just to keep me off balance, like "What do you know about something called S.T.S.?"

I didn't understand the question, so I asked him to repeat what he had said.

"S.T.S. Tell me what you know about it." Kramer's face remained impassive, giving nothing away.

"Uh, not much—the only S.T.S. I know is a tire service," I replied. I was curious to learn what the hell he was getting at with the S.T.S. and Spitz's murder, so I played ball and cooperated. The interrogation dragged on in this vein for a while. Kramer then asked one more time if I knew nothing else S.T.S. could stand for. *How repetitive can one guy be?*

"I'm sorry, but I'm confused. I've already told you the only S.T.S. I know of is a tire service company. It's a large chain and I think I even got a flat fixed there once, but I don't understand why you keep asking me basically the same thing. I'm not sure what you're getting at."

Kramer didn't look up at me, nor did he answer. He kept his head down and continued taking notes. The silence was unnerving, probably a tactic Detective Kramer had learned in his military training. *Suspect Interrogation 101: Ask as many questions as you can so as to confuse the suspect. Write constantly, as if you're taking copious notes. Do not look up at subject. Ignore all requests for food, water, and bathroom breaks. This tactic has shown to be extremely effective in causing the subject to become nervous, to sweat profusely, and eventually blurt out a confession. Case closed.*

I tried to get my point across anyway. "I don't know what happened to James—I only know it had nothing to do with me! You've got to know that questioning me is a waste of time, when the killer is still out there. I had *nothing* to do with his death. For cripes' sake, he was my boss! He gave me a great job, we are—were—friends. I had no reason to kill the man."

"Hmm...really, Mr. Henderson?" Kramer finally looked up at me as he continued. "No reason whatsoever? And you know absolutely nothing about anything that relates to S.T.S.? And you were under the impression that you and Mr. Spitz were friends?"

He proceeded to open a file that he'd brought into the interview room earlier. "Do you know what this is? This is a file from Mr. Spitz's desk. Have you seen this file before?" he asked, not waiting for an answer. "Because I have. And after reading what's in it, I find it hard to believe you and Mr. Spitz were friends. There's a memo in this file that claims a cast member by the name of Armando Quesada was going to be integrated more into the storyline to become the show's new star attraction. It further indicates that with Armando as the star of *Proven Killers*, they planned on diminishing your role after your recent meltdown and lessen your screen time considerably. And by doing so, they could trim costs to help finance their new star's salary."

He shut the file with a flourish. "So, do you still want to tell me you two were friends? Because I know it would piss me off big time if I found out that my so-called 'friend' was up to something like this behind my back." He looked at me expectantly.

I remained calm and acted genuinely surprised by the contents of the memo. "I'm shocked. I mean, I know this is a business and all, but James seemed so sincere and even said he wanted us to brainstorm some ideas for the upcoming season. That was the whole reason for our meeting this morning."

Kramer seemed not to hear me. "This note was found shoved in Mr. Spitz's mouth, post-mortem—that means, after he was killed."

He slid over a sealed plastic bag, containing a crumpled piece of paper so I could see it. All it said was "S.T.S" scrawled in some type of red ink. I picked it up to peer at it closer. "I don't know who wrote this or why. But I didn't. I mean, look at it—it isn't even my handwriting."

I slid the note back to Kramer, who returned it to his folder. He leveled a long, cold stare at me as I tried not to wet my pants. Then, without warning, he said abruptly, "Thank you, Mr. Henderson. You have been more than cooperative. I think we're done here."

"I can go? Really?" After all the intense grilling, his sudden dismissal had me bewildered.

"Well, Mr. Henderson, even a killer like yourself— who acted in self-defense of course—can't be held solely for being in the wrong place at the wrong time. But I promise you that if you did kill your employer, I will get the proof and nail your ass to it. For the time being, however, you're free to go."

Kramer smiled. It wasn't a reassuring sight.

34. NEXT UP

KRAMER TOLD me to go to home to my own apartment for the night because of all the interrogations that were going on in the halfway house, and the crime scene lab also needed to see Spitz's possessions and search for evidence. They had a cruiser take me home, and they even made sure all the paparazzi had left. I sat on my couch wondering if being on *Proven Killers*—and the money I was getting for it—was actually worth all the trouble that had landed on my doorstep. My stress levels were skyrocketing, and the good old days of being a boring grip started sounding better and better. But who was I kidding? My life had changed so drastically, I could barely remember who I'd been before all this crap started. I had gotten way off track and had thrown aside any moral code or values I had. I was turning out to be the very person I railed against. Was it just a few months ago that Mrs. Fox and I would hang out on her back deck, sipping beers while I complained about all the "haves," while the "have nots" (people like me) were left doing their bidding? I remembered Mrs. Fox smiling and saying something along the lines of "grass looks greener on the other side of the fence." At the time, I thought maybe she'd just done too many drugs in the sixties, but now I saw the wisdom of her words. I hated reality stars, and now I was one of them. And was I happy? Not really. Sure, the clothes, nice apartment, and hot car were all good, but I was starting to feel that maybe I wasn't cut out for this life. I really missed my old friends, especially Mrs. Fox and all our heart-to-heart talks. And as much as I tried not to think about it, I missed my mom's calls, when she'd crack me up with the latest gossip from my old neighborhood. I missed the sound of her voice, so much so that I had a sharp pain in my chest.

I had to shut down that line of thought before I completely lost my mind, so I concentrated instead on the murder investigation and the file that Spitz had before he was killed. Was that memo not recent, or did Spitz plan this after we last talked? And what was up with the "S.T.S." calling card in Spitz's mouth? The only possibility that came to mind was whether it could be one of the *Proven Killers* cast members. But if so, why would they want to kill Spitz? I mean—any more than anyone else on that set? Who had it in for him so badly that they'd stuff a signed piece of paper in his mouth and give the cops something to work with?

I knew I'd have trouble sleeping through the night, so I went against my new commitment to stay sober for a while and had a vodka and tonic with a nice soak in the jacuzzi. I'd think about it all tomorrow.

The next morning, the mood on the set was like a morgue. The cast and crew kept their voices low, sometimes even whispering. They stood around waiting, nervous and afraid. Who wouldn't be? The executive producer of the show they worked on had been killed. And what was going to happen to them? They all knew this wouldn't go over well with their parole, not to mention the show and their jobs.

Just then, Victor Klause came through the front door. He was a tall, well-dressed man with blond hair and black horn-rimmed glasses. He carried himself as if he were the star of the show. Klaus had been on Spitz's executive team since the beginning, so you didn't have to be a genius to lay odds that he was our new executive producer. No longer would he be in Spitz's shadow—he was the head man now, taking over front and center. Victor had always talked about having big plans, but everyone was curious to learn if those plans included the *Proven Killers* show.

Victor's baby had always been the first show he took some credit for: *Being Stronge*. Since Petra had been killed, Victor desperately wanted to keep *Being Stronge* on the air. Victor had his own reasons; the rumor was that he was manipulating the Stronge kids for money. He was the get-out-of-jail-free card that those sick bastards needed to ensure the show kept running when the boys found themselves in trouble with the law. Victor would be the one they called for help so no one would find out. He would bribe people to keep things quiet and then would pad the bills to get his cut. His racket was working nicely, but only if *Being Stronge* was still going strong on the air.

With Spitz out of the way, maybe Victor was thinking he'd be able to give the Stronge show another go. Of course, it would have to be revamped, but since viewing audiences tended to skew towards dysfunctional families, it should be easy to gain traction with Sandy and the kids again. Many of us had heard through the grapevine that Victor had always had it in for *Proven Killers*, feeling his show never got the second chance it deserved.

Things, I feared, were going to change. It was our first day back without Spitz and we all could've used some reassurance from our new leader. But as Victor motioned for the cast and crew to gather round, he disabused any notions of providing reassurance or comfort with his little speech.

"As you know, James Spitz, executive producer, tragically lost his life," he began. "While we mourn his passing, we can't forget we have a business to run and work to do. That is what he would've wanted. Naturally, some things will be changing around here, so you can expect a memo in your email by tomorrow with the details. That's all. Thank you."

He turned and left, trying to maintain a solemn, thoughtful expression—but couldn't quite manage it. As the door closed behind him, you could've heard a pin drop. Then there was chaos, everyone talking to each other, or on their phones, preparing for the worst. I kept calling Victor's office to arrange a one-on-one meeting with him, but all I kept getting was a major run-around.

When the email finally came the next day, my fears were proven true. It said the *Proven Killer*s show would be put on hiatus "until further notice." With six episodes already in the can, there was very little time to determine the fate of the show. There was a little good news: most of the on-air "talent" would continue to get paid through the next six weeks, which was the original minimum number of episodes our contracts stipulated. And anyone who didn't have alternate living arrangements could stay on at the house for a few weeks until other arrangements could be made, but only if it met with their parole officer's approval. Some of the cast and crew looked worried, but most of the gang members were smiling. Hell, I'd be too, if I were them. How dope was it to get paid to hang out and do nothing? Sweet setup compared to their alternative.

35. PLAY IT AS IT LAYS

WITH SPITZ GONE and *Proven Killers* looking like it wouldn't get another season, I started to worry about my job security—again. No matter how many times I tried to contact Victor, I was sent straight to his voicemail, and his mailbox was always full. I was left stranded with my own thoughts.

I decided to go over to Victor's home and talk with him in person. Even though he had been the head honcho for only a few days, he was already making changes that could mean the end of my freedom. If I could convince him that canceling the show would be bad for the company's bottom dollar—not to mention how it wouldn't sit well with some of the gang members—Victor might see things differently. If he feared that pissing on the gangs could result in them taking their anger out on him, he may change his mind. There was only one way to find out.

I asked some of the cast members to join me, but they refused. They just wanted to do their time and get out. Couldn't say I blamed them. Plus, Armando had told them that as tragic as Spitz's death was, everything happened for a reason, and they all might be better off without *Proven Killers*. And Benny reasoned, "Why rock the boat when we all getting paid to do nuthin'?" The man had a point.

So there I was, driving solo one more time up Mulholland Drive. It was starting to get dark and I put my headlights on. I finally found Victor's home, a stately and elegant mansion—very unlike The Nest. The driveway had several very expensive cars parked in it, which made me nervous. There didn't appear to be many interior lights on yet. I took a deep breath, parked my car, and got out. As I walked up to the massive front door, I rehearsed what I would say to Victor. I just hoped he didn't have any bodyguards that could throw me out on my ass, or I'd have to talk really, really fast.

I reached for the intercom button but noticed the door to the house was slightly ajar. I looked back at the cars in the driveway and realized that every license plate had "Vic" displayed in some form or another. All the cars belonged to Victor. Great. I knocked, which made the door push open even further.

"Hello?" I yelled into the emptiness. I waited. Nothing.

I went further inside, calling out Victor's name.

Suddenly, there was a noise coming from down the hall. I tiptoed hesitantly towards the sound and looked around, my eyes peeled for the slightest movement. The last thing I needed was a B&E.

As I rounded the corner into what appeared to be the kitchen, there was Victor—sprawled on the floor in a pool of blood. My knees buckled. I was in the wrong place at the wrong time—again! Why did this keep happening to me? This had to stop. Was my karma that bad that I was forced to keep finding dead bodies? Was this God's way of telling me I needed to come clean and if not, that I was destined to be haunted with this bad karma until I did? Crap!

I had to get the hell out of there before anyone saw me. This time I would call no one. I knew enough not to go near the body and get my DNA all over the crime scene. I retraced my steps, making sure I hadn't touched anything but the door handle. I wiped it clean and bolted for my car.

I jumped in, did a hasty U-turn, and started to bolt out of there, when I noticed a Humvee coming down the street towards me. Not one of those fake Humvees either —the real deal, the kind the Hollywood biggies used to drive around town, getting four miles to the gallon. I veered onto the shoulder, put it in a lower gear, and shot past the Humvee without getting a good look at the driver, and hoping he hadn't gotten a good look at me. I did notice one thing, though; it had looked as if there'd been more than one person in the car. Before the Humvee could turn around and give chase, I was barreling down Mulholland and out of sight.

That night, I stayed up all night again, knowing someone had probably seen me or my car in the vicinity of Victor's house. And Victor was dead. You didn't have to be a genius to see where this was heading. I had nowhere to hide, nowhere to go, and the question of "Who the hell was in that Humvee?" pressed in on me from all sides. Then, my only thought was, *That big house had to have one of those security cameras somewhere, right?*

I decided not to wait for the inevitable knock on the door. I called Artie the police detective and told him I needed to see him right away. Seventy-five minutes later, I was back at the now familiar police station. I took a seat in the waiting area—demoralized, depressed, and despondent.

36. THROWN TO THE WOLVES

"THAT IS JUST about the biggest bunch of crap I've ever heard—and I've heard it all." Okay, maybe calling Artie had been a mistake. He obviously didn't believe a word I said. He assumed I was just another egotistical reality star selling some bullshit, eager to generate more press for myself. Artie acted as if I'd let him down in some way. There was a note of disappointment in his voice. Maybe —like everyone else—he believed all the hype and was angry because he thought I had more money and acclaim than he ever would, and it still wasn't enough for me. *Ha! If he only knew.* This time, he sent me to a holding cell and there were no autographs, no joking around with the officers—nothing. This time, I was not to be released on bail, but left to sit and wait for more questioning.

I felt as if I were on a very surreal, very bad episode of *Punk'd.* Let's face it—if it weren't for bad luck, I'd have no luck at all. Spitz and Victor would have loved knowing their untimely deaths had put them in the spotlight, their photos splashed all over TV, the newspapers, and social media. Hollywood was in a frenzy with all the news of a serial killer targeting reality TV personas. Headlines everywhere strongly suggested that the murders had to be an inside job by a disgruntled employee. Everyone in Hollywood knew *someone* who was a disgruntled employee. News outlets were having a field day: "What were the executives of these so-called reality shows thinking? And the latest—*Proven Killers*? You throw a bunch of convicted felons in a house and think it was going to go well?" I couldn't help but think that Spitz was smiling somewhere over all the publicity for his latest creation.

My daydreaming in the cell came to an abrupt halt when two officers arrived to escort me to one of the interrogation rooms. As I entered, Artie was gathering up the note found in James's mouth, along with what looked like a similar note in another evidence bag. *Whoa—had there been a S.T.S. note in Victor's mouth too?* I looked up at Artie, and he could tell what I was thinking.

"Everyone likes to copy what they see in the movies, Mr. Henderson." He then explained that he's seen this M.O. of leaving notes in victims' throats before. But that's not all he offered up—the second note mentioned S.T.S. like the first one, but in a smaller, sloppy print was written: **Seal Team Six.** Whether the same killer had struck twice, or there was a copycat killer out there, either way they were giving clues. Artie stared at me for a long time.

If he was hoping to get some new information out of me, he was barking up the wrong tree. I knew I wasn't involved in James's or Victor's deaths. He gave an almost imperceptible shrug of the shoulders, as if he was giving up on me. He asked a few more questions, but we could both tell he was just going through the motions. Artie ended up where everyone else seemed to end up with me —without enough hard evidence to keep me in jail, and so he had to let me go. It really galled him to do it, and I almost felt sorry for him. Almost.

Proven Killers was now larger than life. In a morbid twist of fate, the show was destined to continue. Audiences were clamoring for more episodes to see if the show actually had a serial killer on it. This was great news for the cast and crew, at least for the ones who weren't too afraid to stay with the show. *Proven Killers* was back to being front and center, except for one major hurdle: we needed yet another new leader. This was going to be a huge problem, considering the track record of what happened to the last two commanders-in-chief on the show.

The studio figured money had to be no object, given they could find the right person. The top brass had no idea if these homicides had come from within or not, so they decided to go outside the company to choose its new producer. They interviewed everyone who they thought had the guts to step into such a landmine, and who was capable of landing the studio a coveted Emmy Award, which now seemed within their reach. Fortunately, they found a new successor, Jonathan Pence. He was an "up-and-comer" with a golden track record. He was highly sought after from all the other studios. His current contract with a competitor was short-term, and it was widely reported he was eager to jump ship. He was especially adept at taking so-so projects and turning them into must-see TV, while securing their syndication and merchandising rights, which was the real gold. He was a hot commodity after a wildly popular run with *Ice Road Truckers*, even when filming had been temporarily suspended after two crew members got frostbite on their hands while filming in Alaska. No doubt about it, Pence had a golden touch, and the studio heads were salivating just imagining what he could do with *Proven Killers*. If this man could take the elements in Alaska, then L.A. should be a ray of sunshine, even with the latest headaches and obstacles.

Pence took the job and got right to work. The first encouraging step he took was tightening up the production. Unlike Spitz's bombastic nature and Victor's cold demeanor, he often chatted with the cast and crew, and insisted everyone call him Jonathan, not Mr. Pence. It wasn't long before he earned everyone's respect—no small feat since everyone was on pins and needles. The studio had been smart in hiring him; they needed someone who was tough yet fair, and someone the cast could relate to. Plus, Pence came from the same neighborhood where *Proven Killers* based many of their location shoots. He was very familiar with the gang scene, having nearly been recruited while he was in his teens. He still personally knew several gang members, and the ones he didn't, he knew someone who did.

Things might've been looking up, after all.

37. HUMMING RIGHT ALONG

JONATHAN and I hit it off great, but then again, he hit it off great with everyone else—especially Armando. Armando was in front of the cameras again—the star—while I was left to languish in the background, basically doing what an ordinary grip would do. I wasn't thrilled about my status, but I was happy being back on the show, plus it was looking like Spitz might not have had a chance to reveal our little secret to anyone.

I may have been coming to terms with not being the star of the show, but I was still plagued by insomnia most nights. I took Benadryl and gummies laced with THC regularly, which were helping less and less, as I was probably becoming immune to them. Alcohol, Xanax, and other "sleep-aids" didn't do the trick either. I paced the floors at night, chewing on every idea that came to mind as to how I could improve my status on *Proven Killers* and keep out of harm's way. But I kept coming up empty.

Suddenly, I heard a siren blaring outside on the street, and I rushed to the window. Even with the security lights on, it was dark out, but I could see the EMT guys race into the building across the street. In a few short minutes, they left, this time with someone on a gurney hooked up to an IV. I kept thinking, *That could just as well be me in that ambulance if I don't get some sleep soon.* Not once did I think about that poor person in the ambulance, though. Nope. Sad to say, I was just worried about me.

As I sat back and watched the lights on the street, Artie the cop came to mind. He most likely kept late hours while working a homicide case, and he was probably losing a lot of sleep over the "S.T.S. murders," as I now referred to them. I had bumped into him on the set one day and he'd looked like a walking zombie, asking the same questions on the set that he had asked a hundred times before, but seemed no closer to solving what the press had dubbed "The Hollywood Homicides." Artie was making everyone nervous because he was coming over to the set a lot lately. Half of us wondered if he just enjoyed being behind the scenes of a TV show, as he was never in a hurry to get back to the station. You could tell he was a little star struck and was probably hoping to get into a background shot or two. Everyone, even hardened police detectives wanted their fifteen minutes of fame.

Then it hit me, the answer: *Proven Killers* needed a cop

on the show. Show the viewing public that LA's finest was on the job, and hopefully stir things up a little. *Bingo!* I got out my laptop and pounded out a scenario for Jonathan to see: *A real-life police detective joins the* Proven Killers *cast to solve the recent murders that have rocked the Hollywood community with the help of Marc Henderson, one of the original "proven killers." This odd, yet intriguing pair make for a unique crimefighting duo as they infiltrate the show to smoke out the killer that may be hiding among the ranks.*

I hit the "SEND" button and waited, hoping Jonathan would love the idea. Then, I took some initiative and sent an email to my favorite detective, one Artie Kramer:

To: Detective Kramer

Artie (I hope it's okay that I call you Artie),

I've got the Proven Killers *show interested in bringing a real-life detective onto the show.*

Before you think this is a joke—it's not. Just hear me out. The newspapers are saying the investigation seems to be dragging. So, what better way for you to get some new info that could help solve James's and Klaus's murders, than becoming a part of the show? I could help you with any obstacles. I could help reach out to people, kind of smooth the way for you. You

solve a double-murder case, the show's ratings go up—
it's a win-win! And who knows, you may even become
a reality star yourself! LOL. So, what do you say?

Marc Henderson

I hit "SEND" again and closed my laptop. As I looked
out the window, I heard a ping from the laptop, signaling
that an email had come in. Looks like somebody else
couldn't sleep either.

Marc: I like the way you think! Let's talk about this
some more. Meet me at my office around 9:15 am
tomorrow morning and see if you can bring the detec-
tive with you. If I like your idea and this guy Kramer
is any good, we'll see about getting you guys set up.
Thx, Jonathan

Another ping.

Henderson: How much does it pay? - Det. Kramer

I smiled and typed back.

Artie, Meet me on the set tomorrow at 9:15 am so we
can meet with our producer Jonathan before he really
gets going for the day.

"I knew this could work," I said outloud to no one. I slept a little better the rest of the night, knowing there was a real chance of getting back on top.

38. BINGO

I WOKE up tired but feeling good about the day. But then I looked at my alarm clock, which must not have gone off. "Holy shit!" I screamed. The clock read 8:45 am. *Oh no, not today!* I thought.

I jumped in the shower and threw on some clothes. The shirt I picked out was clinging to my back because I didn't have time to fully dry off after my two-minute shower. I jumped in the car and headed for the set. I was trying to drive and text at the same time to let Artie know I would be a little late. I lied and wrote that I'd been working on the pitch we were going to have to give to Jonathan. I looked up from my phone just in time to see the traffic light had turned red, and I had to hit the brakes hard. At the same time, I heard tires screeching, but they weren't mine. I looked in the rear-view mirror and saw a truck up close, right on my rear end. My sudden braking must have caused the truck's driver to do the same. I waved to indicate I was sorry, but couldn't see any response from the other driver. *What do you expect in L.A.,* I thought.

I waited for the light to turn green, which seemed like five minutes with that truck right on my ass. I pulled away and looked back into the mirror. That's when I noticed it wasn't a truck, but a Humvee. A Humvee that looked a lot like the one I'd seen peeling out of Victor's house the day he was killed.

I floored it. The Humvee stayed right on my tail. *Uh oh, not a good sign.* I slammed on the brakes to see if I could get a quick look at the driver, then hit the gas again. Maybe wasn't the smartest idea, because he got right on my ass again and was speeding up, obviously trying to hit me.

I braced myself for impact. The Humvee veered and made a screeching turn onto Coronado Blvd. It missed my car by a hair, and that was when I could see the shadowy outline of three people in the mirror. Before they disappeared out of sight, I was able to make out the license plate: SELTMXI.

Then it came to me. SEL TM XI. Seal Team 6. S.T.S. *Shit, that was the Stronge kids!* I'd been so focused on pinning the murders on one of the guys from the *Proven Killers* show, I'd missed what was right in front of me: the Stronge boys. They'd always been walking, talking time bombs, and since their shows had gone down the drain, they were undoubtedly pretty pissed. I just hadn't known how much, I guess. At least I now had some pieces of the puzzle to work on.

After the Humvee bolted out of site and my heart rate returned to normal, I was reeling from this discovery and what it meant. *This could also work to my advantage with Artie.* I had to stop that train of thought and focus. I only had ten minutes to get to Spitz's old office and pitch to Jonathan why a cop on the show would be a brilliant idea.

Yet, with this new information, I was going to have to fly by the seat of my pants at the meeting. How much—if anything—should I tell Jonathan? And for that matter, Artie? I was going to have to revise the ideas I'd pitched to Jonathan earlier. I could handle that. And I felt good, like I finally had something of value to trade—if and when I needed it. I just hoped that after being this late he would still see us.

39. PARTNER

I MADE it to Spitz's old outer office in record time as Jonathan's secretary shot me a silent rebuke from her desk. Artie was sitting on the sofa, looking uncomfortable and drinking coffee. I stole a glance in the mirror to make sure I was as presentable enough after having rushed over.

"You can go in now, Mr. Henderson," the secretary said as she typed away on her laptop.

I stopped in front of Artie, leaned over, and whispered, "Just give me a minute with Jonathan first." He nodded in agreement.

The office had been entirely redecorated since Spitz's death, for which I was immensely grateful. I wasn't sure I'd ever be able to erase that visual from my memory, but I hoped time would help.

"Hey, I'm glad you're here, Marc." Jonathan stood up to shake my hand. He seemed jazzed. "I've been thinking about this cop angle and I think I like it—I really do. Have a seat, I'll have my secretary bring us some coffee."

He sat back down, leaned in his office chair, and got right to the point. He started spewing out all kinds of ideas for Artie's role on the show. I just sat and listened.

"And last, but certainly not least, with these recent murders so close to 'home,' so to speak, having a police detective on site would go a long way to help everyone feel more secure around here," he finished.

He looked more than pleased with himself as he typed a few notes into his phone. "Jonathan, first let me say that your ideas are great," I said. "I mean *really* great, and I'm grateful you want Artie involved. But I might have some new information that could be a game changer. I mean I can't say much yet, but..." I paused until Jonathan looked up from his scribbling, then I hit him with it.

"I just discovered some new information about a possible lead." Okay, that hadn't come out as smooth as I would have liked, but judging by the look on Jonathan's face, maybe it was the right way to have played it.

"What are you talking about? You may know something about the murders?" Jonathan was all ears.

I got up and walked over, perching myself on the corner of his desk, and leaned in. "What I meant to say was, 'Their just might be more than one killer.'"

Jonathan looked confused.

"Like as in killers *plural*."

Jonathan asked his secretary to have Artie join our meeting.

Artie may not have had the total television-cop look Jonathan was envisioning, but I knew he was perfect. He had his own sense of disheveled style, like Peter Falk in the classic *Columbo* TV series, and that weird out-of-the-box thinking thing that picked up what others missed.

"Come on in, it looks like we've got a lot of work to do," Jonathan said, ushering Artie into his office and flashing a cat-who-ate-the-canary smile. I let him have his moment, knowing I was the one who'd really caught the canary. I had to play my hand wisely and not stupidly offer up any details unnecessarily. And most importantly, I needed to make sure I was a major part of this new show idea.

40. PROBABLE CAUSE

YOU COULD SAY that the Stronge boys were a little slow. You could also say they were all fucked up from having a selfish egomaniac as a father and a diva-like, celebrity wannabe for a mother. Sandy Stronge was as narcissistic as her late husband, and singularly focused on obtaining fame and fortune. We all knew she would go to any lengths to get what she wanted. A show of her own with a Kardashian-like following would suit her just fine.

The more I thought about the Stronge boys and their sorry excuses for parents, the more it made sense that they had to be involved in some way. But had they acted alone or did their psycho-bitch mother have a part in it? If so, she could easily have been the mastermind behind it all. The three boys barely had one brain between them, so it fit that Sandy would be the one giving the orders, right? After all, Sandy had harbored a grudge against Spitz ever since she'd learned he had encouraged Petra's flirting with the women on the *Being Stronge* set; Spitz had felt it would generate more sparks in front of the camera. Maybe she'd finally had enough and wanted to teach Spitz a lesson. After all, he did drop her and her boys like a bad habit—if that wasn't a compelling motive, then I didn't know what was.

You see, Army, Navy, and Ranger had lost their moral compasses a long time ago, while growing up in such a dysfunctional family. With names like theirs, they never stood a chance. From the get-go, there was always the expectation for the boys to be tough like their dad, take no prisoners, and kick ass at every turn in life. We all gossiped that they were brainwashed by their father's "my way or the highway" philosophy, but equally influenced by their walking-talking Barbie doll of a mother, who cemented their beliefs that women were only good at being arm candy and breaking the bank, so they could chase beauty and the illusion of youth.

The "Military Boys," as they often liked to call themselves, were in fact the farthest thing from anything remotely military.

But with Petra gone, their mother depended on them even more. They were the men of the family now. Sandy was as pushy as ever, and she constantly nagged at them to "not take this shit lying down." They needed to get back on TV in the worse way. But would they resort to murder?

Maybe the Stronge family was on my mind too much, or my paranoia was kicking in again. But it seemed like everywhere I went, there were the Stronge boys. They kept turning up like a bad penny. I couldn't figure out why the Stronge boys would be following me. *If* they were even following me. Was I their next intended victim? Had Spitz told them of my confession before he was killed? Did they now know I had killed their father, even if it was self-defense? Scenarios were running through my head, and they were all bad.

I needed to find out what was going on and fast. Everyone knew the boys had been royally pissed when Spitz cancelled *Only the Stronge Survive*. The Stronge boys craved fame and money almost as much as their crazy parents. Spitz had told a few of us hanging around the set one day that the boys wanted to "off" Milo while the cameras were rolling. Spitz laughed as it were the funniest joke he'd ever heard, but it could have been more than just wishful thinking on the boys' part. Which gave me an idea. Maybe there was a way to give the boys what they wanted.

I spent the next two days staking out the neighborhood where the alleged Seal Team 6 gang lived. If their comings and goings were any indication, they consumed massive amounts of take-out pizza, beer, Red Bull, and Taco Bell. It didn't take me long to get their routine nailed down. I waited until they were all at home before springing my trap.

I needed some courage, so I took a quick snort of whatever tiny amount of coke was left in my jacket pocket before facing the unholy trio. I knocked on the door, and Navy answered. He took one look at me and yelled back into the room, "You guys are never going to believe who's at our front door, and it ain't the Easter Bunny!" Then he burped. What a charmer.

I swallowed hard as the two other Stronge cretins crammed themselves into the doorway trying to get a look. Knowing the boys as I did, I decided to cut to the chase and set bait before even trying to wrangle an invite into the house.

"Hey guys, I know I'm probably the last person you want to see, but I have a proposition for you. I think you boys should be on *Proven Killers*." I stopped and waited. Their looks went from sneering and disgusted to curious and interested. And before I knew it, I was being offered a Bud Light from Ranger and sitting with them in their man cave.

The room held a king-sized couch with matching recliners and two very large, mounted widescreen TVs on one wall. Empty food, beer cans, and DVDs were strewn all over the place.

"So, what's the plan, Henderson?" The Stronge boys looked interested, but also a little bored—as if they were deciding whether to hear me out or just kill me and bury me somewhere in the La Brea tar pits. I realized then that they could easily make me disappear and no one would be the wiser. No one even knew I was here. Not my smartest move. So, I hurried to get right to the point.

"Look, hear me out. I think you guys know who killed Spitz and Klaus, and for the sake of argument, let's assume I have a pretty good idea who did it too. Now, the only question is: was it one, two, or all three of you boys?"

The boys' faces dropped.

I rushed on, "Now what happened was a bad thing, a *very* bad thing. But there is something good that can come of it. Based on your recent 'work history,' let's call it, you boys would be perfect for *Proven Killers!*"

I shut up and tried keeping my facial expression as neutral as possible. Army stood up and walked over to me, crouched down, and got right in my face.

"Stop calling us boys, you fucking piss-ant. So, let me get this straight. What you're saying is, you can get us on the show, correct?"

"You guys watch the show, right?" They were nodding in spite of themselves. That was a good sign. "You know that Armando dude? Well, Armando hates being on the show, thinks it sends 'the wrong message' to kids. He's on this whole trip against *Proven Killers*, which is having a toxic effect on the rest of the cast, so the new brass wants him off. Pronto. Ever since he got on the show, it just hasn't been the same. Jonathan Pence, the new head honcho, wants Armando gone and is looking for new blood for the show. Sorry, no pun intended."

They seemed to take a long time figuring out what I'd meant by my remark, so I pressed on. "This is where *you* come in. You're naturals in front of the camera and you're already famous."

They appeared to be listening, but also hadn't said anything. I was getting nervous. Let's face it, these boys were stupid, but they were also dangerous. I had to stay calm.

Navy flexed his pecs and cracked his knuckles.

"So, what's the hitch?" Army growled. He was way over his limit on the steroids he'd been taking. He reminded me of Lync, sadly.

"You guys force Armando off the show. And—here's the best part—you do it with the cameras rolling. Think of it as a 'live' audition. It will go viral in a heartbeat and everyone will be clamoring for you to be a part of the show. When the press gets ahold of this, you'll be the most popular stars of the show. What do you say to that?"

I tried not to look desperate, glancing at my watch as if it didn't matter one way or another.

"You mean just bust in and fuck this guy up on camera?" Navy asked.

"Exactly! Embarrass the shit out of him, give him even more reason to hate the show and quit. Rough him up some, let him know that you think he could be the one who killed Spitz and Klaus. Everyone knew Klaus and your dad were friends. And while Spitz wasn't close with your family, Armando wouldn't know that. He hasn't been around long enough to know all that stuff. Think about it—it would be great timing! The fingers would be pointed at Armando because all this murder business started to happen only after he came on the show."

I could practically see the wheels turning in their tiny little minds. Hopefully they were thinking they had a lot more to gain than they had to lose. From their perspective, they had already rid themselves of two major problems, namely Spitz and Klaus. Now, if they literally pushed Armando off the show, it would all but guarantee their ticket back to stardom and riches. They looked at one another, then back at me. The boys looked stoked. I had them.

"Hell, I can see the billboards now"—I paused, motioning to an imaginary ad in the sky—"'*Watch out reality world—the Stronge Boys are back!*'"

That was a whopper of a lie, but I wanted to close this deal and fast.

"Stop calling us boys," Army said, but without any real heat behind it, as he smacked me playfully in the back of my head.

41. THE CON

OF COURSE, I had no intention of any of this really happening. My *real* plan was to have Artie step in right before anything potentially bad could happen, and make sure it was all captured on film. I knew this would thrill Artie with all the attention he would get, plus the added bonus of being the "top dog" at the station, even if for a little while.

I spent the rest of the evening with the Army, Navy, and Ranger, who all seemed more psychotic than ever. They dug through clothes for hours trying to find the best badass outfits for the show. They fussed with hair and military props, and even rehearsed how they would storm the show and confront Armando.

I just sat back and watched the circus, occasionally throwing in a few pointers here and there. Nothing too complicated, just a few tricks I'd learned from being on *Proven Killers*. Once their mania finally wound down, I left the house with my game plan set in motion and D-Day scheduled for an upcoming shoot on set. I got to my car and dialed Artie as I drove away.

When I got back to my apartment, I quickly dialed Jonathan.

"Marc, it's kind of late, do you need something? Can it wait till morning?" Jonathan asked, a bit grumpily.

"I'm really sorry, but I needed to touch base with you tonight. And I need you to trust me when I tell you that I've just worked out a great publicity stunt that should get us the highest ratings yet for *Proven Killers*."

"Okay, hit me with it." He yawned, as he was still trying to wake up.

"I just spoke with these guys who gave me some new information about James' and Victor's murders. After what they told me, I think they have inside knowledge of what happened. We can either just dump this all in the laps of the police and walk away"—I hesitated—"or, we can play this out and reap the rewards. These guys either know who did it and have withheld the information from the police, or they were a part of it. They were kind of buzzed, so it was a little difficult to pin down the details, but they know things no one else seems to. Anyhow, I've convinced them to come to the set on Thursday to audition for *Proven Killers*, but really, we'll try to get them to talk about what really happened. I've already cleared it with Artie, so he's up to speed and will be ready to step in and make an arrest...if it comes to that."

No response. I rushed on.

"The way I've set it up, these guys think they're auditioning for roles, so they won't be on their guard."

Still more silence. I started to sweat. *He's not going for it. Crap! Did I come this far just to have it all come apart at the seams?*

"Marc, I'm not sure what you're up to, and I'm even less sure that you know what you're doing. But on the off chance this crazy idea even half works, I'd be the laughing stock of Hollywood if I missed out on it. What do you need from me?"

I let out the breath I didn't realize I was holding. "The crew needs to be on point Thursday. You need to make sure they keep filming regardless of what happens, so that when the whole thing goes down, it's all caught on camera."

"Done. What time will these 'guys' arrive?" Jonathan asked.

"Nine o'clock Thursday morning. And Jonathan? Thanks," I said, and hung up before he could change his mind.

42. THE BEST-LAID PLANS

ARTIE and I spent much of Wednesday night finalizing our game plan for nabbing the Stronge boys. I felt a little guilty about keeping Jonathan somewhat out of the loop by not letting him in on the entire plan, but the less people who knew what Artie and I were really up to, the better. Hopefully all would be forgiven when Jonathan made TV history. The ratings from this episode alone would catapult *Proven Killers* into the stratosphere. And Artie would be as happy as a pig in turds when his mug made front-page news for solving not just one, but *two*, very high-profile murders.

Thursday morning came with Armando already on set, with makeup and wardrobe people buzzing all over him. He looked calm, cool, collected, and totally unaware of what was about to go down. Artie had secretly positioned police around the neighborhood, which included a couple of SWAT team snipers just in case, which I only found out about later. Then, the cameras started rolling and everything seemed to happen in quick succession.

Just as Artie was being introduced as the newest cast member, I faked a pulled muscle and motioned to Jonathan that I had to step out back for a few minutes to walk it off. I went out through the side door and looked up and down the street. *What the—?* There was no sign of the Stronge boys anywhere. I'd specifically told them when and where to meet me before their "audition." Crap! This was so not good. Those boys could not be trusted. I raced back inside, frantic.

Channel 26 News was the lucky media outlet selected by Jonathan to do an official interview with Artie and talk about his new role on the show. The reporter was one of their best, and she knew how to coax information from Artie, while putting him more at ease in front of the camera. As they chatted, Artie kept an eye on his surroundings. He saw me looking terrified and he slid me a questioning glance. I shrugged, not knowing what else to do. Then Armando silently appeared, standing patiently just out of camera range, waiting for his entrance.

That's when all hell broke loose. The Stronge Boys came crashing through the front door, screaming orders, waving guns in the air. They were imitating moves straight out of *Tropic Thunder* and chanting, "We're the Dudes, playing the Dudes disguised as some Dudes," one of the more memorable lines from the movie. These boys were definitely on something. Their eyes were bugging out of their heads and it looked like their jaws where moving a mile a minute; they were off the rails. Everyone stopped what they were doing to stare, not sure if this was scripted or what.

Artie went into full cop mode, grabbing a walkie-talkie out of his pocket and ordering the SWAT team onto the property. I started to panic when I realized that the boys were pushing right past Armando, who hadn't moved from where he was standing. Army was leading the charge.

In what seemed like super-slow motion, Army raised his gun and pointed it in my direction. I was crammed between one of the staging lights and a huge dolly filled with equipment, so I was pretty well trapped. All I could think of was, *I'm going to be killed by a Mutant Ninja Turtle wannabe. How pathetic is that?* Then I heard a scream. I think it might have been me.

In a flash, there was Armando, who stepped right in front of Army and began to unleash a series of dizzying Kung Fu moves that made everything blur together. We'd all known Armando had martial arts skills, but who could've guessed he was another Bruce Lee? The next thing I saw was Army on the ground, breathing heavily and struggling against the lock hold Armando easily had him in. By now, the L.A. police had stormed in alongside the SWAT team, who had pinned the other two boys to the floor and were securing the area and checking on everyone's welfare.

Armando, sensing the threat had been neutralized, eased up on the pressure he was applying, allowing Army to assume a more comfortable, sitting position. Army—who clearly had more brawn than brains—made yet another bad decision by making a grab for his gun, but Armando got there first. They wrestled for the weapon briefly before the gun discharged. Armando's face fell into shock as he rushed to hold onto Army, who was slipping back down to the floor. Army looked like he was in shock, eyes glazed, his skin pallor gray.

Armando, with tears in his eyes, gently laid Army on the floor. Army was trying to say something. Armando leaned over him, trying to catch his faint words. Everyone gathered around, looking stunned. Jonathan, sensing an Emmy Award within reach, motioned to the cameras to get as close as they could. Artie had radioed for an ambulance, and sirens could be heard in the distance.

"Am I going to die? I really wanted my brothers to...be on the show...get back on top." Army took a shallow breath. "We weren't after you, man. It was Henderson, he wanted you out ...." His voice cracked and then he was gone. There was more wailing, but I couldn't be sure if it was the sirens or Navy and Ranger, grieving for their dead brother.

Before I could gather my wits about me, Armando got up from where Army was laying, as the EMTs came in to take over. He said a few words to the police and pointed at me. They nodded and then Armando walked straight towards me. I wanted to run, hide, be anywhere rather than here, but I was frozen to the spot. Out of the corner of my eye, I spotted Jonathan shoving the cameraman in our direction.

Armando got right up in my personal space and stared hard into my eyes. The beleaguered cameraman was there, ready and waiting. I closed my eyes as I steeled myself for a punch or kick, or whatever punishment Armando planned to dole out. I so deserved it. But instead, he simply embraced me.

My eyes popped open, arms dangling at my side. I was utterly confused and shocked.

"I know it was you," Armando whispered quietly, with his head turned towards mine so the cameras couldn't pick up what he was saying. Then Armando pulled back and held me by the shoulders so we could be face to face. He had tears in his eyes, but he didn't seem to notice. I felt my own eyes begin to water. The cameraman zoomed in on Armando as he hugged me for the second time.

Armando whispered again, "I forgive you, man. I know what you were doing, and I forgive you. We're good."

I was stunned. He pulled back again to face me. He said in a louder voice that the mics could pick up, "Don't blame yourself for what happened to Army. No one is to blame. It's a tragedy. But this is the price of all this distorted reality TV. This is what I've been trying to tell everyone all along. It's a drug, man, as addicting as heroin. It consumes you, changes you, and makes you do shit you can't even imagine."

I just stood there, spent and shaken. Armando looked at me questioningly. I nodded dumbly. He smiled and gave my cheek a reassuring pat. The police and TV reporter swarmed around him, all wanting a piece of him. Normally I would be seething at the amount of attention he was getting, but now, I could feel nothing except humbleness, gratitude, and maybe even a little peace.

I turned and saw my buddy Greg, who gave me a quick, hard hug. "Come on, let's get you something to drink." I nodded my agreement and thanks.

We passed by Jonathan, who winked and gave me a thumbs-up. I smiled shakily and kept walking. I heard him whisper to the cameraman, "Kaitlyn Jenner my ass —*this* is reality television!"

Artie was over in a corner, already being interviewed by Channel 26 again, this time about how he felt being one of the heroes of the day. Artie was trying to look serious and humble, but I knew on the inside he was already planning his guest appearance on *The First 48*.

43. KILLING REALITY

ARMANDO WAS happy to leave the police station in record time. He had spent more than his fair share of time being scrutinized over homicides. The killing of Army Stronge clearly was an act of self-defense, and one that was backed up by all witnesses. The same couldn't be said for Navy and Ranger Stronge, who were booked on numerous charges and being held in the county jail.

Sandy Stronge retained a lawyer who tried to arrange bail for the boys, but was denied due to their complete lack of remorse. This infuriated Sandy to the point where she went out, proceeded to get drunk, and drove her Mercedes into a guardrail. She was arrested and brought to the police station, and had to call the lawyer again, this time for her own bail.

Meanwhile, Armando was all over the news. While he may not have loved being in the spotlight, at least this time, Armando used it as a forum to reach even more people, using his newfound fame to demand changes on set. In its rebooted format, *Proven Killers* now consisted of a camera crew following Armando around the rougher areas of L.A., where his streetwise-style of evangelicalism proved to be a hit. He became front and center as the savior of the show, and the paparazzi couldn't get enough of him.

Even though no one suspected that I had anything to do with what had happened that day, the camera had caught me on camera acting like a coward. The "Armando Effect" had not extended to me. Any acclaim I held in the public eye from saving people's lives at Lync and Paul's fatal party was but a dim memory. Jonathan gave me my walking papers, shook my hand, and wished me well. Only he and Greg showed any concern, whereas everyone else seemed to give a mental shrug and get back to business. Truth be told, I probably would have done the same if I were them.

I didn't even try to get another grip job. Let's face it, people in the business now associated me with words like *catastrophe*, *death*, and *disaster*. And the shooting on *Proven Killers* left me feeling hollowed out and questioning everything I had previously assumed to be true. I was aimless, not sure who I was anymore or which direction I should be going. The only positive thought I had was that it looked like my secret with Spitz remained quiet.

I passed by a church one day while out walking and

stopped to listen to the faint organ music playing inside. I
wished I had something that could anchor me like faith
did for countless others. While I couldn't muster up the
courage to go in, I couldn't stop thinking about it, even
when I returned home. I tried to pray, using the only
prayer I remembered from my youth, the Lord's Prayer. I
couldn't remember anything after the first line, felt silly,
and gave up. I began again, this time just plainly and
sincerely asking God to forgive me of my sins. I closed my
eyes and thought of everything I had done, and all the
good I had sacrificed, just for the chance of being in front
of the cameras. I didn't know what else to do, so I
repeated this mantra again and again. The brunt of what
I'd done hit me with the force of a Mack truck. The pain
and remorse I felt ran deep. I was scared. I was physically
shaking.

———

Days later, I was sitting on my couch channel surfing, still
morose but still keeping up with the praying. TMZ was
doing a spot about *Proven Killers* and its newest star. The
piece focused on Armando's capacity for forgiveness, and
how it lit a fire for the show on the streets of L.A.
   Armando was walking the talk, no doubt about it. And
this walked him right into a church of his own, as well as
a spin-off show entitled *Saving Grace*.
   The tabloids depicted Armando as a New Age "spiri-

tual vigilante." And viewers, perhaps tiring of all the self-aggrandizing of the Real Housewives, the Kardashians, and the like, were eating it up. The show's concept was helping people understand that seeking fame and fortune were not the real truth. Having stuff didn't mean much, but living a good life, helping others, and knowing God loved them, was.

I started seeing t-shirts worn by young kids with "Armando" emblazoned on them, with him crouched in a Bruce Lee-like fighting stance. These littered every middle school playground in L.A. Armando memorabilia was huge. A video of Armando's takedown of Army Stronge was number one on YouTube for weeks.

As happy as I was for Armando, I felt even more ashamed. I didn't want to show my face anywhere, and no matter how often I tried to be inconspicuous, people invariably pointed at me and whispered. My money was running out, too. My prayers continued to go unanswered. It was once again time for desperate measures.

One Sunday, feeling restless, I was about to jump on an eastbound bus, just to go anywhere and get out of L.A. for a few hours. As I paid for my ticket at the kiosk, I turned and looked up. There, across the highway, like a sign from God, was a billboard advertising the Saving Grace Church and its namesake show. Armando was smiling that million-dollar smile of his, hugging his followers. A sudden wave of raw emotion fell over me. I knew where to go, so I changed plans and got on a bus for the Saving Grace Church.

I walked the final few blocks to get to the rundown church. As I turned the corner of Petaluma Ave, I could hear sounds coming from within, signaling that a service was underway. Not wanting to be seen, I snuck in the back with a dozen other homeless people who had littered the packed service. I kept my head down.

Armando's voice came through the mic clear and in command. "God is Love."

People were chanting "amen" and "praise Jesus."

"There's a song that goes: love is all we need. Well, it's true. Love is what changes a person from the wrong path to the right one: the road to loving others, helping others as Jesus did. I know this. I know sometimes it's not easy, it's hard. But God never lets me forget that all I need to do is love others, even and especially, my enemies."

Armando ended with an emotional "Amen" as the service erupted in clapping and a universal chorus of "amen." I felt something in me that I really didn't recognize. Whatever it was, it felt good. Maybe I was feeling that "peace that passes all understanding" that Armando always spoke about on set.

Time slowed. Sounds died down and that peaceful feeling engulfed my whole being. I briefly closed my eyes, savoring the moment. As I opened my eyes, Armando was saying, "Communion is for everyone."

Parishioners stood and began forming a line that

headed straight to the altar where Armando stood. Some people were somber, heads down, hands clasped, while others held their hands open in the air, murmuring "praise Jesus." I wasn't sure what to do; I knew only that I wanted this feeling to continue, so I slowly stood and got in line with the others, thinking, *Maybe this is it, maybe God has forgiven me and shown me mercy.* I felt a sudden rush that everything might turn out okay.

The line was moving slowly towards Armando, who was giving out something that looked like a cracker. I was three people away from him when I saw a rush of movement coming out from the back of the altar. Behind Armando—coming fast—was Benny with something in his hand and a determined look on his face. It was the same face I'd seen when he'd threatened to shove my gun down my throat.

Armando was in trouble and he didn't even know it. I was scared shitless, but I knew I needed to stop Benny. Now. I pushed the man in front of me to the side, who was about to give me grief, but stopped when he looked up and saw Benny charging with the gun. The sudden commotion got Armando's attention, and he saw me moving quickly towards him.

Armando looked surprised to see me, and a little concerned. But with his cat-like reflexes, he was able to quickly move out of my path.

That's when Benny fired.

Armando quickly assessed the situation and made a

grab for me. As I stumbled toward the ground, I felt a fire begin to burn in my stomach. Armando motioned one of the parishioners to stay with me, and another to call 911. Then, he went after Benny. Benny was armed but bulky and slow. I hoped Armando could use that against him.

As I lay on the tiled floor, I started to get dizzy. A very nice lady, who smelled like jasmine, was holding me, trying to staunch the blood flow from the bullet wound with a towel. She spoke to me softly, "You're going to be all right, sweetheart. Just hang in there."

As I tried to stay conscious, I noticed a flash of something way up in the back, among the balcony. I spotted a few people from my old crew, who had been filming Armando and the service the entire time. I stared at the grips, who were once my friends. Even as mayhem ensued, all the noise around me started to fade. Mercifully, I blacked out.

44. A STAR IS BORN AGAIN

I AWOKE IN A HOSPITAL BED. God-awful fluorescent lights. I looked around and saw I was in a private room. *Nice.* I tried to move but quickly realized I was strapped to the bed. There was a lot of commotion outside my door that sounded like people arguing. Then the door flew open and Artie stormed in. I could see behind him that there was a mob with cameras and microphones, all pushing and shoving. There were a hundred flashes in that split second. I was literally blinded by the light.

Artie turned back to the crowd, clearly pissed. "Look, if you people don't behave, I'm going to have my two sergeants here start tasering any and all of you. *Capeesh?*" That seemed to subdue them, at least for the time being.

Then the door flew open again. This time it was Jonathan.

"Thanks, Artie." Jonathan said.

Artie responded with his customary grunt. He and

Jonathan proceeded to pull up chairs alongside my bed. Man, my head hurt.

"You were beautiful, Marc." Jonathan beamed, like a proud parent.

Whoa. What, did I miss something? Am I still unconscious and dreaming?

Artie, who sensed my confusion, gave me a quick debrief of what had transpired. That helped fill in some of the gaps, but not all.

"What about Armando? Is he okay? Before I blacked out, he was going after Benny," I said worriedly.

"Don't worry about him, kid. Armando is fine, more than fine. Benny was no match for him. But the real story is *you*. You're a hero. Hell, you're like the damn Energizer Bunny. Just when everyone counts you out, you come bouncing back."

I looked to Jonathan, who was smiling so broadly that I thought his jaws would crack. He then told me his good news.

"Marc, everyone is calling me—they all want interviews with you! Wait till you see the footage. It's incredible. We're going to sell it to everyone. I'm going to make TMZ pay out the nose for what we put together. The producers of *The First 48* want to do a documentary on this whole thing!"

I saw Artie's ears perk up at that.

My head was swimming and I wasn't sure it was just from the bullet wound. This was all too surreal. And I was exhausted, even though I had only been awake for a few minutes. They must have noticed the tiredness etched on my face, because Jonathan said, "Marc, get some rest. We'll be back in the morning to see you."

I dozed on and off, for how long I couldn't say. The pain meds they had me on must have been good, because the realization of what transpired hadn't fully dawned on me yet. When I did manage to stay awake for more than a few minutes, I kept playing the scene at the church over and over again in my head. What the hell had made me do that? It was like an out-of-body experience. Taking a bullet for someone? That was *so* not me.

Nurses came in periodically during the night to check my pulse and take my temperature, always making all kinds of "hmm" noises. I think a few came in just to check out the patient who'd caught a bullet on live TV. At one point, my door opened, and a female voice spoke softly. "There he is. Poor guy, he looks exhausted. And shorter than he does on TV."

Once again, I was all over the news. Nurses would sneak in newspapers and magazines with me plastered all over the cover. They read "Untouchable!" and "Henderson Takes A Bullet" and on and on. I could do no wrong. If only they knew.

45. SNAKES

A COUPLE OF DAYS PASSED. I was still sleeping a lot, thanks to the pain meds the doctors had me on. I awoke from another nap to find Jonathan sitting in the corner of the room with a beautiful woman. She wasn't a friend, but I knew who she was. Anyone who watched *Entertainment Tonight* on TV would, as well. No doubt Jonathan had cut a deal with her for an exclusive to my story. I wondered what his asking price was.

Sheila Cox was more beautiful in person than she was on TV, if that was possible. Jonathan and Sheila looked to be very buddy-buddy, which had me wondering what else she had to do to get this interview. Jonathan started the introductions, but I cut him off.

"Sheila and I know each other. She did a piece on me right after I was acquitted for Lync's death—she screwed me on that piece. Everyone knew it is was self-defense, but no, not Sheila. She said it was too coincidental that three reality stars were killed around the same time and wondered why the police didn't consider me as the prime suspect in all three incidences. She lied to me then, and she'll lie now. Isn't that right, Sheila?" I looked to her for confirmation.

"Marc, Jonathon and I have a deal. I can understand your frustration over how we handled that interview, but my producers call the shots, not me." She smiled like the snake she was. "Besides, we have a deal, you or Jonathan try anything, and they will sue your collective asses so fast, you won't know what hit you. Be reasonable. I can be your greatest ally or your worst nightmare. Let's just move on and get this interview behind us. So, what do you say?"

I talked to Sheila for a good two hours off and on, with a little light dozing in between. I relayed some of the information Artie had shared with me over the past week. During questioning, Benny had admitted he'd been ordered by his gang leader to kill Armando because he was causing too much trouble. According to Benny, after his arrest some of the gang members tried approaching Armando about cooling it a bit and to stop recruiting members to "his club," but Armando refused to listen. When Armando got his church and the *Saving Grace* spin-off show—which now included members of numerous gangs—it was too much. *Proven Killers* had been bad enough and they needed to put a stop to this once and for all.

I was exhausted and hoarse by the time I got to the point in the story where Benny busted into the church. I told Sheila I was getting tired and needed my pain medication. I asked her if she could finish up the story with Jonathan. She seemed happy with what I'd given her, apparently satisfied she'd gotten her money's worth. I was just glad to see her go, and glad it was over.

46. A FINE ROMANCE

I SPENT a few more days at the hospital, while they weaned me off my meds and kept tabs on my vital signs, and then I was finally discharged. I was wheel-chaired to the exit, where I painfully eased myself into the limo that Jonathan had graciously provided for me. He also included a bottle of Moet et Chandon champagne and a box of DeLafee Switzerland Gold Chocolate. *Oh boy*, I thought, *here we go again*. I was so tempted to crack that ice-cold bottle and drink up, but something stopped me. All I could think about was the clarity and peace I had felt at the church that day, and I knew I wanted to keep feeling like that. So, I passed on the bubbly but did enjoy a few of those amazing chocolates.

The limo dropped me off at the front of my apartment building. I went inside, expecting the good feeling to stay with me. Instead, I felt very alone. My mom had called me incessantly while I was recovering in the hospital and wanted to fly home from her yoga retreat in India, but I persuaded her to stay. She wouldn't be home for another few days, and international calls were expensive, but I needed to talk with somebody, someone who was on my side, who always had my back and made me laugh. Mrs. Fox came to mind. It felt like it had been years, not months, since we'd last spoken. I was instantly ashamed for neglecting our friendship and treating her so poorly. I definitely needed to make amends.

I got my car out of the garage, stopped by a liquor store to get the ingredients for making her favorite margaritas, threw some chips and dips in for good measure, and headed to the old neighborhood to see my "best girl," Aud. I just needed to hear some of her stories and see what has been happening in her life. I thought about calling first, but I decided to make a surprise visit. I knew she would forgive me of my sins and never hold a grudge. Besides, she loved my margaritas. If I was lucky, we'd even get out with Daisy for a while. I parked the car in front of the apartment complex and got out, nervous as hell.

I knocked on her door a few times, but there was no answer. While I was standing there, I could hear what sounded like Daisy barking, but it wasn't coming from inside Aud's apartment, but rather my old apartment. *What the—?* I moved over to my old apartment door and knocked, wanting to see if that really was Daisy. Maybe Aud was out and her new neighbor was dog sitting for her. A really pretty girl in her mid-twenties answered. Wow, I mean she was beautiful.

"Hi, can I—?" She stopped mid-sentence as she opened the door and saw me. "Oh my gosh, you're Marc. I mean, of course you are! It's just that Audrey always"— she stopped for a moment, flapping her hands—"sorry, I sound like an idiot. Let me start over. Hi, I'm Lisa, it's so nice to meet you." She looked flustered but in an adorable way.

I said hello and the next thing I knew, Daisy came bolting out and practically jumped into my arms. "Daisy, behave!" Lisa scolded her and laughed. She started to explain that Daisy doesn't usually jump on people. I said, "I know," and Lisa caught on, remembering that I'd lived here before her. We smiled at each other. I explained that I'd come to see both Audrey and Daisy, but that Audrey must be out on the town with her peeps.

Lisa looked shocked, which was confusing, but she invited me in and asked me if I wanted something to drink. I told her water or soda was fine, if it wasn't a bother. She motioned for me to follow her into the little kitchen, where I sat at my old kitchen table. It felt weird being back in the apartment when I didn't live there.

Lisa seemed reluctant to talk while she retrieved two Coke Zeros from the fridge and placed them on the table. She sat down to join me, but I sensed something was up.

"I hate to be the one to tell you this, Marc, but Mrs.

Fox passed from a heart attack just under a month ago," she said, her eyes full of sympathy.

I felt my heart shatter. Lisa's eyes were welling up. I could tell she'd adored Audrey too. How could anyone not?

She said Mrs. Fox's estate wanted to keep everything quiet and private. She also went on to tell me they'd wanted to put Daisy in a shelter. Lisa had learned this from Mrs. Fox's attorney, who also notified her that Mrs. Fox had left Lisa a bracelet of hers that Lisa had always admired. Lisa told the attorney that no way in hell was Daisy going to a shelter—she loved Daisy almost as much as Mrs. Fox did, and that she would be Daisy's family from now on. Lisa was getting worked up all over again on Daisy's behalf. I could have married that girl right then and there.

We were both hurting and before the mood got too low, she started telling me stories about how Mrs. Fox would go on and on about our weekly margarita happy hours we had, and how proud Mrs. Fox was to know me before I got so popular, Aud had said she loved those times. I got a little teary-eyed when Lisa told me that Mrs. Fox had missed me, but still always hoped everything would go well for me.

I felt like I'd just swallowed a huge stone. I did what was starting to come natural for me—I said a quick prayer under my breath, "Please God, watch over my Aud. And tell her I'm sorry and that I miss and love her."

Thankfully, before I got too maudlin, Daisy started jumping up and down, yapping, going crazy. It was her signal to go for a walk. Lisa said she was sorry about having to be the bearer of bad news and that she knew Mrs. Fox had really loved me.

She then changed the subject and told me she was working at a vintage clothing store that sold secondhand high-end brands like Gucci, Valentino, and Chanel, but hastened to add that it was a temporary job while she pursued her acting career. We chatted for a few more minutes, but Daisy had had enough of not being the center of attention. I finally worked up the guts and asked Lisa if she wanted to go grab a bite, and I'd tell her some of the more outrageous things that went on behind the scenes of the reality shows. Lisa said, "I'd like that," and dazzled me with that smile of hers. I told her I'd take Daisy for a little walk by the river and be back in half an hour or so.

We set off, and Daisy was thrilled to be out and walking by the water. It brought back memories of a better time, a simpler time, when Aud and I would come here and throw a Frisbee around for Daisy to catch. As heartbroken as I was about Aud's passing, she'd be the first to give me a good shake, kick me in the ass, and tell me to snap out of it. She was one in a million. The more Daisy and I walked, the more I couldn't get Lisa out of my head. I hoped she liked me, as I felt we had made a real connection. *Wait till I take her out in my car*, I thought, and then laughed at myself.

We came to a beautiful old tree along the water's edge, one that Audrey loved. It seemed like the perfect spot to say goodbye to Aud and give her a proper send-off. I sat down next to the tree, thanking God for the blessing that was Aud. I also asked for His help with this nice new girl I'd just met, knowing Aud was smiling down on me. It was peaceful.

Then I heard a loud yelp from Daisy. Turning, I saw Daisy just lying there, half in the water and half along the embankment. I turned to go help her, but not fast enough. Something hit me in the back, knocking the wind out of me. The blunt force spun me around to see Benny's sidekick Eddie with a baseball bat in his hand, with Sandy Stronge next to him. *What the hell?* Eddie and Sandy? How had these two ever gotten together? My mind scrambled to put the pieces together. Revenge!

I couldn't dwell on any of that right now. I only knew I was in deep trouble and that I had to save Daisy. I had lost Aud, but I sure as hell wasn't going to lose Daisy. That first blow had done something to a few of my ribs and they hurt like a mother. I tried yelling to Daisy but still hadn't gotten my breath back. I was standing up when Eddie charged at me with the bat like a battering ram, knocking me into the water. Now I was struggling to breathe *and* needed to get myself out of the water. Daisy was also trying to move, but she must have sustained an injury as well and couldn't roll over enough to get traction. I crawled over to her but was stopped—this time by Sandy, wielding the bat and shoving me hard on my shoulder. Luckily, this time it knocked me a little towards Daisy, and as I was falling, I grabbed Daisy and threw her with all my might. I only managed to throw her about five feet, but it did the trick. She was out of the water and hopefully out of danger.

I was in shallower water now, which helped me regain my footing. I stood up just as Sandy took another swing. She swung with all her might, but this time, she lost her footing and missed. She had counted on a direct hit, and the momentum carried her clear into the water. *Thank you, God, I really needed that.* I finally caught my breath as Eddie picked up the bat from where it had fallen from Sandy's grasp when she'd swung and missed. Eddie was short but wiry and strong, if his first hit had been any indication. I knew his next hit was probably going to do me in if I didn't do something quickly. Eddie raised the bat over his head, screaming like a banshee, and came at me. I was able to get a little traction with better footing. I remained in a crouched position, hoping Eddie thought I was still unsteady and struggling to get back on my feet.

At the last possible moment, I got up and under Eddie, half tackling, half lifting him up off his feet. The impact jostled the bat out of his hands. It must have been all that adrenaline pumping through my system, for I knocked him a good two or three feet into the river. Eddie was flailing around and coughing, trying to keep his head above water, just as I had moments ago. *How does it feel, asshole?* But Eddie didn't go down easily—he was already making his way back to the embankment with a murderous look on his face. I knew I couldn't keep this up much longer; the adrenaline surge was going to drop any second. I had to finish this before he or Sandy—who by this time, was also heading towards the embankment—had another chance to kill me.

Fortunately, when Eddie had dropped the bat, it had landed close to me. As Eddie stood up and climbed out of the shallow water towards me, I crouched down and took a few crab steps closer to him, keeping my new weapon under the water and out of view. I closed my eyes and swung with all my might. I heard the not unfamiliar sound of a heavy crack. Before even opening my eyes to see what damage I had done, I knew I'd gotten him good.

I turned, checking to see how Daisy was holding up. As I did, Sandy was coming at me with something in her hand. I didn't wait around to find out what it was. I still had the bat in my hand, so I took a three-quarter swing and hit a line drive off her mid-section, and she went down for a second time. I dropped the bat, stumbling and falling back into the water. I could hear Sandy screaming in pain as I crawled my way back up the embankment towards Daisy. When I got to her, she was barely moving but still breathing. I thanked God. Again.

Scooping Daisy gently up into my arms, we made it

back to the grass under the tree, where I collapsed, spent. It was then I heard the police sirens. Who would have thought I, of all people, would love to hear that sound? But at that moment, it was music to my ears. Daisy gave my cheek a weak but encouraging lick. I hoped it was Daisy's way of assuring me she'd be okay. I sighed with immense relief and would have cried if I hadn't been so damn tired. The sirens grew closer, and as I slowly passed out, I thought, *Here we go again.*

THANK YOU

People say it takes a village to raise a child.

Well, it took a village to help me write this book.

I first want to thank my family for encouraging me to continue with one of my goals on my bucket list. Especially Mike and Pat, for putting the wind back in my sails so I could have the ability to get this book started.

I want to thank...

Maya Christobel, for helping me believe I could actually write this book and for helping me get started.

Ayanna Tillman, for giving me her perspective and helping me to keep it moving forward in a positive way.

Thanks to Karissa for giving me the idea for the book. Even when she didn't know it.

Kristen Forbes of DeviancePress, my editor, whom I would recommend to everyone. She did a brilliant job.

Alexander von Ness, thanks for a great cover.

Lastly, my wife, Lisa. I am so lucky she is so talented. She made this book "cool."

Made in the USA
Middletown, DE
05 August 2019